Riding
with the
Hides
of
Hell

♥

Stacia Leigh

DEDICATION

To the usual suspects: George, Bianca, and Ruby
To the *un*usual suspects: Tango & Tilly

* * *

Cover design and photography
by Espial Design
www.espialdesign.com

ISBN: 0692797270
ISBN-13: 978-0692797273

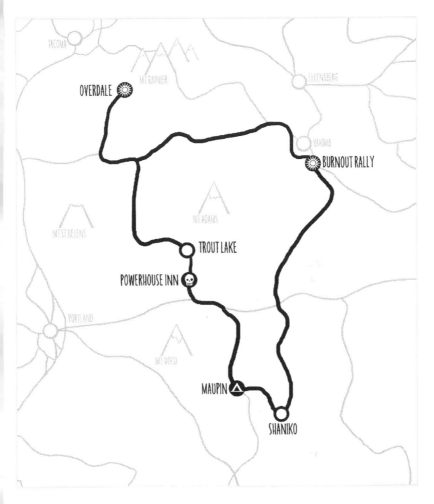

Overdale, Powerhouse Inn, and Burnout Rally are fictitious places and events meant only for the imagination.

CHAPTER 1

A COLD ONE

Whenever Will heard his mom's brusque voice in his head, it was time to crack open a cold one.

Will, this is your mother speaking.

Like now.

Eleven months ago, she'd been killed, and in the beginning, he'd cried gallons of tears until his joints ached from dehydration. But it didn't take him long to discover the beauty of getting drunk and passing out. Since beer was mostly water, it was hydrating, right? Water that buzzed his brain, so he could stop all the crying and go unconscious through the night. It was sort of like sleeping, but better because his mind turned into a vacant tube with no dreams and no voices.

When he wasn't drunk—or drunk enough—she'd sneak up on him and interrupt his thoughts in the same way.

Will, Will, Will. This is your mother speaking, speaking, speaking.

It was like his mom sat on the cushion of his brain with a bull horn. Her tone rang out crisp and clear, like the good old days when she'd harp at him to load the dishwasher or to ask for the loaf pan from the top shelf. He'd gripe about it, and she'd tell him to be thankful he

1

had long legs. She couldn't reach anything. Will, the world wasn't made with short people in mind, she'd say.

"So, leave the top empty." Will used to tell her. "Or better yet, get a stool."

"Why?" She'd shrug. "When I have you?" Then, she'd pat his forearm, and the subtle gesture would infuse his system with belonging and love. Sometimes, he'd grumble all the way back to his laptop, and other times, he'd smile and rinse out a bowl or two.

Will, this is your mother speaking.

He wanted to yell at her, Of course, I know it's you! But he couldn't because she wasn't really there. If he yelled at his mom, he'd be yelling at himself, and it would mean he was bat guano crazy, something he didn't want to think about.

Will, I was wondering if Helmet ate his dry food this morning. Did you check it? Have you seen him today? He doesn't look well. Maybe you should take him to the vet again. Take good care of him, Will. I love you.

Not now, Mom. I'm busy!

He clenched his back molars tightly and tried to focus on his game. He was playing Goblin Strike online with his buddy, J.J., and Will could barely focus on the ogre kicking the red pixels out of his character.

Things were getting blurry, but even so, it sounded like he needed another beer.

While Mom lamented front and center about the health of her polydactyl cat, J.J.'s laughter boomed through the headphones. Will pushed his long bangs back and rubbed at his temple where a thudding headache threatened to crash the party.

"Man!" J.J. hooted with glory. "Did you see how much swag that ogre was carrying?" His loud voice echoed deeply into Will's ears. "Two magic scrolls, a morning star, and a wedge of cheese. Sweet."

"Oh, yeah. You're kicking butt," Will said. His heart wasn't in this game. Was it beer time yet?

The wire trash basket next to his desk sat half-full—or was it half-empty?—of drained bottles in various colors: clear, green, brown. He wasn't picky. He couldn't be really, because he raided whatever was left in the fridge after his dad's biker buddies stopped by. The guys were relatively tame. No more getting smashed, brawling on the living room floor, and ratcheting up the music. Those antics were saved for the clubhouse.

Will, remember when the guys broke my pink lamp? It was your great-grandmother's, and I told them no more parties at the house. You boys had school the next day, and how could anyone get a decent night's sleep with that ruckus going on?

One more beer. If he could sneak another one tonight, he'd be set, and then he could hit the sack with his mother turned off. She was getting way too chatty.

"So…" J.J. drawled out.

"Dude, I hate it when you do that. 'So…'" Will mimicked him and dropped his head back to study the finger smudges around the light switch. "So…" meant J.J. had something on his mind, something he needed to chat about, and Will wasn't in the mood to listen. Not tonight.

"I've been wondering about something you said a while back. We were at a bonfire, the one in the meadow. Remember?" J.J. asked.

"Uh…" Will frowned, and the chair squeaked as he leaned forward, wracking his melon for incriminating things he might have said while under the influence. He was barely conscious that night. Besides, it happened like two months ago.

"You mentioned Zombie Lips—"

"Dude!" Will dropped a heavy fist on his desk. "Are you serious?"

"Last I heard, she flung her bikini top in your face, and it was like a year ago. You never mentioned her again until the meadow. You babbled something about how she was only after your body. What am I missing here, man? Like, what the hell happened? Not sure what's up with the nickname, but the rest of it sure sounded good."

Oh, my God.

Will pinched the bridge of his nose until it started to tingle. He could *not* talk about Zombie Lips right now. Not her. No way. "When did you turn into such a gossip queen?" Will muttered.

"When did you get such a tight lip?" J.J.'s voice crackled over the line. "I'm not trying to ride your biz, man, but your mom's been gone a year—"

"What the hell do you know, Rad-boner?" Will asked. J.J.'s last name was Radborne, so any chance to call him a *bo*ner was a *bo*nus. Will narrowed his eyes at the glowing monitor. With a couple clicks, he could hack J.J.'s character into chunky salsa. "You try losing your mom. Then you can tell me all about it."

"Hold it. Not what I meant." J.J.'s deep voice vibrated in Will's ear canal. "C'mon, man. I'm only wondering if Zombie Lips is part of the problem."

"What problem?" Will snapped, pulling the keyboard closer. Get ready to die. Chunky style, dude.

"Man," J.J. said tiredly. "You wanna go out less and less, and when you do, you're tanked all the time. If you

4

turn into an alcoholic, you're going to kill your liver or worse. Trust me. You know I've seen it in action."

True. J.J.'s uncle was a raging alcoholic who'd turned into a fist-wielding, family-robbing, drug-addicted asshole. Will pushed the keyboard back, sparing J.J.'s onscreen life, and slumped into his chair. He closed his eyes, trying to see inside himself, but it was cloudy and dark in there.

"I don't want you to pull a Chill Will on me," J.J. said. "You don't want to talk about it? Fine. But it had to be said, man. And if I need to punch you in the face, I will. Because that's the kind of friend I am. We good?"

"Sure," Will said and conjured up a sizable belch to lighten the mood, a juicy one, too. He wiped his thumb over the mic on his headset.

"Thanks. No, seriously. You gassing my ear gives me a thrill," J.J. chuckled on his end of the receiver, followed by soft clicking and shuffling noises. "And speaking of thrill, I gotta call my girl."

"Be sure to tell Suzy her ol' man says 'hey.' After all, she was my girl first."

"The hell she—"

"Later, dude." Will laughed loudly and ended the call. Boom! He got the last word and the hang up. J.J. was the master, but this time, Will got him good.

Will's eyes drifted back to the dirty wall. He used to like Suzy. Sure, it was brief, but enough to ask her to junior prom. He even tried the "I saw her first" claim, but J.J. swooped in with some cockamamie story and—water under the bridge—Will stepped aside. His head and heart were numb, and deep down, he couldn't fight for her. Good thing, too, because Suzy and J.J. were the real deal.

Besides, Will had his mom in his head. What could he offer a sweet girl like Suzy?

He drooped and his eyes closed. Maybe he'd had enough to drink, after all. He was comfy here in his office chair with his chin tucked into his chest, and his dark bangs drawn like a curtain. Already his mind hung like a humid cloud, not raining, not floating, just there.

Will, please wake up and check on Helmet. He's my soul kitty, and he needs you. Did he eat? Did he drink? Has he moved from the kitchen chair?

Will lifted his head and struggled to peel up his eyelids. Game over. His computer screen had turned black, yet there was his phone, blinking with life. He had a text message.

Z-LIPS: It's been a while. Hope ur doing okay.

Well, well. Someone's ears must have been burning. J.J mentions Zombie Lips and look who's texting again. Will shoved away from his desk, catching the corner to steady himself. What was the tally up to now? It had to be around twenty-something. He scrolled through the messages. He had no idea why he kept them, but the count was exactly twenty-three since he'd last spoken to her. Why wouldn't she leave him alone? No clue. More importantly, why hadn't he blocked her number? Too much hassle? If she sent him twenty-three more texts, maybe he'd forgive her. Yeah…maybe.

He opened his bedroom door to a haze of smoke, swearing, and laughter, which meant the beer-drinking Hides of Hell bikers were still here. Didn't they have their own homes to go to?

Will used to consider these hairy, tatted up guys his family until after his mom died. Their world went back to normal way too soon for Will's liking. For the Sullivans, things stayed the same. Dad pored over photo albums and played the "remember" game with Liam, who openly sniffled like the sensitive bastard he was. Will preferred to sit on the floral couch and let the days drift by...

Will, don't just stand in the hall with your teeth in your mouth. Go check on my cat!

Yeah, yeah, check on the big-pawed kitty. Who didn't love his mom's littlest badass? He left dead birds on the porch, fished wet cigarette butts out of plastic cups, and scratched and farted with the rest of 'em. Good ol' Helmet.

Will stepped around the corner into the kitchen, and the guys sitting in the attached living room fell quiet. He could practically feel their concerned eyes pelting the back of his head and wished the hood of his sweatshirt were big enough to engulf him. Why were they here again? They could hang out at Mook's place or Flossy's garage or—hey, here's a great idea—go hang out at the clubhouse with the rest of the leather backs.

"Want some grub, Will?" his dad asked tentatively.

"I already ate," Will muttered without looking over his shoulder.

He scuffed across the cold slate floor in his bare feet to Helmet's ceramic bowl. It was piled high with dry kibble, the water hadn't been touched, and the orange fur ball was still curled up on the padded kitchen chair. He was off in dreamland—busy plucking feathers out of birds with his six toes—sleeping like he always did with an arm covering his eyes.

But, he hasn't moved in the past five hours, Will.

7

He hasn't?

The floor tilted, and Will grasped the edge of the table. "Helmet," he whispered. "Hey, buddy. Wake up."

His hand shook as he stroked Helmet's soft head.

It was cold.

CHAPTER 2

DARK AND LIGHT

Miki's hair hung straight and sleek all the way to her waist. Everyone loved it, her friends as well as her frenemies, and it wasn't because she had the longest hair in the junior class. Nope. Try the entire high school. Well, she used to. It also used to be a shiny black, the same as her dad's.

Not anymore.

The plump hairdresser, decked out in polka dots and pinup heels, whisked the dark cape away with a flourish, then combed her painted fingernails through Miki's tresses, as if she couldn't let go of her masterpiece, her baby. Miki stared wide-eyed into the mirror and even after three grueling hours in the swivel chair, she still didn't move. Finally, with tentative hands, she sifted through the blunt ends that swung around her shoulders.

"You like it, don't you, honey?" The hairdresser's thinly sculpted brows edged up into her bumper bangs. "It's what you wanted, right?"

It was. Mermaid Blue like the picture. Aqua ends that graduated up to her natural black roots.

"Is it the color? Is it the length?" The hairdresser clacked her glossy nails together. "Because thick hair like yours grows fast."

"I could kiss you." Miki jumped out of the chair, sending the woman back on her heels. "I love it." She beamed in the mirror and fluffed her hair again. It was different, beautiful even.

More importantly, it wasn't long or black.

Dad would be pissed.

Miki'd raced from the salon all the way home to pluck her brows, fight with her mom, and stare holes in the front door. She flicked her eyes at the clock above the mantel again, then back to the same spot on the door, the one her dad should have knocked on forty minutes ago. Some birthday.

Normally, she embraced the virtue of patience, but since he hadn't bothered to see her in six weeks, her eager anticipation slowly turned into festering dejection. Why'd he even bother to call if he was only going to stand her up?

No. He wouldn't. He's the one who said, "It's my day. I'm taking you to lunch." Visitation rights and all that. It was her birthday; he'd remember.

Miki checked her phone again and waited. She spun the black, woven bracelet on her wrist around and around, staring even bigger holes in the door. She yawned—

Boom! Boom! Boom!

—and jumped at the loud pounding on the door that only a meaty fist could make. She breathed in through her nose, fluffed her dye job, and flung the door wide with a beaming smile.

10

"Hi, Dad," Miki said brightly and lifted her hand to flip at her hair, but her dad pressed into the room with his broad shoulders and looked around.

"Hey, Miki-Lou. Your mother here?" he asked gruffly.

"Upstairs." She let her hand drop. "Why?"

"Good!" Dad turned on his boot heel. "Let's get outta here before she comes down. Your brother's waiting in the truck."

That was that. No double-take. No wide-eyed gasp. No screeching, *You paid how much?* No wailing, *Your beautiful hair!* And certainly, no begrudging compliment, *I'm sure I'll get used to it, eventually.* All that had been reserved for her mom.

She climbed into the extended cab and wedged herself between a pile of balled-up hamburger wrappers and an errant set of jumper cables. Her brother, Owen, slouched in the front seat, barely acknowledging her. He was five years older, twenty-two, and thought he was God's gift to society; he couldn't tear his eyes off Mr. Good Looking in the side mirror.

"Guess who's in the hospital this time?" he muttered at the passenger window as he stroked his chiseled jaw.

Hospital! Who cared? Probably another case of rally road rash or monkey-wrenching elbow.

"Wait...is that what we're doing?" She flung her hands out and gaped at the back of her dad's head. His black hair curled damply along his neck as if he'd stepped out of the shower and toweled it dry about ten minutes ago. He turned the key in the ignition, and the truck rumbled at the ready. "I thought this was my birthday lunch."

She was a Gemini, so she appreciated the unusual, but please-please-*please*, for the love of God, don't let her celebrate turning seventeen by eating packaged food in a hospital cafeteria!

"Calm down, Mik," Dad muttered and tapped the brakes at a four-way stop. He cranked the steering wheel into a sharp left turn and gassed it up Pill Hill toward the hospital. "It's only a pit stop. Then we'll be on our way. Badger Paw burgers like we said."

Surely, they knew they were playing with fire. Lack of food made her irrational. Nobody escaped her wrath, so they'd better be prepared to throw in a double order of onion rings and a large strawberry milkshake because she was starving. Miki rubbed soothing circles over her empty stomach. The lunch hour had come and gone.

The truck bounced over a speed bump as Dad swerved into a parking space near the broad awning that marked the hospital's main entrance. He stomped on the e-brake and slid out.

"Hey, Dad." Owen planted his feet on the asphalt and turned back. "What are the deets on the ride Bill's pulling together?"

"Later." Dad leaned into the truck. "Mik, hand me my cut, would ya?" Miki hefted his worn leather vest over the seat and watched him slip into biker mode. He patted the front pocket of his jeans for his keys, like he always did and then grabbed the door, ready to shut it in her face.

"Hey! A little help here!" Miki yelled and rattled the headrest. Those two were going to leave her behind like an old hamburger wrapper. Thanks a lot, Dad.

"What?" His face warmed with a laugh as he levered the seat forward. "You thought we forgot about the birthday girl?"

Uh, yeah. She did. Miki scowled as she squeezed out from behind the front seat, and for a little *extra* satisfaction, she slammed the truck door a little *extra* hard.

She quickened her pace across the parking lot to keep up and glared at the fraying club patch in front of her as the sliding-glass doors whirred open and closed. The patch was a spiked-out motorcycle rim embroidered with thick, gold threads against a black background. The flaming wheel represented the Hides of Hell Motorcycle Club, and it mocked her from the back of her dad's leather vest as she trudged after him and Owen like a second-class citizen.

Not even Owen said anything about her new look. Didn't blue hair warrant a second glance, a nod, or at least some kind of comment? Long black to short blue was a big change, and those two seemed oblivious.

Well, apparently just oblivious to her, because they clomped right past the reception desk and jumped on the elevator like they knew where they were going, and of course, she followed along like she had a bull ring in her nose, which she did not. Not yet.

Her dad jabbed the button for the fifth floor, and while the elevator creaked up and up, Miki studied her brother's pin-striped back. He wasn't decked out in his black leathers today but instead wore his signature charcoal vest. The rest of the suit was long gone. He'd torched it in the parking lot after he'd gotten fired from his sales job over a year ago. Story was he'd grabbed a "pencil neck" by the throat and threatened to kill the guy for stealing leftovers from the fridge. When security escorted Owen outside the building, he'd stripped off his clothes and lit them on fire while everyone stared in horror out of their office windows.

The elevator groaned past the fourth floor, and Miki shifted her eyes to her dad's patch. He beamed at every opportunity to recount his version of the story, like how he'd raced his bike ahead of the cops to pick up Owen, who'd stood in his tighty-whities and in that same tailored vest. Miki could totally picture him with a cigarette between his lips and the lighter in his hand. Dad couldn't have been more proud of his son than on that day.

Owen flipped off corporate America and slid into the Hides of Hell like he was riding on an oil slick. Dad, a.k.a. Leo the Lion, was the H.O.H. president and welcomed his son with open arms. Their love was a beautiful thing.

Gag!

The elevator chimed, and the doors creaked open on the fifth floor. The soles of their heavy boots clunked against the light-gray linoleum and resounded off the equally gray walls in the hospital's sterile corridor, and she followed along in her own boots like a minion.

"Who are we here to see again?" Miki asked, scanning the rooms for a McDreamy doctor or a nurse serving Jell-O shots. Last time she'd been at the hospital was six months ago when she'd driven Flossy, the club's mechanic, here. He'd crushed his thumb between a V-twin engine and a hard place, and it'd burst like a cherry tomato. He'd wailed so loudly she almost ran his car into the ER. Good times.

Dad stopped abruptly, and Miki face planted with his flaming wheel patch inside a dimly lit room. It was eerily quiet except for hushed voices in the hall, swishing fabric, and soft pinging noises. She peered around her dad's shoulder to see a pasty-white body lying against an even whiter pillow. Her heart somersaulted.

Will Sullivan!

Miki pushed past her dad and Owen and clutched the bedside bars next to Will. His dark lashes cast long, spiky shadows down his pale cheeks, and his lips hung lax and open, even as she bumped the hard splint on his arm like a klutz. His discolored fingers, reddish-purple and green, poked out the end. No more green survival bracelet; it had been replaced by white cotton and gauze.

She still wore her black one and slowly twisted it around her wrist. It had been nearly a year since she'd seen Will. It was last summer when his mom died. Since then, he'd managed to drift out of sight for good.

"Hi, Will," she murmured and watched his lids, waiting for them to blink open to show her those melty-licious brown eyes. But he didn't move.

"The jerk-off is lucky," Owen said, stroking his skull cap of black hair. "His face is pretty banged up. Reminds me of the time I roughed him up for ya. Remember, Mik? You were crying." He chuckled like this was the time or the place.

"I cried because you beat him up," Miki said and studied the scabbed gashes from Will's temple down to his cheek. Standard biker fare; it looked like he'd used his face to wipe up some asphalt. She leaned over and touched his jaw lightly where some bruising had turned a sick yellow. What happened to him?

"Oh, it wasn't so bad," Dad said.

"He was thirteen!" Miki glared at her dad as he stepped closer to the bed. How could he stand there and defend Owen? "I don't think a high schooler should hit a little kid—"

"Owen popped him one and gave him a bloody nose is all." Dad loomed like a tower, rubbing his black whiskers while his dark eyes roamed over Will's feeble body. He pursed his lips and circled the bed. "Will's gonna be all right. It's a rough patch, and the brotherhood's gonna see him through it."

"He deserved the lick he got, believe me." Owen grunted and kicked out a plastic chair, dropping his weight onto it. He tucked his hands into his armpits, and his unbuttoned vest fell open over a white dress shirt. The cuffs were rolled up to his elbows, showing off lean forearms and his ornate eagle tattoo. "He never bothered you again, did he? Huh?" Owen's eyebrow twitched in one of those cocky smirks. "No, I didn't think so."

"You're right. He never bothered me again." Miki rolled her bulbous skull rings against her palm like they were a set of brass knuckles instead of silver-plated jewelry. If she could slug her brother in the face *and* get away with it, she would.

Why did she have to be related to Owen, again? Oh, right. Because if Mom would have divorced her dad when she'd wanted to, Miki would never have been born. Thankfully, her mom stuck it out for makeup sex. Unfortunately, Miki'd been brought into a crazy, dysfunctional family with a chauvinistic biker dad, a brother with anger issues, and a bitter mother who complained about the first two all the time.

Miki yearned for normal, and Will with his scratched-up face and broken arm was…okay, not normal, but his roots ran deep. Not to mention, he had the tall, dark, and broody thing going on. He carried an internal strength, even though currently he had the external look of a puffed marshmallow. Will knew what he wanted...or didn't want in her case. If he opened his eyes right now, he would definitely say something about her hair. Good, bad, or indifferent. But he would notice.

She hadn't seen her crush for nearly a year, and with his scabbed body and his matted hospital hair, he still gave her goosebumps.

"I'm here, Will," she whispered into his face, waiting for a sign like an eye spasm or a finger twitch. "Can you hear me?"

"Leave the poor guy alone," Dad said, then pointed to a cluttered side table with a pink barf basin. "Bill and Liam must've brought his stuff. Gameboy, chargers, some music gizmo...a laptop."

"Gadget freak," Owen muttered.

Dad picked through a basket of comic books and candy. Then he opened his jacket and pulled out a thin paper bag the size of a magazine. He tucked it under the rest of the stuff, making sure it was covered, and with a sly smile said, "That'll keep him entertained."

"What is it?" Miki frowned. Was there a card? Because no one asked her to sign it.

"Nothing you'd be interested in." Owen shifted his dark eyes to Dad, and they snickered into their palms like mischievous children. Those two really were the same, but instead of two peas in a pod, they were two ball bearings in a crankcase.

Miki lost interest in their innuendos and inside jokes and let her eyes roam Will's marred skin. The only unscathed places with no scratches, no scabs, no bruises, and no gauze were the very tips of his fingers. She touched them gently.

17

After the memorial service, Miki had reached out to Will with a text or two—okay, more like twenty—to draw him out from under his rock to show him people cared. To show him *she* cared.

Nada. He never wrote back. He never called. All she heard was the cracking of her own desperate heart. It was like he'd fallen into a black hole.

Or maybe she had.

CHAPTER 3

LIMBO

William Robert Sullivan! If I catch you even taking a sip of beer, I'll ground you for the rest of your life! Goodbye laptop, goodbye Internet and all your video games. I'll take your phone away, too, and I'll never make apple pie for you again!

His mom's voice broke on a sob, and Will squinted through a blur, half expecting and mostly wanting to see his mom there. He could almost visualize her standing at the foot of the metal bed with her hip cocked out and her finger wagging, a familiar vision of pissed-offedness. How many times had he been grounded for life? Too many to count. So what'd he do this time?

It wasn't the beer because it was like a staple in his family. The bikers drank it along with their wives—for the most part—and the kids took turns sneaking a can or two. Nobody batted an eye. So what was this really about? Helmet? He'd been a very ripe sixteen-year-old with kidney failure. It wasn't Will's fault her old cat died. If anyone should be fuming mad, it should be him. She's the one who croaked and left him, Liam, and Dad to splinter like a broken bottle. Then her damned cat had to go—

Mom…wait!

I'm sorry.

He blinked, and the room came into focus, gray walls, metal trays, white sheets. A woman with a short cap of blonde hair like his mom's hovered over him.

"Mom." Will tried to reach out to her, but his right arm was trapped under a boulder. When he did manage to lift it, a shard of pain ripped through his forearm like a bolt of lightning. His entire body caught on fire, and he fell back against the pillows.

"Will, are you in pain? Can you describe it for me? Zero being no pain and—"

"Ten." Will groaned again. It hurt inside and out. While everything below his neck fried, everything above froze as if he'd plunged his head into a cooler of ice water. Suddenly, it went dark.

Then it was light again.

Will couldn't keep track of the time or the faces. People wearing bright cotton filtered in to nudge and prod at him, followed by a wave of dark leathers, who scratched their beards, dropped f-bombs, and evaporated back into the light. Somewhere in between it all, Will hovered between deep sleep and trying to wake up.

This time, he broke through the film and opened his eyes. He smacked his lips with a grimace and slowly inhaled a mixture of chicken broth, orange Jell-O, antiseptic, and Band-Aids. Oh, God. His guts roiled.

"There he is," a gravelly voice said. Then Dad stepped up to the end of the bed, but instead of wagging his finger like Mom would have done, his hands were tucked into his front pockets. He stood with his elbows jutting out like wings on a gigantic furry moth. His salt-and-pepper hair was loosely scraped back while his matching beard hung banded down his front like a long, segmented rope.

"Dad?" Will's voice cracked, and he tilted his head for a better view.

"I'm here, too," Liam said from a corner of the room.

"Dad, I don't feel so good. I...I might hurl."

"Here." His brother materialized and pushed past Dad to set a kidney-shaped bowl next to Will's neck. He wore his familiar camo baseball hat over short brown hair and an unfamiliar—Will squinted. What the...? It looked like a caterpillar had crawled under his nose. Was Liam trying to grow a 'stache? If so, major weak.

"Welcome back," Liam said. "We were all starting to get worried, like maybe you'd slipped into some kind of coma. After you get outta here, be prepared to have your ass kicked for the stunt you pulled. You could've killed yourself drunk driving, you prick, not to mention you totaled your bike." He threw his hands up. "Now what? The rally starts this weekend."

Rally? Who cared? Will never went to those things anyway.

"I got somethin' to say, Liam." Dad announced, pulling his hands free. "I want to get it out there quick, before Will conks out again."

"Okay, Dad." Liam scrutinized a nearly empty water bottle on the side table. He picked it up. "Go ahead. I'll get Will some water."

His brother headed for the bathroom, and a triangle of light spilled through the doorway, illuminating the gloom. The blinds had been pulled down, and it seemed like whatever sky was on the other side had turned to twilight. It could be time for an early breakfast or maybe a late dinner for all he knew.

Will rolled his head slowly back to his dad. He had something to say?

When their brown eyes connected, his dad nodded.

"Alright." Dad cleared his throat and lowered his gaze. His ram-like shoulders grew even bigger as he sucked in a huge breath. When he looked up, he'd turned into a mountain, and his eyes focused somewhere above Will's head. This was the look of impenetrable force. He'd made up his mind about something, and there would be no negotiations and no changing it. This was the precursor to the standard "Sit up and pay attention because I'm not sayin' it twice" talk.

Will shifted and tried to get more vertical, but his head spun. He reached up and stroked the edge of the barf basin for comfort before sinking back into the pillow with a grunt.

"Will, my son, things have to change. It's time to move on. I met this woman, and…" He cursed under his breath and rubbed his forehead as his brown eyes scrolled down to meet Will's head on. "Not like what you're probably thinking. Nothing serious. We talked, and something she said made me realize—It's just…" He turned away to holler toward the bathroom. "What was it your Aunt K said?"

"Just tell him about the ashes, Dad," Liam said with the water bottle in his hand. He came around the bed and set it down.

"We're taking Mom's ashes when we head to the rally. This will be her last ride, son. We're *all* going, and we're setting her free, understand? And the damned slice of apple pie is coming with us. You hear me, Will?"

The hell it is. If only he could sit up, shake his fist, and yell, but he couldn't even move his pinkie. "No," he croaked. Plain and simple.

Dad lifted a stocky finger and pointed it at him. It shook slightly, and the words "Don't tell me no" were written all over his face. "Yes," he said, his voice dark and full of emotion.

"My apple pie." Will closed his eyes.

"Shit, Dad. He's stoned. Is he even going to remember this conversation?"

"Will! I'm serious now. Your mom's ashes and apple pie. There's no going back. Wait…Will! Liam and I are leaving early in the morning. We have to make a drop off, and your Aunt K's planning…can you hear me?"

"I think he passed out," Liam muttered. "Now what do we do?"

His dad sighed wearily. "Call your Uncle Shorty, I guess."

The last word Will heard before drifting off was another f-bomb.

"Hey kid. Who are you?" A man's voice said quietly from the mist.

Will pried his eyes open, expecting to see a male nurse or maybe even a winged angel hovering above his bed. But instead of teal scrubs, the unfamiliar dude was dressed all in black and was ugly as hell with a tuft of bleached hair on top of his bald melon. Hey, it's Mr. Clean wearing a kitchen sponge. Funny, but Will couldn't laugh. His heart was too busy accelerating with a punch of adrenaline. Somehow, it seemed like fight or flight time, only he couldn't move to do either.

"What's your name?" Ugly Dude grinned, and his teeth were bright like stars as if he'd double-downed on the chemicals to whiten them. Or maybe he'd bumped into someone's fist one too many times, and they were all fake. "I bet you're somebody important, aren't you?" he whispered, sounding kind of creepy.

"No," Will rasped, trying to keep his mind focused and to stay out of the misty cloud.

"I dunno. You've had a lot of interesting visitors. You're popular," he murmured, his crystal blue eyes leaving Will's face to rove around the room. He pinched a get-well card from the side table and read it. "Will," he said. Rubber-soled shoes squeaked down the hallway, and the guy cocked his shaved head toward the door as he carefully set the card back, either listening or waiting.

Was this guy lost? Will tried to swallow past the growing lump in his throat. Or was he about to get suffocated by his own pillow like in a mobster flick? His eyes slid down to the guy's battered hands where bluish skeletal tattoos marred the backs of his fingers along with the letters PS.

Pulver Skulls.

Oh, God, this was it. He was gonna get his ass pummeled. Will closed his eyes and let the morphine take him away.

Will unhinged his jaw and tried to pry his thick tongue off the roof of his mouth. Water. Just a drop. Sounds filtered into his consciousness, a creaking chair, swishing fabric, rubber soles on the floor. Then there was the comforting smell of vanilla, like perfume. He wasn't alone.

Was it the nurse?

"Will. Are you awake?" A woman's soft voice drifted through the fog into his ears. "Here, drink this." Gentle hands lifted his head and cool water dribbled across his lips.

He sipped slowly and opened his eyes to a familiar face surrounded by wispy gray curls peering down at him, his behavioral science teacher.

"Mrs. Norton."

"Oh, stop it, Will." She shook her head, and her hair shimmied against her shoulders. "School's out. You have an entire summer to call me Aunt K again. I'm glad to see you haven't lost your sense of humor." She pushed up her round glasses and smiled. "Listen, the nurse had to dial the morphine back quite a bit, okay? Seems to me you've been asleep way more than you've been awake, so I think you might be sensitive to it. But that should be fine since we want you off it today, anyway. How's the pain now?"

"Aunt K, I think I have to take a piss—"

"Oh, dear, of course! You'll need some help in case you're light-headed. Have you had a bowel movement yet? If not, I'll ask the nurse about a laxative. Try it on your own first—"

"How's it going, Willy-boy?" A voice boomed from the doorway.

"Hey." Will eased up on his elbow and grinned at his Uncle Shorty while thanking God for the interruption.

25

Holy crap…laxatives? Aunt K may be his dad's sister, but he wasn't going to discuss taking a dump with her, no matter how perky he felt.

"You fared better than your bike, at least," Uncle Shorty said and stepped into the room, looking like his usual spiffy self with a clean-shaven mug and closely trimmed white hair. He was a professional tax accountant by day and a hardened Hides of Hell biker by night. Following him was a rumor he could break a man's face with his middle finger. So even though he stood at five-foot-seven, calling him Shorty was the extent of the height jokes.

Aunt K stepped toward her husband, and the beads at her wrist jangled as she rested her hand on his sleeve. His polished leather hung unzipped over a tucked-in gray t-shirt with a pocket on the front for his smokes. She whispered something into his ear, and he pulled her in close as his eyes flicked from Will to the bathroom door and back again. He nodded affirmative.

"Okay," Aunt K said loudly, giving Uncle Shorty an affectionate pat. "I'm going to find the nurse and a strong cup of coffee in that order. I'll see you two down in the lobby whenever you're ready. Take your time."

"Let's find out what needs to happen for a quick checkout. You're ready to bust out of this joint, aren't you, Will?" He dropped his palm onto the blankets covering Will's lower leg making him clench down on a queasy groan. Uncle Shorty jerked his hand back. "Sorry. Forgot about the road rash. Hell of an accident, Willy-boy. Listen…" he glanced back over his shoulder, watching as Aunt K left the room before scraping a plastic chair closer to Will's bed.

He sat and leaned forward like something weighed heavily on his mind. Will mentally crossed his legs and searched for the ever-elusive happy place he heard other people talk about while his bladder screamed for relief.

"Here's the thing." Uncle Shorty tapped his steepled fingers together, his large knuckles flexing as he studied Will's face.

"The thing?" Will raised his eyebrows as he reclined, ready to exercise good listening skills and patience.

To hell with it. His bladder needed immediate attention. Emotionally prepared to bolt, hobble, or crawl for the john, he threw the covers aside and stopped. Thick scabs covered the length of his left leg, and if he bent his knee, those things would crack wide open. Will's stomach slipped around his insides, and he panted to keep the scant water in his belly.

"Willy-boy, you okay?" Uncle Shorty murmured. "Are you in pain?"

Sure, he was sore, but what got him were the crunchy abrasions woven into the dark hair from his thigh to his ankle. That sharp turn onto Cat-O'Mountain Road did this to him. He should have slowed down, worn his leathers, a helmet, gone to bed, or better yet, skipped the last bottle of beer. It was the horde of bikers at his house, laughing it up and having a good time when they should've still been mourning. It was those damned cat kidneys and the vet who said, "There's no cure." So the answer was yes. He was in pain.

"I'm gonna explode. Could you help me?" Will dropped his chin and squeezed his eyes shut.

"In a minute. I wanted to tell you that the Hides of Hell is a brotherhood, and even though you're not a patched member—"

"Or a prospect...or a hang-around...or *interested*—"

"Okay, I get it. You're none of those things, but you're still family. So when you're down, your dad's down, and the brothers, we feel it, too. So in essence, your bad attitude directly affects the club. Your dad is ready to let your mother go, and so is Liam."

"Liam, too, huh?" What a traitor. Will narrowed his eyes and looked away. So they were all ganging up on him, trying to force him to feel something he didn't—to bury his memories and forget his own mother.

"That's right. They both want to get back to the land of the living, so it means all eyes are on you. We're all standing behind your dad. It's time for you to move on... and guess what? We're all on board to see that you do."

"So all you badasses have nothing better to do than to stand around talking about me? How you gonna do it, Uncle Shorty? What's the plan? Tie me up in the torture chair and beat me with a baseball bat until I start thinkin' like you?"

"Worse." Uncle Shorty sat back with a grin plastered across his face. "You have a choice. We're not complete barbarians, after all. Come to the rally with us. The ride is dedicated to your mom and will be a special event all around."

"What's the other option?" Will had to take a leak so bad he shivered. Fight the urge, dude. Just hold it.

"You either come with us, or I'm leaving you here with your Aunt K, and believe me, she's got big plans for you. Rehab, AA, intensive outpatient programs...you should see all the brochures piled up on our kitchen table." He blew out a low whistle.

"I'm not an alcoholic," Will muttered. Some choice! Snivel with a bunch of soft-boiled psychiatrists or take an asphalt trip with a pack of gossiping mongrels. His eyes burned as he wiggled his foot to keep from pissing himself. How long was this conversation going to take, anyway?

"Your Aunt K thinks you need help, and she's prepared to make everyone's life a living hell over it, and I'm married to the woman! Whatever you decide, I'll be hearing about it, got it? Big problems are brewing with the club, yet your name is the one always bubbling to the top. Every chance you had to get your shit together, you foundered. Now, it's our turn. We're gonna get your shit together for you. How does that sound?"

"Like you're assuming I'll ride with you guys." Will lifted his cast off the bedding to awkwardly cross his arms, and it sat hard and heavy on his chest. Rides and rallies. Will scoffed. The Hides of Hell crew grabbed at any excuse to let loose and party. His mom's death was not something to celebrate.

"Come on, Willy-boy. Don't be stupid. You're lucky you're gettin' this opportunity."

"Let's say I do decide to go…" Will lifted his plastered forearm, and his fingers stuck out the end, yellow and green from left-over bruising. "I can't drive with one arm, and I'm kinda sure after horizontally parking my bike, it's in no condition for a long haul."

"We've got a ride lined up for you. You come to the rally—"

"Who…my dad? No? Then it's Liam. Bet he loves that…" Will spouted—talk about cramping his brother's style—then frowned when Uncle Shorty shook his white head.

"Bill had to leave early for important club business, and Liam went with him. They were both here yesterday to see you. Don't you remember?"

Vaguely.

"Better not be Caboose 'cause I won't ride with him." There was no way Will would wrap his arms around a barrel of a guy who had fuzz growing out his nooks and crannies, from his ear holes on down to his plumber's crack. Caboose wasn't a patched member or even a prospect...just a hang-around. Then, there was Flossy. He wouldn't even consider it, and Owen would kill him for shits and giggles. Leo? No way. Trip? He was a prospect. So sure, Trip. Maybe.

"Jesus, Willy-boy. You'd be lucky if Caboose'd let you ride bitch with him. We all love ya, kid, but nobody wants you on the back of their bike, so check the attitude. You're gonna spread your mom's ashes like your dad wants, and however we get you there, is how you get there. Got it? Now, that's better than sitting in a room, spilling your guts into big ears, isn't it?"

Will grunted.

"Good. Our job is to make sure you get to the rally safe and sound. Everything else is taken care of. Remember, when your Aunt K pumps you for info you're on board, you're going to quit drinking, and this is your big turnaround. So embrace it. It's gonna happen." He kicked his legs out and relaxed into the plastic chair. His leather jacket fell to his sides, and he reached in for a pack of Marlboros.

"I need to use the bathroom," Will said, trying to keep the desperate thread out of his voice.

"All you need is some fried chicken and a gallon of water. Then, you'll be right as rain." Uncle Shorty stood, poked an unlit cigarette between his lips, and patted his leather pocket. "What I need is a smoke. I'm gonna find your Aunt K, and we'll see about getting you discharged for good behavior." He chuckled, and his boots knocked against the linoleum floor as he left the room.

CHAPTER 4

NICE TOUCH

Checkout didn't happen as efficiently as everyone anticipated. Uncle Shorty was called in for some SNAFU at the club, and Aunt K couldn't reach Will's dad when signatures were needed, and insurance cards had to be dealt with—and, and, and.

Will didn't care. He didn't want to leave, anyway. Was it wrong to prefer staying in a place where he didn't have to do anything but sleep, watch YouTube, surf the internet, and check out the nurses? Sure, he was lazy, unmotivated, and a sidekick in his own story. So what?

Not to mention the drugs. Oh, yeah, they were a nice touch. It kept Mom out of his head along with everything else. He might have heard her voice once or twice, but for the most part, the morphine days were spent drifting through a mind-bending fog where things were blissfully vacant. A lot of time went by unaccounted for. It was hell.

Not really...it was awesome.

He was going to miss this place.

Of course, all good things had to come to an end, and the bad news? Yesterday, they'd dialed back on the juice, so it was only a matter of time before things went back to normal. Mom would get chatty, and now there would be Helmet to contend with, too. He'd probably yowl every night around dinner time, per his usual.

The good news? Will had a prescription for pain meds that read, "Do not operate heavy equipment." Oh, yeah. Sounded about right.

He eased his scabby leg over the side of the bed and stilled while his brain got settled in the vertical position. No more lying around. It was time to get dressed. Uncle Shorty had made a brief appearance, dropping off some fresh clothes, but he didn't bother to stick around. What if Will fell on his face trying to get his underwear on?

When both feet touched the cold floor, he sucked air through his clenched teeth because not only did he have road rash down his back and leg, he had asphalt ass, a bruised spleen, a cracked ulna, a sprained thumb, and a broken pinkie toe—and the little mother hurt. He could practically hear his buddy, J.J., saying, *You're chunky salsa, man.*

No argument here, dude. Will studied his purple toe and knew he looked as bad as he felt, like a hot mess.

Getting dressed was going to take forever.

"Dude." He held up a pair of baggy green sweatpants. He was gonna look like a class-A dork. The next six weeks of summer were going to suck. With this green cast on his forearm, there would be no swimming at the lake, no sunbathing in the sand, no video games with a bum thumb, and he probably couldn't type on a keyboard either. He would be reduced to a book-reading, TV-watching, house-bound hermit.

Hmm, it didn't sound so bad.

After a ten-minute struggle getting his boxer briefs and sweatpants on, he gave up on the t-shirt in favor of a five-minute break. Surely, the nurse would take pity on him. Somebody had to.

"Need some help, Will?" Speak of the devil. The curvy girl with the pretty face pushed a wheelchair into his room. She was a super-sweet redhead with freckles reminding him of Suzy, a girl he used to like. Briefly. Suzy didn't wear leather. No, she was reserved and classy with long hair piled on top of her head. She was the type of girl he wanted to like, someone as far from the biker world as possible.

"I'm going to miss this place," he said. "I bet no one ever says it, but it's true."

"Lift your arm. Here…" She tugged the white t-shirt sleeve over his cast. "Everything will be fine once you get home. Your body needs to heal, Will, and to do that, it needs lots of rest. Go ahead and sit in the wheelchair. I'll put your socks on."

Her warm fingers were gentle on his elbow as she guided him, and he smiled. He sort of had a thing for nurses. He used to love playing doctor with the girls at the clubhouse when he was a kid. The boys would run off to play jailbreak, while Will pretended to moan in pain, loving the soft hands poking and patting him. *Where does it hurt, Will? Here or here? Hmm, it's a bad case of hairy-mole-itis disease. Looks like surgery. Bring me the wrench!* Music to his ears. Surgery was the best, followed by a sponge bath and a fake cast.

"I want to remind you…you have a bruised spleen, so take it easy, and no heavy lifting or jarring activities. Here." She handed him a ream of papers and cupped his shoulder with a nurturing touch. "This covers follow-up appointments and activities to avoid. Watch out for chest pain, dizziness, a bloated feeling in your stomach…read this. Okay?"

"I don't want to go home," Will muttered. Who would take care of him? Poke and pat him and ask him where it hurts? No one, not even Helmet.

"Hey, you're going to be fine." She nudged the wheelchair brakes with her toe. "You're a quick healer. Amazing, really. Your aunt and uncle are here to take care of you, and I can tell you're in good hands. Ready?" He took one more look around the room. His uncle had packed off the wicker basket of cards and magazines along with his electronics. The room wasn't his anymore. It was empty, and he was being kicked out of his comfy nest.

"You could always adopt me. I don't do yard work, but I'm good with pets. Animals love me." Will turned to give the nurse a pleading look, and she laughed, a sound which lightened his spirits infinitesimally.

"Oh, Will. We'll miss you around here." She stepped behind the chair and eased him out the door, gentle and sure.

Like the drugs, she had a nice touch.

Once outside, Uncle Shorty pulled into the loop with his one-ton truck, all gleaming white and polished chrome. Will carefully bent his leg while hefting himself up into the passenger seat with no help from his uncle.

"All set?" Uncle Shorty climbed into the cab, turned the key in the ignition, and drove the eight yards it took to pull into the first parking spot. Then, he cut the engine.

"What're you doing?" Why were they parking at the hospital when they should be leaving it?

"I need a smoke," Uncle Shorty said and nodded to the bikers lurking in the shadows.

Another one? C'mon, they were only three miles from his house. Oh, well. Did it really matter? He could sit in the truck as easily as he could sit at home.

"Can you at least crack the window before you go? I need some fresh air."

"You barf in my cab, I break-a-your face." Uncle Shorty laughed like he was joking. Right. Will wasn't worried though because even at his drunkest he managed to blow it outside. Just ask J.J. who had to clean it off the side of his truck on more than one occasion.

The window rolled down as his uncle muttered something about being quick. He eased out, slammed the truck door, and crossed the short stretch of parking lot to the sidewalk of waiting leathers.

Leo the Lion stood there with a couple other guys in the shadows, greeting Uncle Shorty with a round of grunts and chin nods. Leo used to be the V.P. but was now acting president since Dad sorta checked out. After Mom died, Dad couldn't perform his presidential duties, like sorting out the drama queens, griefing on the rivals, and attending to sketchy club business. What was Leo doing here anyway? Surely, he had more important things to do than hang around the hospital.

Uncle Shorty lit his cigarette, then casually blew out a stream of gray smoke like he was about to hang ten with his buddies, yet all the while, his blue eyes covertly scanned the parking lot. The others stood with low brows over dark shades. Things looked a little tense over there.

Will tilted his head back, closed his eyes, and thought about puking. Not here and now, but all over J.J.'s passenger door the last time in the meadow. Must have been real fun scrubbing chunks off the paint job. Did he ever apologize for it? Did he have to? Probably not, because J.J. got it. He understood that if the tables were turned, Will would have his back. That's what friends were for.

"The drop-off went smooth. He called in, said he had a tail, and we haven't heard from him since." Leo's words drifted by. "And coincidentally, a couple P's were seen milling around here. I'm getting a bad vibe. Not good."

Will opened his eyes and studied the air vent on the dash while he focused on what the guys were saying. Who hadn't they heard from? Who were they talking about? P's was short for P-Scum or P-Skulls, all nicknames for the rival club, the Pulver Skulls.

It took a while before Uncle Shorty acknowledged that he heard Leo. Then he said, "Anything else?"

"So what're we gonna do?" another voice murmured.

"Not here." Leo's voice rumbled. "But I'm looking at an earlier departure."

"Agreed," Uncle Shorty said. "I'll get my side together, and you—

"Yup. I'll do the same." Leo cut in. "We'll meet later."

Will strained to hear the grunts of acceptance followed by a cryptic discussion on preferred hardware, women, and who was going to the rally.

The rally. Will closed his eyes again. He didn't want to go. He'd have to ride on the back of someone else's bike like an old lady. God, he'd never hear the end of it. What's more, they expected him to let go of his mom's ashes, her last slice of apple pie, and he'd have to quit drinking. They'd make him remember what he wanted to forget and make him forget what he wanted to remember, and he didn't want any part of it.

What he did want was to be left alone.

Spending a week with thirty, fifty, maybe even a hundred bikers up in his grill sounded less and less appealing. If he stayed behind, he could have the entire house to himself, negotiate the AA meetings with Aunt K, and bluff his way through any therapy she might have planned. One or two meetings a week sounded way better than 24-7 with a bunch of dudes in leather. As it turned out, Uncle Shorty sucked as a nurse. Who would take care of him? Aunt K, that's who.

Will started to drift off when the truck door flew open on the driver's side, and Uncle Shorty dropped in on a cloud of Marlboro smoke. He raked his teeth across his lower lip and slung his wrist over the noon-spot on the steering wheel.

"What's up?" Will pulled out of his slouch.

"Does your phone still work, Willy-boy?" He didn't look at Will but watched Leo and the guys mount their bikes and gun it out of the parking lot. Their engines roared like a giant beast leaving behind a wake of fear and excitement. "Just wonderin' since it was all beat up."

"No, the screen's shattered, and it won't hold a charge. Why? Is everything all right?"

"You bet." He turned the key in the ignition and shifted into drive. "We're going to make one stop, so you can pick up your pain meds and anything else you need for the road. Toothpaste, fresh socks, deodorant if you wear it, whatever. Then, I'm dropping you off at home. You got a bug-out bag?"

"Sort of."

"Pack the essentials. Keep it light and tight. Got it?" His lips were set in a grim line in parallel with his brows. "Don't forget your mom's ashes and the container of apple pie. We all know about it, and it's makin' the trip."

Will glanced down at the bright green cast wrapped around his arm and thumb. A nap in his own bed sounded way better than a five-hour bike ride, playing shield in the wind, in the dust, in the bugs, cross-country in someone's bitch seat. And with these guys, he'd probably be hanging on for dear life the entire time.

Going on this ride? Not gonna happen. But by the look on Uncle Shorty's face, now wasn't the time to tell him.

"Right..." Will needed to steer the conversation into a more tolerable direction. "So...uh...where's Aunt K?"

"She's taken care of," Uncle Shorty said.

Will lifted his brows. Was the guy serious? What was "taken care of" supposed to mean? "What...like bound and gagged?"

Uncle Shorty chuckled, and the mood lightened. "You know the saying about catching more flies with honey, not vinegar?"

"Hey." Will lifted his good palm. "I don't want to know what you guys are into."

"Now, I'm not saying your Aunt K's a fly. No, no, she's one hot mama—"

"Dude." Stop. Will shook his head with disgust.

"What I'm saying is...women like sweet talk." He glanced across the cab. "Remember my words when you're picking up chicks."

"Right. I'll add it to my list. One, find a chick. Two, add some honey."

"All you need to know is she's on board. She knows the value of the brotherhood." He flipped the blinker on, guided the truck into an easy turn, and braked in front of the pharmacy. "You can thank me later. Now..." He dug into his back pocket and pulled out a flattened leather wallet. "Here's a twenty. Get in, get out. We've got places to be."

"I've got a bruised spleen and a broken arm. I've been out of the hospital for twenty minutes, and you want me to go in there and buy my own shit?" Will held up his cast and frowned.

"Like I said, get in, get out. You need to toughen up, Willy-boy."

CHAPTER 5

TAIL PIPES

The peach floral couch with matching throw pillows or his own bed wrapped in Gram's denim quilt? Decisions, decisions. God, it was good to be home. Everything was the same, except poor Helmet wasn't here taking up space, and Dad and Liam were gone. Probably at the rally by now, setting up an art tent.

Liam spent the last year refurbishing old helmets and Harley gas tanks with a fresh coat of metal flake paint and custom art. His apprenticeships, one at Candy Coating Paints and the other at Blinky's Tattoo, were paying off. Now, he had his own stash of merchandise to sell under the Burnout Rally big tents. The vintage biker crowd loved that stuff.

Why hadn't Dad called? What about Liam? It seemed sorta rude, but of course, his phone was broken. Maybe they'd tried. But c'mon, one hospital visit, then taking off before he was even conscious seemed kinda cold. Uncle Shorty said they had "club business," and Will knew not to question it—but still. Couldn't the club business crap wait until he was fully functioning? He could have died.

Will eased down onto the floral cushions, letting his scabs crack and sting while they readjusted. He lounged his bare feet on the armrest. First, he'd call Dad after a snooze—let him know how he wouldn't be making the trip. Then, he'd call Aunt K to make sure everything was square. Uncle Shorty may have whispered sweet nothings in her ear, but once she understood Will would actually *agree* to see a therapist...well, old Shorty wouldn't stand a chance. All Will had to do was say the word.

Yep, it's all he had to do. Will relaxed his muscles and sighed as his cast sank down beside him. *I missed you, peach floral couch.* He blinked at the ceiling, tensing and waiting for Helmet to jump on his gut like he always did, fifteen pounds of love.

But there was nothing.

Earlier, when Will had walked through the door, the first thing he'd seen were Helmet's filled bowls still in the kitchen, then the Hair Chair in the living room still covered in orange fur. But two things had changed. The litter box had been moved out, and Helmet's collar and tags had been hung on the key hook by the door, right there at face level. Will couldn't miss it if he'd tried.

And, God, did he try, but he couldn't think about it right now. Not when his eyelids felt like they'd been pumping iron. Those "Don't operate heavy equipment" meds were kicking in, so just a quick nap and then he'd...yeah, some shut-eye was all he needed.

Will, this is your mother speaking. I heard a noise, and it wasn't Helmet. I think someone's in the house. Hear that?

Oh, great. Mom was back to her chatty self.

Meow.

Helmet? Will's eyes sprang open, and above him hovered a wiry, red beard and eyes as dark as midnight. Jesus! Will scrambled clumsily to his elbows, clamping down on the jets of pain shooting through his cast, his gut, his toe, and—

"Hallelujah. He's alive," Flossy said to the room as he tilted back on his heels. He stepped away to lean against the wall.

"What are you guys doing here?" Will scowled and went to rub his forehead but instead smacked his nose with the cast. Dammit! His brain spun a doughnut from sitting up too fast.

He looked at all the faces in the room. Flossy was the mechanic whose daily uniform consisted of bright white t-shirts and thick turquoise jewelry. He had wavy red hair to go with his beard, and his sinewy arms were crossed while he chewed on a toothpick. Trip, a muscle-bound prospect, had a very cool fake leg, all chrome to match the pipes on his bike. He didn't have much to say, which was the direct opposite of Owen, the pack's biggest a-hole in a pin-striped vest.

In the middle of the room stood Leo the Lion. Normally, he had a mane of black hair, but sometime today, Leo met with a pair of clippers. He looked less like a lion and more like an insurance salesman with his short cut hair and clean face. Will inhaled and almost coughed. Was that the woody smell of Lucky You cologne polluting his living room? Must be some hot date Leo's got later.

This was his dad's crowd, Liam's crowd. One guy was missing, though. "What's going on? Where's Uncle Shorty?"

This doesn't look good, Will.

No, it didn't.

Leo didn't answer because he didn't have to. He was the Hides of Hell president, *acting* president, and all-around bad dude, who stood in his living room, looking ominous and...well, he was hard to read. He was a hot temper, a cold shoulder, and a funny bone all rolled up into one.

"We ask the questions here, Gadget Freak," Owen said, wide-legged like he was ready to kick some ass. "Why aren't you ready, and where's your bag?"

Jesus, did he ever take it down a notch?

"Gadget," Flossy chuckled softly. "I like it."

"No," Will cut the air with his palm. He wasn't ever going to be in the club. He wanted to go to college, get into game design, something fun. He wasn't going to be a thug, so he didn't need some stupid nickname. It was time to get real. "Listen, I didn't get a chance to tell Uncle Shorty, but the nurse said...uh. Well..." he held up his new friend, the green cast. "I've got this, and a bruised spleen, and turns out I need a lot of rest. Some peace and quiet, you know?"

"Now," Leo said in a placating tone, "I'm no doctor, but I've seen plenty, so trust me when I say you'll be just fine. As for Shorty, club business. So he's staying behind to...man the fort, so-to-speak. I know you were expecting him to ride along, but plans change, and you're with us. We're leaving in..." He pulled out his phone. "...ten minutes."

"Uncle Shorty isn't going? But we're still meeting up with my dad and Liam, right?"

"We'll talk about it on the way. Get your stuff together, which means everything…" Leo cupped his hand around his ear at the deep rumbling of a motorcycle pulling up outside. "…because it sounds like your ride finally made it. Right on time."

"Cutting it kinda close, isn't she?" Owen muttered.

"She? She who?" Then, Will jerked like he got smacked in the head by a two-by-four.

Owen and Leo's she, as in Miki? If they were talking about him riding on the back of her bike…absolutely not gonna happen. He wouldn't do it.

No way, no how.

* * *

"Hop on!" Miki hollered over the roaring motorcycles—boom, boom, boom, boom—as she tilted her black Suzuki cruiser upright and released the kickstand. This was the first time her dad had invited her on an official ride. She was surrounded by the guys in their leathers, the polished metal, the clouds of exhaust, and it made her heart accelerate. Boom, boom, boom, boom. Now she knew what it felt like to be a part of it, to be a part of the pack.

She flipped up the visor on her helmet and looked back at Will in his forest green hoodie and matching track pants. He looked ridiculous, like a Leisure Suit Larry. No wonder the guys stuck her with him. She didn't care. She couldn't wait to feel his arms around her, even if it was through her leather jacket. A girl could dream, couldn't she? Fortunately—or *un*fortunately—he looked the same, like a moody grump.

45

"How am I supposed to strap this thing on with one hand?" He said loudly, holding out his half-shell helmet, a skid lid painted a smoky gray like the plumes of ash from Mount Saint Helens. It was Liam's handiwork for sure, from the high-gloss finish to the words *Third time's a charm* scrolled along the back edge. She was pretty sure it referred to Will being the third William in his family.

So there was his face, all bruised and scabby, yet his helmet didn't have a scratch on it, a telling sign. Will hadn't been wearing it when he wrecked his bike. Smooth move, Ex-Lax.

Hers was a full-face with a tinted visor. It was also scratch free, but not because she didn't wear it. It was brand-spanking new, a late birthday present from her dad when he'd invited her along. Some might consider it a bribe, but she chose to see it as a thoughtful gift. Matte black, too. So cool.

She and Will were both rockin' it. Except for his leisure suit. He even had the sleeve cut to fit over his cast. *Très* nerdy, but she'd forgive him.

She pulled the front jaw of her helmet down, so her voice could be heard. "You're going to cramp my style with your gym suit." She smiled. Now, if only he'd do the same back. Just once.

She watched him hobble closer, raking his long, brown hair away from his face. He stood next to her handlebars and set the skid lid down on his head, then lifted his chin, waiting for her to clip the straps. His throat was exposed. If they were going out, she'd kiss him right there.

"Believe me, I hate this as much as you do," he said above the rumble of engines.

"I doubt it." She shook her head. He really had no idea. "You should feel honored. At least you get to feel me up…again. What do I get?"

He lowered his eyes to hers and glared.

Miki blinked at him sweetly. They'd kissed and groped each other once in a coat closet at the club house. While the parental units were busy having their own party outside, the teens were inside, exploring the options on a pair of erotic dice she'd found. Combined with Truth or Dare and a dark room, things had gotten interesting with Will—fast. After seven short minutes of doing the tongue tango with a lot of cupping, squeezing, and sighing, they'd stepped out with eyes the size of moons. Before the closet, she'd gotten his number—

"Well?" he said, flicking the chin strap impatiently.

After the closet, he'd told her to erase it and never talk to him again.

She reached up and clicked the buckle ends together, trying to touch him as little as possible. No sense torturing herself. She turned away to face the flaming back patches and spewing tail pipes in front of her.

"Thanks," he grumbled. "Oh, and by the way, don't worry about me enjoying the ride." He held up his cast and wiggled the ends of his fingers. "I popped some pain pills, thank God. Soon, I'll be flying high as a kite, and hopefully, I won't remember a thing."

Will inched his leg over the seat, hissing and ahhing, until he dropped his weight down behind her. Miki steadied the bike's balance, waiting for his arms to slither around her, but he sat back there like a cold stump. Right. Guess she'd have to gun it out to the road. Then, he'd have to hold on. That's what the guys did to their old ladies. She smiled. Can I get a *Hell, yeah*?

In a short while, they'd be in their own little world. With his arms resting on her hips, maybe it would remind him how much heat they could conjure up in seven minutes.

Sigh.

As if Owen could read her thoughts and felt the need to douse 'em, he coasted to her side—boom, boom —then dropped his feet to the gravel, walking his bike closer. His full-faced helmet sat sleek and black in his lap.

"Hey, Mik. All set?" Owen yelled to be heard above the revving engines.

Members were pulling forward with Dad and the road captain in the front, leading the pack. Her last count was thirty-two, a lot of bikes to keep in a tight formation. She rubbed her palms up and down her leathers and nodded, hit with a sudden case of thick tongue.

"You're in the back of the lineup with the friends and family and the hang-arounds. Some of the prospects are back there, too. Flossy said first stop on highway twenty-three is Trout Lake. Gas and snacks, then punch it all the way to Maupin. We'll get to the campsite around six and still have daylight hours to burn. Got it?" Owen flicked a look of disdain at Will. "You're carrying some serious dead weight, sis…got your phone handy in case you need it?"

Miki patted her front pocket as a hard ball formed in her throat. This was it. Time to show her dad she could keep up, that he should be proud of her.

"Got everything you need? Sunscreen, water?" Owen pulled on his helmet and adjusted his shades. "See you in Trout Lake." He shut his visor and pulled into the throng of bikes. The engines thundered as each motorcycle crept forward into the lineup, then accelerated down the street, leaving Will's white house in a billow of fumes and dust.

Will's green cast rested on his leg, hard at her side, but his other hand inched around her waist. It felt good, natural.

"You ever ride with these guys before?" Will asked loudly from behind her shoulder, his voice muffled through her helmet.

"No."

"Me, neither," he said and hugged her with one arm.

He might have simply been holding on, but it felt like an affectionate gesture to her. His body warmed her back, and confidence surged in her gut. She gassed it to catch the tail end of the Hides of Hell and smiled when Will clutched her tighter.

She might be riding the tail pipes of the pack, but these were her wheels, her ride, and Will was in her bitch seat.

Boom, boom, boom, boom.

Hell, yeah!

CHAPTER 6

GOOD & PLENTY

Will lied when he told Miki he'd popped his meds and would be flying high as a kite. For the past three hours, his asphalt ass chaffed against the tiny seat cushion, and now his guts were on fire, and his arm throbbed. He hadn't planned on riding with the hairy bunch, so he'd popped his pills early, and now it was late.

Will, this is your mother speaking.

Yep.

Remember when you had your tonsils out? The nurse gave you a special root beer popsicle because you were the bravest boy she'd ever seen. Not a single tear! I knew you wanted to cry, but you were so proud. She said it was important to stay ahead of the pain.

Thanks for the newsflash, Mom. He was totally behind the pain now. The label said take two every four hours as needed, so he'd take three at the upcoming stop to make up for it.

Ahead, tail lights glowed, and the bikes looked like scales of a long, slithering dragon. The group slowed, and Will caught the flash of a green and white highway sign: Trout Lake, 1 mile.

Thank you, Baby Jesus.

By the time Miki pulled up next to the pump, the core members had filled their tanks, fed their faces, and puffed their cigarettes. They waved and yelled, "No stoppin' 'til Maupin!" and "Let's ride!" before roaring off down the road.

Will hefted his weary butt off the bike and watched as Miki did the same. Three hours of riding, and they still had two more to go. His back was screaming tired, and he felt like a tattered flag in the wind. He wasn't cut out for this crap. How did those old guys do it? Some of them bragged of thousand-mile tours, two-wheelin' it day and night. At only a hundred plus miles from home, Will was ready to hit the sheets for some round-the-clock shuteye.

Miki unscrewed the gas cap and poked the nozzle into the tank. He tugged his helmet free and leaned against the washer fluid stand while his manhood took a hit. Here she was, taking care of business while he stood around, trying not to focus on that itchy spot under his cast. It was driving him insane.

Your dad always kept my car tank full. The day I married him was the last day I touched a grimy hose at a gas station. He held the door, took in the groceries, and replaced the toilet paper roll just the way I liked it, like a true gentleman.

Yeah, well. Wasn't Miki always telling everybody how she wanted to be a mechanic? She must like to get her hands dirty, so let her. It's not like they were going out. It was her bike, and he was the dead weight along for a free ride, according to her brother.

Maybe he should grab a quick snack. Taking pain pills on an empty stomach might not be a good idea.

"You want something?" Will asked, pushing the sweaty hair off his face. Miki pulled off her helmet, and he half expected to see her shake out that long black hair like a super model. Instead, it was chopped off shoulder-length and the ends were as blue as a dime store slushy. "What the hell happened to your hair?"

"I got it cut. Do you like it?" She swished her fingers through the dyed ends. She wore big silver rings on her fingers and together with her blue lid, she looked like a hipster-doofus.

"Is it permanent? Because if so, that is seriously too bad. I liked your old hair better."

"Good news...hair grows back. Bad news...you look like Ghetto Gramps in those track pants, so I'm happy to report your opinion doesn't matter." She turned away to hang up the nozzle and tear off her receipt. "To answer your question, yes. I'll take a cold water. Thanks."

Ghetto Gramps. Ha! Will ground the cement grit under his heel and headed toward the store. The amazing thing was that he even owned a sweat suit because he never ran anywhere or lifted heavy objects. Generally speaking, he never broke a sweat unless he was eating a spicy burrito. A bell dinged above the door as he pushed inside. He offered a standard chin nod to a group of familiar biker faces waiting in line at the cashier, then headed to the back cooler. Will grabbed a couple chilled waters and took a turn through the candy aisle. Was she a salty nuts, a sour balls, or a chocolate kind of girl? He opted for a box of Good & Plenty. Black licorice oughta make her happy.

He added spearmint gum, two Snickers bars, and a box of Lemon Heads to his bounty, and after paying, crossed the sidewalk to Miki, who'd parked her bike and now leaned on it. Her helmet dangled off one handle bar, and her leather-clad legs were stretched out in front of her.

Whoa.

He hated to admit she looked good, but her short blue hair kind of ruined it for him. It used to be thick and straight, and he could imagine her whipping it back and forth like a long-necked headbanger. So cool.

"Ready?" she asked and pushed off the seat to stand in front of him.

"I got you something." Will tucked his skid lid under his arm and hooked the plastic bag over his cast to dig out the box of pink and white coated candies. Her face lit up.

"I love black licorice," she said, studying him with her big brown eyes.

"I know."

Oh, Will, that's so sweet. But I always pictured you with a nice girl who liked shabby chic antiques, baking desserts, and the color pink. Someone more like me. I had no idea you had a thing for Leo's daughter.

I did. No, I didn't...I mean I don't.

"Remember when you called me Zombie Lips?" Miki smiled, and her voice quavered a bit like this was the most touching gift anyone had ever given her, and he suddenly felt awkward and weird.

"It's no big deal," he said firmly, though his face felt warm. "They were just sitting there, so I grabbed a box. Look..." He held the sack open. "I bought other stuff, too."

"Oh. Okay. Thanks." Miki took the bag and peered into it. She pulled out the bottle of water and popped the cap, then held it to her lips. Her blue hair fell back, and Will's eyes followed the line of her throat down to the "V" of her t-shirt under her leather jacket.

He scowled and turned away, plopping his helmet on and pulling the strap under his chin. This time he'd left the ends clipped together, so he wouldn't have to ask her for help again. She was going to be a problem.

This whole trip was going to be a problem.

How could he push her away when he had to hold on tight at every curve?

Every time he blinked, a mile marker or two would go by. Okay, maybe he shouldn't have taken the extra pill. His head kept falling forward, and now he'd clanked helmets with Miki's again. He'd already yelled "Sorry!" twice, and if he wasn't careful, she'd curb him. In his condition, it might make for an extra-long walk to anywhere.

He bit the inside of his lip hard, and his eyes opened. Okay, pain worked. Then…eyes shut. He pinched his leg…eyes opened, and he could see the yellow lines on the road again. Good. He could totally do this for the next ninety miles.

His eyes closed, and he tried to slowly erase Miki's backside snugged to his front and his one hand doing the wraparound at her hip, her waist. Was it really only a year ago when they'd started looking at each other funny? He had a clear vision of her at the Lemon Squeeze Snack Shack where her hair was long and black. She'd licked her lips and laughed, and he'd sort of smiled along with her while staring at her teeth…

Zombie Lips

Why would anyone want to a kiss a mouth like that? He did, and for some reason, he couldn't tear his eyes away. Her lips and teeth had turned a freaky, grayish-green color.

Then she stuck out her black tongue.

"Sick," Will said, his eyes coasting up to Miki's big brown ones. They were fringed with thick, dark lashes. She was cute. "I don't see how you like that stuff."

Miki swirled her dark-stained tongue around the ice cream nearly as black as her hair. Hair, which was one-length and shiny with the ends brushing her waist. She was a mutt, probably a mix of Native American, Italian, and Greek with a splash of Gypsy. Who knew? What he did know was every time she was around, bad things happened.

His teeth—white teeth after a normal, white-chocolate cone—sat on edge, waiting. What would it be this time? Where was Owen?

"Black Licorice is my all-time favorite. Right up there with Banana Blitz." Her zombie lips turned up into a grin. Yep…still cute. Sweet, too. But horrible taste in ice cream.

Will narrowed his eyes, then looked over his shoulder. "Where's your brother?"

"Don't worry about him. He's preoccupied with unhitching the boat."

He studied the tattooed group milling down at the dock, but what he didn't see was her hot-headed brother, Owen. If something didn't follow his script, he introduced some muscle and made it so. A terror in pin stripes.

"So can I call you sometime?" Miki wiped at the sides of her mouth with a tiny napkin, tilting her head in a coy way.

Shy, she was not. And those black-smudged lips? Hey, anise wasn't his favorite flavor. In fact, it didn't even rank on his top twenty list, but he still wanted to kiss her.

Dude…chill the hell out.

"Could I stop you?" Will raised his eyebrows and gave her the look he'd perfected back when he was a sophomore. I'm too bored-lazy-comfy-cool to bother-listen-act-care about whatever it is you just said. He didn't even like her—

Okay, so he did, but he didn't want to. They were complete opposites. She was fast, extroverted, motivated, and a biker wannabe. He, on the other hand, was none of those things.

"God, Will. You make me feel like the guy here. I chase you, and you play hard to get. So give it up already."

"Give what up?"

"You're number, you idiot. Here, type it in." She held her phone out. He took it and quickly entered his number before passing it back.

She smiled again, and—what would her kiss taste like anyway? Maybe licorice wasn't so bad. The thought quickly vanished when Will's Spidey sense told him he was being watched.

Where was Owen again?

Queue the end of the fun memory.

When did things stop being normal? Back in the day, Will and Miki were playmates, part of the biker brat-pack. While the adults partied it up, they played at the clubhouse: hide-and-seek, tag, dodgeball, and video games. When did he start checking her out? It seemed like she'd always been on his radar, but one day, it was like...Hey, she's looking back at me.

When she'd chosen him to go into the coat closet for some touchy-feely dice game she'd made up, her eyes said, *Let's go for third base.*

Oh, yeah. He liked her, but she was a package deal. With her came Owen, and his look always said, *You're dead, bro.* Being with Miki meant dealing with her big brother, dealing with trouble, and the last thing Will needed was another bloody nose...

A searing pain, like a stinging nettle, ran up Will's thigh. Or was it a bee? His helmet clanked off Miki's again, and he tried to peel his weight off her back. The drone of the engine, the constant wind, and the lack of back support were killing him.

"Ouch!" He clumsily slapped at his leg only to realize that Miki had been twist-pinching him. His good leg was going to be black and blue because of her. He couldn't keep going. They had to pull over because at the next bend in the road he'd most likely roll right off the fender of her bike and hit the pavement. Since they were doing sixty, it would be a fine red mist, dude.

She must have read his mind because she shifted down, and the bike slowed until they coasted to a stop on the side of the highway. With her legs dropped at each side, she kept it steady as a couple cars zoomed by at top speed, shaking the bike at each pass.

She flipped her visor up and half turned on the seat to look over her shoulder at him. "Will, you're wearing me out. I've slowed down so much already I've lost sight of Mook's cousin."

Damn, they really were sucking wind because that guy was a three-hundred-pound big boy who rode a hog like he was on a Sunday drive. No problem—it was Will's speed, too, low and casual—but it did mean the slowpoke was always at the end of the pack. Will knew this because Mook's cousin had earned the nickname Caboose, and he wasn't even in the club, just a hang-around.

"I need a break. I...I can't ride." He was tapped without a microgram of energy left to even open his eyes. So he simply sat there in doze-mode. The bike shook again as another car whipped by.

"Will! I'm talking to you. What is wrong with you?"

"Huh?" He rubbed his eye with the heel of his hand while his cast hung limp. "I took an extra dose, probably shouldn't have."

"Why would you do that?" She growled with frustration. "Oh, never mind. Just hang on...and if I dump my bike because of you, I'll kick your—"

Why was she so pissed off? He'd only gotten out of the hospital this morning, and now look at him. He drank, he drove, he almost killed himself, and now he was at the mercy of a blue-hair on a bike.

The engine revved and the Suzuki pulled forward onto the road. Will squeezed Miki's waist like a body pillow. He closed his eyes and pretended he was horizontal on his favorite couch. Oh, yeah. He could sleep right here.

* * *

Punch it all the way to Maupin, that's what Owen had said, and here she was, failing her mission twenty minutes out of Trout Lake. What would her dad say?

Normally, Will's body all over hers would have sent her shooting for the stars. His long arm wrapped around her, sort of possessive and needy like. Yeah, it would have pushed her straight into heaven...if they weren't on *her* bike with people to see and places to go. She wanted to show Dad how she could be a part of his life, keep up, and make him proud. He'd invited her along for a father/daughter trip, yet he was in the front of the pack, and she wasn't anywhere near the end of it. Why, Will? Why'd you have to get doped and screw things up?

His helmet clanked with hers for the hundredth time, but she couldn't be mad at him. He was holding on to her, and he needed her strength to be safe. Right now, Will should be at home recuperating, not on the back of her bike. What was Dad thinking? What were any of the adults thinking? It was just wrong.

At this rate, if she kept driving she'd spill her bike and turn them both into road jelly. Was Will's life—or her own—worth the risk to please her dad?

No, it wasn't. Screw it. She slacked off the gas, putting more distance between her and the bikers. Even if she could catch up to Caboose, what help would he be? He'd probably tell her what she already knew: pull over and play it safe. Dad would agree with that, wouldn't he? She'd find a hotel room for the night and catch up with everyone at the rally in Burnout. Nothing was happening in Maupin anyway, except tent camping with a rowdy crowd. Her dad probably wouldn't even notice if she were there or not. He hadn't bothered to wait for her at the gas station. Why would he suddenly care now?

She flipped the blinker on and took the first exit advertising gas, food, and the Powerhouse Inn, which turned out to be a single level motel with a faded blue-and-white sign: Vacancy, Comfortable Rooms, TV-Phone-Wifi. On the opposite side of the parking lot sat a rustic log tavern called Knotty Knoll's with a couple beat-up cars parked out front and a rusty dumpster.

The road grit crunched under her tires as she coasted to the motel's office. She cut the engine in time for Will to slide off the back end into a pile. He clunked his helmet on the asphalt and groaned.

"Will Sullivan..." Miki leaned her bike onto the kickstand and swung her leg over the seat to stand in front of him. "I think you finally scratched your helmet, and now I can't like you anymore."

If only it were that easy. A simple button to push for on or off, for hot or cold, for ramming speed ahead or putting the skids on. Even though she was annoyed, tired, frustrated, and sore after a hellish ride, and even though Will grunted and made a wimpy attempt to stand, she still...*still* couldn't unlike him.

"Why, you ask?" She shook her head. "Because you're an idiot. Stay there, Will, or you'll hurt yourself. I'll get us a room and come back for you." She rolled her eyes and headed for the glass door. "Idiot."

The office was painted a warm country-yellow but was as chilly as standing in front of an open fridge. The air-conditioner unit hummed loudly in the window and rattled the picture frames against the wall, all color photographs of mountain flowers. It was sunny and bright above the pine wainscoting and heavy and brown below it with chunky furniture and drab carpet.

The room was a contradiction, as was the girl behind the counter. On the outside, she looked like a live-and-let-live kind of dread-locker who smelled like swamp mud and black pepper, but her brown eyes were filled with suspicion.

"That your bike out front?" she asked, peering past Miki's shoulder. "Who's the guy laying out there? Your boyfriend?"

Miki turned to look out the window at her black Suzuki and the pair of long legs stretched out beside it. Green track pants, what a sight. She turned back to the desk clerk. Her name tag said Pinecone, and she looked really young, like she might be a freshman in high school or something. Miki narrowed her eyes right back at her.

"Yeah, he's with me. He's real tired. You got a room?"

"Overnight or hourly rate? Cash or credit?"

Hourly? Was that an option? Miki glanced back over her shoulder at Will's boots. It was nearly five p.m. By the time Will rested, and they had dinner across the way, it would be dark. Riding a bike in the dark to sleep in a tent on the ground while listening to barrel-chested guffaws...well, none of it sounded very appealing. "Overnight." Miki tapped the edge of her dad's credit card against the counter, then slid it across to Pinecone.

"Are you from...you know. Around here? Or do you have a discount?"

"A discount?"

"You know, a password. What're your last names?" Pinecone looked at the card in her hand, and her brow lowered. "Leo Holtz."

"It's my dad's card. I'm with Sullivan. He's the one taking a dirt nap out there." Miki pointed her thumb over her shoulder.

"Sullivan," Pinecone said and cleared her throat. "The name sounds kind of familiar. Is he friends with Smiley?" She lifted her thick eyebrows. "If he is, I could probably give you a deal on a room."

"I don't know." Miki shrugged. "Maybe Will knows him, but unfortunately, he's not in a real talkative mood right now."

"Will…William Sullivan." Pinecone didn't blink an eye as she clicked the end of her pen.

Click. Click.

"That's right. Do you know him?" Miki squinted. She didn't want to feel jealous over a girl who had a couple squirrel pelts for eyebrows, but what if she and Will had some kind of sordid, long-distance past? It was a small world after all. Please-please-*please* don't be Will's type.

"No, I…I only need it for the reservation, that's all." Pinecone fumbled with a stack of papers on her desk, then dropped Miki's credit card on the floor and swore under her breath.

"Is everything okay?" Miki studied the desk clerk with a quirked brow. Something didn't smell right here, and it wasn't Pinecone's spicy eau de cologne. Why was she acting so weird?

"Sorry, too much caffeine this afternoon." She slid the key card and Miki's credit card across the counter.

"Room number eight, the honeysuckle room, on the end. Checkout is noon."

Honeysuckle? Oh, baby, she could handle that. At least it wasn't the bleeding heart or the touch-me-not room. Miki tucked the plastic cards into her back pocket and pushed out into the parking lot to stand over Will. His mouth was slack, and his eyelashes rested on his cheekbones. Miki sighed. Why'd she have to like him again? She nudged him with her boot. Gentle, since he hadn't even been out of the hospital a full day.

"Water," he croaked.

"I can't carry you, Will. Get up, so I can help you to the room."

He took his sweet time easing into a sitting position and pulled up his knees. When he finally stood, Miki wedged herself under his right arm and hugged his waist to keep him steady as they stumbled out of sync down the breezeway.

She'd finally have Will alone in a room all to herself, but instead of getting her honeysuckle on, she'd probably sit there like a lunatic and watch him as he slept. Or watch bad TV until the sun went down. Or worse, worry about Pinecone's multiple problems from her matted hair to her cagey behavior when she heard Will's name. Miki did a mental shrug. Maybe she'd do all three, simultaneously.

Miki keyed into the room and guided Will to the queen bed. Of course, the first thing he did after tossing his helmet was crawl across the brown bedspread at an angle, hogging the whole thing. Oh, well, guess they'd have to snuggle. A real hardship.

"Feelsh good," Will mumbled into a pillow as he turned onto his side with the dirty soles of his shoes hanging over the edge.

Great. Stinky foot duty. Will's sweaty socks had to smell better than this place. It reeked of trapped exhaust fumes and old dirt from a vacuum cleaner. She tugged his boot free and dropped it beside the bed.

The room was dark and small with heavy brown drapes blocking a single window. Outside noise, like cars whizzing down the freeway, someone showering in the unit on the left, and bed springs bouncing from the unit on the right, made their room seem like a cozy cubbyhole. A calm spot surrounded by activity.

Miki traced Will's sock up his pant leg and peeled the top down slowly over of his rough, scabby skin. She stopped at the sight of his dark purple pinkie toe.

"Thanks, Cute Nurse," Will murmured with his eyes closed.

"What?" Miki pulled her hand back. "Hey…Will." But he was dead to the world, snoring softly.

She eased away from the foot of the bed to stand next to him. He had such a baby face with no whiskers, only smooth, flawless skin and a beauty mark on his cheek that any girl would kill for. How'd he get so lucky? She stooped and sifted her fingers through his silky soft hair, and her heart fluttered in her chest like a million helicopter seeds falling out of a maple tree.

She'd always liked him, ever since she was a little kid. She did everything to catch his attention. First she'd told him dirty jokes. Then she'd tried to make him jealous by "liking" other guys. Then she'd worn tight tank tops with short skirts. She'd tried flipping her hair this way and that, and she'd caught him looking at her a couple times, but he would never take it to the next level. Why not? What'd a girl have to do?

She wanted to throttle him more than she wanted to let him nap, but the saddle bags had to be hauled in, and a pizza had to be ordered. They could rest, eat, then maybe hit the road, dark be damned. Pinecone fumbling around behind the desk, acting like she didn't know Will, it all seemed sort of peculiar.

Miki had definitely been hanging around the Hides of Hell clubhouse too much. Now she was starting to think like a biker, and her radar said something was off. Discounts and passwords? What was all that about? And who the hell was Smiley?

CHAPTER 7

LUCKY BREAK

Will rolled over, and a spring poked him in the back. Where was he? This wasn't his bed at home, and it wasn't the peach floral couch, either. When he breathed in, hints of anise filled his nose. A Miki dream.

She giggled, and it echoed somewhere in his head. Through the fog he could see her smiling and holding out something in her palm. A pair of erotic dice she'd found somewhere in the clubhouse, but she refused to say where. What if they were his dad's? Stop!

His dream, his rules.

Okay, one die had actions: Kiss, Suck, Lick, Spank, Bite, and Rub. The other had places: Lips, Butt, Nipples, Thighs, Ankles, and Ears.

The closet dream. Will rolled the dice and…

Spank ankles?

No, he would roll something sweet and normal because it's the kind of guy he was, not someone who spanked or even licked ankles. It was a leg joint, a basic body part. What was so erotic about them anyway? No, it was Miki's ears. Her thick hair always covered them, but once or twice, she'd pulled her mane back into a ponytail, and he'd witnessed her earlobes, dainty and soft. They rarely saw the light of day like forbidden flesh, and being a sweet guy, they're where he'd start. Then he'd work his way down. Oh, yeah.

The dice clattered around in his mind, coming to a stop on Bite and Ears. Finally, something he could work with.

Last time they'd been in the closet, they'd been vertical, leaning against the wall. But now he was horizontal, and he had Miki tucked in close. He rolled his head toward her, and his nose met her hair. It smelled like some girly shampoo. Something flowery, but he'd call it black licorice because this was his dream, and even though he didn't necessarily prefer the taste or the smell, he liked it on her. Her tongue swirled around the heaping scoop of black ice cream.

Whoa. This was the closet dream, not the Zombie Lips dream.

Okay.

He puckered his lips and nibbled his way deeper into her hair until he found an earlobe. He sucked it between his lips. She sighed. Or was it a moan? Oh, God, this was getting good. He sucked again, and she giggled. He smiled. Her ears were perfect.

He rolled into her, his leg bending to entwine with hers. Ow! Pain, cracking scabs. They were probably bleeding.

Don't worry about it. Get back to the good stuff.

Right…

His hand coasted up her hip, nice and round, then up over her t-shirt to her ribs. He rested it there in neutral territory. Should he head to the front for more forbidden flesh? Or stay sweet and head to her back? This was his dream, so he could do whatever he wanted, right? In the closet last year, she had let him touch her, so his palm drifted between them and cupped her boob while her hot little hands roamed under his shirt, over his back, to his stomach, then down the front of his pants...

"Oh, God." Will opened his eyes, and the room was dark except for the street lights glowing through the gap between the drawn curtains. He was on top of the real Miki, panting in her face. "I'm sorry," he said, his cheeks flaring with heat. He tried to roll away, but her arms hugged him.

"Don't be," she whispered. "Do you have a condom?"

"A what? Oh, uh..." Seriously? He was getting the green light to go to fourth base? His first time. With Miki Holtz. And...no rubber. Will turned onto his back and groaned. Wow...some bad luck right there. "No. No condom," he said, staring at the water stains on the ceiling.

"We could do other things, you know." Miki scooted closer. Her warm breath touched his neck, and her lips followed. She kissed him. It was so sweet.

Will tilted his chin to study her dark eyes, her tousled blue hair against his shoulder, the v-neck of her t-shirt. Oh, yeah. Color him interested. He did a mental check on his well-being. His guts felt fine, his arm was kinda heavy, and his scabs were...crispy. Okay, they might be a problem, but otherwise, he could totally get busy.

Will, this is your mother speaking.

Or not.

Remember what happened after the closet? Remember how she made you feel? Now, I wasn't there, and I know absolutely nothing about it, but I'm a part of you, Will. You thought she liked you! You're nothing special to her. Seconds after the closet door opened, she humiliated you in front of everyone. What will happen this time, now that she's got you in a hotel room, panting on all fours—

Try three-point-five, Mom. I've got a cast.

Don't get smart. Find yourself a sweet girl, Will. Someone you can trust.

"Miki…when we're in the dark, everything's great. No lie…it's hot." He couldn't move away because she was nestled tightly under his arm between his ribs and his cast. "But what happens when the lights come on?"

"I don't know. You tell me." She leaned on her elbow and smiled down at him.

"I think we want different things. You're like the eye of a storm—"

"Oh, my God, Will." Miki pressed a palm to her face. "Please tell me you're only playing." She dropped her hand and sat up. "Are you seeing someone? Do you know a girl named Pinecone by any chance?"

"Pine what? No, I'm not seeing anyone. I only mean I'm a low-key kinda guy, and it seems like being with you is not easy."

"How can you say that? I'm the easiest person you can get, Will, I'm right here. God." She shook her head. "I feel like I've been chasing you forever, and if you'd stop running and open your eyes, maybe you'd see the real me." Her voice hitched, then lowered. "Well, it doesn't get much easier than that, does it?"

"There's your problem. You're using up a lot of energy chasing guys who don't want to be chased. Haven't you ever heard of the law of least effort?"

"Laws." She snorted.

"Okay, so why'd you cut your hair and dye it blue?"

"I wanted to piss off my dad." Miki shrugged. "What does that have to do with anything?"

"Figures." Will scoffed. Here we go, back to President Leo and the biker scene. "You made it all about him and not yourself. Did he even care?"

"No." Miki frowned. "He didn't seem to notice."

"A lot of effort for no return."

"You know what? I happen to like my hair," Miki snapped.

"I'm not judging." Will opened his palm to her as a sign of peace. "All I'm sayin' is it seems like you try too hard. Your dad only gives a crap about—"

"So in your world, how would I get your attention? Huh? Are you telling me to pretend I don't care? Pretend I'm not interested? Been there, done that."

Rule number one—he didn't chase anyone. If someone liked him, all they had to do was show it, and if he liked them back, he'd do the same. Boom. Easy. Not to mention a little loyalty went a long way. It wasn't too much to ask for, now was it?

"No," he said warily. He was lying on his back at her mercy and at a serious disadvantage and…what the hell were they talking about anyway? His world consisted of his mom popping into his head right in the middle of a good time. It only proved he was crazy. "Uh…I'm not ready for this. I can't…" Will shook his head and leaned up. He inched away and flung out the first thing coming to mind. "You might not believe this, but liking you only invites trouble."

"Trouble! How can you say that?"

Boom!

The room echoed. What the hell was that?

Boom!

The door shook and splintered.

Wham!

It flew open, bouncing off the flimsy wall, and Miki screamed as chips of wood fell onto the carpet.

"Jesus!" Will yelped and pulled himself up on his elbows. The lights flicked on, and he raised his cast to block the eye-burn from the lamp. He blinked and blinked again, then dropped his arm and glanced around the room, taking in all the hairy faces. What the hell were they doing here?

"Miki, I'm gonna kill you!" Owen huffed and puffed and lunged toward the bed. He grabbed her ankle and jerked her across the brown spread.

"Hey!" she yelped and kicked out.

"Careful, Owen. You touch her when you're mad, you'll regret it," Flossy said easily with his thumbs hooked into his belt loops, casual, like busting into a hotel room was as routine as a coffee break.

Owen dropped her bare foot, leaving her sitting on the edge of the mattress, mussed up and freaked out. His voice shook. "Mind telling me what you're doing here? You know how long we've been looking for you? Driving all over Pulver Skull territory? Thank God we got a call. Otherwise, we'd be searching every exit, while you're busy getting into Will's pants."

"Hey, now..." Will frowned.

"You're lucky I don't..." Owen's face tightened, and he dropped his fists, then his chin. He stood quietly in front of her, staring at the brown, matted carpet, as if he were trying to get his emotions in order.

"Enough talk." Flossy stood wide-legged before them like a warrior. He combed his fingers down his coppery beard, and his turquoise and silver jewelry glimmered. "All our bikes are out front. Get your stuff, and let's move."

Will eased his legs over the bed and pushed his long bangs off his forehead while he gathered his wits. Trip blocked the door, Flossy had his back, and Owen was inside ready to kick ass. Why the big freak-out? Before these a-holes showed up, there was only one bike out front. Even a P-skull wouldn't look twice at a single bike.

"Dude, we had to pull over." Will glanced from Flossy to Owen. "I kept falling asleep."

"Sleeping?" The dragon lit up behind Owen's eyes. "I caught you with your filthy hands all over my little sister. You two ever hear of a phone? I mean we're settling into camp, and I see Caboose pulling up. He's the last of 'em, man. What're we suppose to think?"

"Dude, I—" Will turned and looked at Miki. "Why didn't you text 'em?"

"I left Dad a voicemail." Miki rubbed hands over her eyes, then pushed her hair back. She glanced around the room. "Where is he?"

"You did?" Owen gaped. Then he swore and slapped the brass lamp off the desk. It thudded against the wall, and the shade rolled across the carpet. "Dad is...he's with someone, and they're in Maupin at some hotel." Owen swore again and clutched his head. The pits in his shirt were stained with sweat, and he smelled like campfire smoke and motor oil.

"He told me this was a father-daughter ride," Miki said.

"Dad is..." Owen dropped his arms. "He's dad, alright? You keep hoping he'll change, but he keeps on staying the same. When're you gonna figure it out?"

Will sat quietly, not wanting to draw attention to himself because Owen was a geyser. Didn't the Holtz family know anything about keeping their cool and staying chill?

"We need to get where we're going. I feel like a sittin' duck here." Flossy glanced past Trip to the parking lot. "Get your shoes on, kids. Double-time."

Will fumbled with his socks, then slid his feet into his boots. Why were these guys so jittery? What was going on with the Pulver Skulls? They were a smaller club than the Hides of Hell. They didn't have as much muscle, did they? Maybe Miki should skip the rally and give him a ride back home. If there was biker trouble, they certainly shouldn't be in the middle of it. She was tough, but no match against a meathead in leather, and Will was nowhere near a bruiser even though he was covered with 'em. Throwing punches required breaking a sweat and it simply wasn't his M.O.

"You hear what I hear?" Trip said from outside the doorway. The shredding sounds of motorcycle engines could be heard prowling in the distance.

"Hit the lights," Flossy said, pulling the curtain aside with one finger. The room went pitch black, cut only by the yellow fluorescents glowing from the breezeway.

"Maybe Miki and I should head home. I'm awake now, so we'd be fine," Will said and looked at the digital clock. He'd caught plenty of z's since it was already after ten.

"That's what I was thinking, too." Miki nodded.

"Shut up. I'm still pissed at you," Owen growled at her, then leaned down to pick up Will's backpack. "Unfortunately, there's no going back," he said and launched it at Will's head.

73

Will deflected it with his cast, and it plunked down on his little toe. The broken one. He winced.

"We're gone," Flossy said and stepped away from the window. "But let's play it safe. Miki in the middle…gun it around the backside. Will, you're in a new bitch seat."

"Not it," Trip said.

"Man, you spoke up too soon." Flossy nodded his wiry beard at Will. "You're riding with Trip. Now, hustle. It's time to hit the road."

Will slung his backpack on, grabbed the last of the cold pizza off the nightstand, and followed his new ride out the door. He maneuvered onto the back of Trip's vintage Indian Spirit with a backrest—thank you, baby Jesus—and in between bites of pepperoni and cheese, his mind reeled with questions, like why was he even here? Why were they running from a bunch of P-skulls?

Why hadn't he heard from his dad or even his brother? Mom's ashes and the slice of apple pie were in his backpack, but what was the plan exactly? And what about the line of crap they'd all fed him about needing to move on and let go?

Mom?

Yes, dear?

Why'd you have to die anyway?

I love you so much, Will. I died loving you.

CHAPTER 8

A HOT ONE

The four motorcycles hit the highway with Owen in the lead and Flossy pulling up the tail. Miki leaned into the curve with her headlamp trained on Trip's back tire and Will's rear end. Sixty minutes of staring at his green butt with another sixty to go. Torture! *I'm a low-key kinda guy.* Jerk. *Being with you is not easy.* Idiot. *Haven't you ever heard of the law of least effort?* She'd have to look that one up later…in private.

So she had Will pushing her away, Owen yelling in her face, and her dad completely ignoring her. Talk about man troubles. At least Owen seemed genuinely concerned about her even if he was pissed off beyond recognition. Dad, on the other hand, hadn't bothered to return her call or to let anyone else know her whereabouts. Instead, he found himself a hoochie-mama, and—

Didn't she matter to him at all?

Miki's heart clenched.

And what about Will? She was ready to tear her clothes off for that guy, yet he couldn't get away from her fast enough. *In the dark, everything's great.* Yes, yes it was. When she'd had her hands on his back, she could feel his warmth. Smooth, soft skin on one side, rough and scuffed up on the other. He could have killed himself laying his bike down like that with no helmet.

Idiot.

With at least another hour to go, she needed to think about something more uplifting, something other than Will smeared across a two-lane highway. She studied the width of Will's shoulders as she glided around yet another bend in the road, and a smile tugged at her lips. How about that time last year at the Hides of Hell Family Picnic? Oh, yes. It had been a hot one.

A Bikini Summer

Ninety-one degrees slow-cooked Miki's skin like the crock pot of baked beans that no longer existed. There wasn't a thing left unturned on the red-and-white checkered picnic tables after the hungry bikers threw in the flag on flag football. After hours of rough play, they devoured mountains of baked beans with pork belly, potato salad with dill, bratwursts with yellow mustard, entire bags of salty chips, and whole watermelons. They stuffed and chewed all the way down the line only to freeze with their hands in the air in front of Cindy's All American apple pies. Will's mom was club-famous for them—tart, sweet, and with the perfect crust every time.

One rule surrounded the pies and was strictly enforced by muscle: Will's dad, Bill, got the first slice. Always. Or blood would flow. The guys panted and waited with shifty eyes while Bill calmly cut himself a civilized wedge, then stepped out of the fray to watch the crumbs fly. Later, the guys dropped like walruses on the beach while the poor women cleaned up the unholy mess, and the kids scattered like birdshot.

Since Miki didn't want to be on kitchen patrol, she firmly agreed to be in the kid category and picked her way around the dotted bodies on the beach in her new, shimmery bikini. Her long, black hair brushed against her back—swish, swish. She scanned the ice cream counter at the Lemon Squeeze Snack Shack, the oiled up sunbathers on beach towels, and the little bobber-heads in the swimming area, until...

Target located. Will Sullivan had the floating dock all to himself.

Will usually lazed around like a moody grump, like everyone was wasting his time, but she knew better. Even though they didn't go to the same school, they hung out plenty at the club family functions. She liked what she knew and knew what she liked. Will, Will, and more Will. And...if she could guess? He liked her, too. More than once she'd caught his melty-licious brown eyes following her.

So if he thought she would give up on him because he was peeved, he'd be very wrong. She'd knock him out of his shell before the summer was over, and he'd know exactly what hit him. Yep... that's right, Miki "Hot Bod" Holtz.

Now if she could only get the nickname to stick.

Miki waded ankle deep into the warm lake, then knee to thigh deep and dove under. She torpedoed through the blue water with ease while she sculpted a plan of attack, one that ended with Will's undivided attention. She bubbled to the surface like the Swamp Thing, her seaweed hair plastered to her skin. A thick, faded rope hung off the platform, and she gripped it, raking the tangles out of her eyes. Trip sped by in a white boat, towing Owen behind on a wakeboard. Owen jumped over a swell, tilted the board to spray a rooster tail toward the dock, and missed. Not even close. Then the two roared off across the lake in search of another victim.

The water lapped and sloshed against the platform, rocking it like a baby's cradle. She quietly pulled herself up to peek at Will, a long-limbed starfish spread out in the sun. He wore cheap black shades and had a forest green survival bracelet clipped to his wrist. Everyone had one; it was all the rage. Hers was black and boring, but his matched his swimming trunks. It was hot...and so was he.

Miki sank back into the water and scanned the beach. It was far enough away so nobody would see anything, and Owen was merely a speck on the other side of the lake. The coast was clear.

She held onto the side of the dock with one hand and groped behind her back with the other, unhooking the clasp on her bikini. The fabric fell loose in front of her, and she tingled with wild liberation. Biting her lip to keep from giggling out loud, she glided around the dock's corner with her turquoise top trailing after her. Will's damp hair hung over the edge, so she drew in a long, silent breath and slapped her wet top on his face. She plunged under the surface with long, powerful strokes and then breached the water about ten yards out. Slicking wet hair off her forehead, she laughed up at the sky. Nudity, sun, and Will. This was the life!

"Miki!" Will bellowed, poised on the corner of his island. He shook his fist. "I should've known it was you. Why don't you leave me alone?"

Not a chance. She saw progress with him, and there was no way in hell she was letting a little joke, a misunderstanding, throw a wrench in it. She'd apologized all over the place yesterday, and he needed to get over it. Pronto.

Commence Project Will. She slapped the water with the flat of her hands.

"Help! Help me, Will," she yelped with glee as she flailed and splashed. "I lost my swimsuit." She bicycled her legs in the water with her bare shoulders bobbing, relishing Will's slackened jaw. He slowly un-bunched the fabric and held up two triangles. Now, didn't *that* look say apology accepted?

"Oh, you found it." Miki giggled. "Well, don't just stand there, big boy. Help a girl out."

Will's grouchy face broke into a broad grin, just as she'd planned. Could she call 'em or what? She'd have him eating out of the palm of her hand before this club picnic was over.

But the script she'd written in her mind involved him laughing at her wild-child antics and tossing the top back to her, like a gentleman, or possibly even swimming over with it. Instead, he dropped the turquoise swatch at his feet and peeled off his sunglasses. They clattered across the sun-dried wood. Then he sprang off the corner, curling into a cannonball.

"Yeehaw!" He hit the water like a giant boulder, sending a wave in her direction. It smacked her in the face and shot up her nose.

She sputtered and wiped her eyes just as the familiar blub-blub blubbing of an idling boat poked her consciousness. Uh, oh. Red flag alert. It was Owen and Trip.

Plan gone awry.

"Will, no!" Miki shouted at the sparkling ripples while she frantically searched the deep-blue that surrounded her.

There was no Will…anywhere. She dove under and paddled farther away from the dock, hoping to circle back and nab her suit before her brother, Will, or anyone else caught her. Great plan, except a hand gripped her ankle and gave it a tug before she broke the surface. Miki kicked her foot free and swam upward to catch a breather, coughing on a mouthful of lake water.

Will popped up two arm-lengths away and laughed, an infectious sound really, if only she had the time to fully appreciate it. Why did Owen have to come around and ruin this?

"Now what are you going to do?" Will wagged his brows and smirked, like he was pretty sure he had her. If only.

Miki gritted her teeth and with one finger made a cease-and-desist slicing motion across her throat. Will inched closer, but he cocked his head and frowned.

"Will!" She shook her head quickly. "My brother is—"

"Miki!" Owen barked from the boat. He peeled off his fluorescent-yellow life vest and propped his foot up on the rail. "What the hell? Are you skinny dipping?"

Trip raised his eyebrows as he cut the engine and let the boat drift toward them. He had bulky muscles covered in intricate, Day of the Dead tattoos: red roses, blue script, and black skulls. He was one of Miki's favorite guys since he was sweet, kind, and a little mysterious with being an orphan, a high school drop-out, and an amputee. The most amazing thing about him was he kept quiet, whereas Owen had a ginormous mouth.

Will treaded water as the boat eased closer, but his contagious grin hardened into a dark scowl. The walls of his personal tower erupted around him, and Miki watched as he turned back into a moody grump.

"Here." Owen tossed his life vest overboard, and Miki grabbed it, holding it close to her chest. Apparently, wakeboarding was over and now, so was fooling around with Will.

"You having fun, Little Willy, harassing my sister?" Water dripped off Owen's nose and made plipping noises beside her. "I'd kick your ass, but I'm done playing in the water."

Trip puffed out a tired sigh but kept his eyes front and center behind the steering wheel.

"Dude…" Will curled his lip. "I'd like to see you try."

81

"Duly noted, you punk." Owen glared back and slowly cracked his knuckles. "I'd love to give you another bloody nose. Give me a reason, and it doesn't have to be a good one."

Will cast her a wary look. "It's always trouble with you," he muttered before dipping underwater.

"Will..." Miki pleaded at the ripples he left behind. Her heart turned into a lead weight, and she sank against the life vest.

"Miki, what are you doing?" Owen growled down at her, his eyes as dark as night. "This is a family picnic. There are little kids running around, and you're not impressing anybody."

"I dunno. I'm impressed," Trip muttered with a shrug and wisely averted his gaze to the bow.

"Shut up, Prospect," Owen said as he watched Will heave himself out of the lake and onto the platform. "Hey!" Owen hollered. "Toss her swimsuit over, asswipe!"

Miki churned the water with her legs while trying to ignore Owen. He was seriously killing her buzz. What would Will have done once he caught her? Goose bumps sprang up her arms, and she shivered under the ninety-degree sun rays. So close. She almost had him, but Owen always seemed to be minding her business. He was only five years older, not twenty-five. He wasn't her dad...thank God.

She gulped as Will bent down and scooped up her bikini top, his swimming trunks riding tight over his butt. He was so fine she almost fainted.

"Here, Miki." Will dropped it into the water right at his feet.

Now why did he have to go and be like that? It wasn't her fault she had a jackass for a brother. She and Will had made a little progress with some eyebrow ogling and a couple laughs. Now it seemed they were back to square one.

Will jerked his chin up at Owen and tapped it with his middle finger. Then he arced off the side as sleek as a dolphin and performed a perfect crawl stroke back to shore.

"Get your suit, Mik, and let's get out of here," Owen said and slid a pair of mirror shades onto his slender nose.

"I came with Dad." Miki flashed him a smile, clutching the neon vest closer. Sorry, sucker, but she had her own plans.

"Unfortunately, you're with us. Dad left with the Lemon Squeeze lady an hour ago."

"Why would he leave with her?" That girl wasn't a day older than Owen. What was she, twenty-one? Twenty-two? Miki glanced back at the beach to the brick and mortar snack shack, a place that served up an array of ice cream flavors from black licorice, her personal favorite, to white chocolate, which happened to be Will's.

Trip raised a sleek brow and gave her a mocking look as in *You're a big girl. You do the math.*

"Listen, Mik," Owen pulled his foot into the boat and glanced across the water. After a moment, he looked back down at her and rested his hands on his hips. "This divorce, it's really gonna happen, alright? Dad's already checked out."

Yeah. Good, ol' Dad, living the bachelor life at the clubhouse in one of the spare rooms, same as

Owen. Now, Dad could chase anything that wiggled, an old man picking up young chicks. Just gross.

That day was supposed to mark the start of an awesome summer, but it had foundered at the bottom of the lake, sort of like her turquoise bikini top. Not because her brother caught her topless and chased off her crush, not because her dad flaunted his sex life like a horny high school quarterback, and not because her mom stoked fires in the backyard using Dad's lucky bandana collection.

No. It had been the worst summer ever because Will's mom left the picnic that evening with a carload of dirty crock pots and empty pie tins. She'd tapped out a text message, and before she could hit send, she'd wrapped her Honda Civic around an oncoming truck in her lane, four miles from home. She died of blunt force trauma to the head and a punctured stomach. Later, Cindy's phone was recovered, and so was the text intended for Will.

MOM: I saved you a slice.

Worst summer ever.

CHAPTER 9

BIG V

You don't try hard enough.

Will's heart raced, and he blinked up at the tent. So weird. He stuck his pinkie in his ear and twisted it back and forth. It tickled inside like his mom was right here next to him, whispering.

Boom-boom-boom-boom.

A motorcycle pulled into the campsite, and if he could guess by the boom-boom, it was Leo. His chopper had Big Growl, double-barrel pipes, which sounded cool as hell. Leo the Lion took the "Loud and Proud" badge he wore very seriously.

Unfortunately, even the rattling beast on the other side of the tent wall couldn't drive out those questions bouncing around in Will's head. He'd done a lot of thinking and worrying last night. Where the hell were Dad and Liam? Why wouldn't anyone give him a straight answer? "Club business" wasn't going to cut it anymore.

Leo had some 'splainin' to do.

Will nudged the sleeping bag open, a stinky old thing reeking of onions and gas, a clubhouse special, and unzipped the flap. It felt like eight or so in the morning, and Caboose was still snoring like a locomotive somewhere

85

nearby. Good. Everyone was sleeping, the perfect time to put the screws to the ol' prez wannabe. Will stepped out shirtless, wearing only his Ghetto Gramps and waited for Leo to kick off.

Only Leo wasn't alone.

An Amazon woman who was round top to bottom from her high cheek bones to her big toes peeping out her sandals—not to mention everything in between— eased off behind Leo. She wore tight denim jeans with strategic rips in the thighs and a billowing white shirt. The scooped neckline was low enough to show off a whole lot of cleavage. Not too shabby.

She smiled at Will, and suddenly he wished he'd put his wrinkled t-shirt back on. What if looking at his crusty scabs or the new pink skin made her want to throw up a little? Things were drying and healing, which was good, but what if something fluttered off? Talk about sick, wrong, and just freakin' gross.

But he couldn't miss this opportunity to corner the boss.

"Hey, Leo." Will covered himself by cupping his opposite shoulder with his good arm while his casted limb hung like a plumb weight.

"Father-daughter trip, huh? Who's this?" Miki stepped out of her tent, looking dark and rumpled with a bad case of blue bed-head. She wore an oversized t-shirt long enough to cover her butt but not her knees. Tan legs, flip-flops, candy-coated toenails. Yeah, he noticed. It didn't take away from the fact she was stealing his air time, though.

"Come here, babe," said the newly showered-and-shaved Leo, but he wasn't calling to his daughter. He held his arm out to the tall blonde, and she stepped forward, wearing a glossy smile meant to warm the planet. "Valentina, I want you to meet my kid, Miki, and this beat-up one here is Bill's son, Shorty's nephew...and probably someone's cousin, William the third."

"It's just Will," Miki grumbled, all tight-lipped and stern, looking an awful lot like her brother, the geyser. Scary.

"Hi, Just Will. You can call me Just Val." She laughed easily, like not much was going to ruffle her feathers, especially not her biker boyfriend's snot-nosed kid. She made duck-lips at Leo, who made duck-lips back.

What the...? Will gave a sideways look at Miki and raised his brows.

She glared back at him. "Is that what you meant by 'trying too hard,' Will?" She turned on her flip-flopped heels and stomped to the road, heading for the bathrooms.

Will opened his mouth, then closed it again. Part of him wanted to follow her, vacate this suddenly awkward, adult love-fest, but a bigger part of him needed a word. "Leo, we have to talk. Like, why haven't I heard from my dad?"

Leo studied him for a moment, then nuzzled Val's ear. "Babe, why don't you go find Miki. Get to know her better."

Wrinkling her nose like a rabbit, she whispered, "I got this," and stepped out of Leo's embrace to strut her stuff in Miki's wake. Will shook his head. Nothing good would come of it.

"Sit down, Will." Leo gestured to the weathered bench at the picnic table. He kicked his boot onto the opposite side and rested an elbow on his knee. His black leather vest hung open and Lucky You cologne misted the air directly under Will's nostrils.

Damn, dude.

"We've got problems." Leo rubbed his bottom lip.

"We all do, so tell me. What's up with Dad and Liam?" Spit it out. Will picked at the edges of his cast. He wasn't here for the small talk, dude.

"I'm gonna give it to you straight. Your dad and your brother...they went off the grid days ago, and we don't know where they are. We have reason to believe the P-skulls are in retaliation mode, and Bill and Liam were targeted."

"Targeted? How? As in kidnapped?"

"There's a shit-storm brewing," Leo said with his dark eyes trained on Will's face.

"What do you mean? They're alive, right Leo?" Oh, God. How would Leo know? The dude was half checked out with Big Val while Will sat here, probably a complete stray, his entire family dead. Dead! "But you don't really know." Will cleared his throat. "Do you?"

"I do, and we're going to get them back safe and sound. You'll see."

Leo's confidence was amazing. No wonder he grabbed the president's chair when Dad went numb. Leo was an emotionally vacant, heartless prick who was more than ready to take over while telling everyone Cindy died, but we didn't...remember her, honor her...blah, blah, blah...let's live on for Cindy. Now pass me a beer!

Or something close to it.

Will didn't care what the exact words were, but he did care how Leo was the one who wanted to "move past this" and "get on with our lives" as if he were as affected as everyone else. Last time Will checked, Leo wasn't a Sullivan. He wasn't blood, no matter what those bikers said about being brothers.

"How're you gonna get it done?" Will stood. "Do you even know where they are?"

"I've got a couple rats—"

"And what'd they say?"

Leo gave a dismissive wave. "It's club business."

"I'm sick of hearing those two words, dude." Will could hear the quaver in his own voice, but he didn't let it stop him. "I want to know what the P-Skulls want, Leo. Money?"

The Lion dropped his boot down and straightened. "They wanna die, son."

Live...die... The words pounded between Will's temples like drum beats in a heavy metal riff, like something from a Five Finger Death Punch album...*the art of a lie.*

Hadn't he been through enough already? How could he lose his dad and his brother, too? Why'd life have to be so damned precious? How could he keep anyone safe in a world where one moment she was smiling up at the sky and the next, she had dirt in her eyes and up her nose? If they'd buried Mom, she'd have nothing left to look forward to, except for earthworms and roots.

He couldn't imagine it, and neither could Dad or Liam or even Aunt K. They'd all agreed to have Mom cremated, baked in an oven, just the way she'd've liked it, reducing her to a gritty pile of dust.

"I'm going home," Will said, trying to keep his voice normal. How could he have a proper breakdown in a tent where everyone could hear him? What would the bikers say? Would they yell about how real men don't cry? How death is part of the cycle of life? So get it together, man. The good die young.

Did they even care two of their own were missing? While Leo was busy sappy-lapping with his new gal, the rest of the guys were sleeping off a long night. Will clenched his teeth until his molars ached. Who was looking for his family? Why didn't they tell him earlier? Why all the secrets?

"Listen to me," Leo's big paw clutched Will's shoulder. "It may seem like we're not doing much, but appearances can be—"

"Deceiving, I know." Will twisted out of Leo's grip. This conversation was going absolutely nowhere. It was clear the good ol' Hides of Hell president didn't have a plan. All he was doing was blowing smoke.

Will trudged to his tent and stepped in. He couldn't slam the flap shut, but he could rip the zipper down. Unfortunately, it wasn't nearly as satisfying. Slamming his bedroom door used to grate on his mom's last nerve…

Will, this is your mother speaking, speaking, speaking. Forget the door! If your father is dead, you'll be adrift in this world. If your brother is gone, too, you'll be alone. Alone, Will. Worse than now. Think! What can you do?

Stay out of my head…stay ahead of the pain. He unscrewed the cap on his pain meds, tipped out three, then downed 'em with a big gulp of water. He face-planted onto the sleeping bag while erasing all thoughts of Dad and Liam and the sick feeling churning in his gut. He couldn't…wouldn't think about his mom, either. If he had to dream about death, it would be of the time when his cat dismantled a possum in the house. What a sick mess.

Good ol' Helmet.

* * *

Miki slammed out of the bathroom stall and jerked to a stop in front of the sinks. Valentina stood with a designer-denim hip cocked out and her arms folded under a tremendous chest. She dominated the space with not only her giantess height but with her confidence, too. Miki eased her shoulders back, hoping to gain an inch, but she still felt like her little seventeen-year-old self, inconsequential and immature.

Miki scowled and stepped to the sink to wash her hands. There was no soap in the dispenser, and the water was ice cold. What next?

"Okay, you followed me in here, so you must have something real important to say. Something brilliant, I'm sure." Miki huffed. Great. Her black survival bracelet was sopping wet, and the paper towels were jammed. She flapped her wet hands over the trash barrel, flinging water droplets against the concrete wall.

"I know your type, a jealous daddy's girl who needs to be the center of attention. Believe it or not, babe, I'm not here to take him away from you, got it?" She dropped her arms and softened her voice. "Listen, Miki, I'm here to tell you to move over and get used to sharing the spotlight. I like Leo, and he likes me, and that's the way it is. Why fight it? Accept it, and it'll make your life easier...trust me."

First of all, Miki wasn't jealous or a daddy's girl, and she didn't need a lot of attention, but a little would be nice. Maybe, instead of pacifying her with expensive gifts, Dad could say something important and meaningful for once, like I want you in my world, Miki-Lou. It could be that simple...that easy.

But Val's talk of *It is what it is—just accept it* sounded very similar to Will's half-cocked idea about effort or the lack of it. Miki didn't want to accept the status quo. She fought for what she wanted and tried to change things. Look where it got her, though. Nowhere she wanted to be. Was she her dad's pride and joy? No. He barely had time for her. Did she have Will's undivided attention? Did he like her? Only in the dark it seemed.

So maybe Will and Val were right.

Effort, why bother?

"You do know you're one in a long line of women, don't you? Let's see..." Miki glanced up at the dead bugs in the light fixtures and ticked off her fingers. "There was Ellen, uh...Mary Ann...then Dixie, Jo Jo, and Heather...someone named 'Wild Wilma' and of course, the big one, Flossy's ex." Her dad was a pig.

Poor Valentina. She was nowhere near the beginning of the line and probably nowhere near the end of it. In fact, just a couple days ago, Dad had been stroking the arm of a nurse with an arm full of bed pans while Will was laid out, flat as a pancake. For the past year after the divorce, it seemed all Dad had to do was sit back and crook his finger. The easy girls flocked to him, and it didn't matter who they were or what they looked like, his type of woman was the type who said yes.

Didn't any of them have a sense of self-worth or dignity?

"And once..." Miki lowered her gaze. "...much to my mom's regret, he came over for 'old time's sake,' so—"

"That's ancient news, hon." Valentina shook her head with mock sadness. "For me? I get what I want, and for six-straight-weeks I've been getting Leo. See what I mean? We're working toward something long-lasting," Valentina said.

She was pretty sure of herself, standing there with her golden tan, ash-blonde hair, and her trendy outfit. Miki really did want to root for her, wanted Val to get her man, to win. Because deep down, she wanted to be the same, be the type of girl who homed in on her target and bullseye! But instead, Miki spent a majority of her time pining and losing. The law of least effort was starting to have some appeal.

"You know what? My dad's never going to change, and when I look at you..." Miki let her eyes travel down the length of Val's jeans to her sexy leather sandals and back up again. "...do you know what I see?"

"Oh, I can't wait to hear this," Val smirked.

"I see someone who can do a lot better than him."

* * *

You don't try hard enough.

There it was again, the tickle in his ear canal like someone was right here with him. Why was waking up so difficult? His entire body felt thick and heavy like a glob of swamp mud. Stagnant. He could stay here like this forever.

"I know you're awake," Miki whispered.

Will's eyelids peeled back immediately. The tent glowed with the high sun, and the heat inside turned stifling. He shifted to look at Miki with her big eyes and her blue hair pulled back in a stubby ponytail. The tops of her ears were showing.

"What are you doing in my tent?" he croaked, sounding like a bull frog. "God. What time is it?" He eased up slowly, hoping to avoid a head rush and searched for his water bottle.

"Here." Miki handed it to him. "You've been sleeping for hours. It's after noon."

Noon, huh? So if he had his math right, and one pill equaled ninety minutes of sleep, he would need to take three more to get to happy hour. Then another ten to get him through to the next morning. Within a day or two, he'd either be an addict or brain dead. He may be a lazy gob, but getting fried wasn't part of his life plan. Besides, he couldn't imagine putting Dad or Liam through that kind of ringer. They were alive; they had to be. The Pulver Skulls wouldn't—

They wanna die, son.

"I gotta get out of here, Miki." He cranked up the intensity as he studied her brown eyes. "I'll do whatever you want if you'll take me home."

"The stuff of dreams. Too bad I don't like you anymore," she said before lowering her voice. "They're not going to let us go home because the Pulver Skulls are out there roaming. Remember the ugly P-Skull patch nailed to the wall in the clubhouse? It's in the room we're not supposed to know about."

"What room?" She didn't like him anymore? Why?

"You know...the one in the basement." He shook his head because he had no idea what she was talking about. She rolled her eyes and sighed heavily. "Never mind."

"What does this have to do with you and me?"

"I think it belonged to one of the P-Skull guys who killed your mom. They were drunk or stoned when they hit her, and the one guy..."

"Wait." Will held up his hand, letting the fog clear. What was he hearing? "It was a Pulver Skull driving?"

"Will..." Miki lowered her chin. "Are you serious?"

His breaths became shallow like a beer keg sat on his chest. Last year, when he'd gotten the news about his mom, all he'd retained was a drunk driver, her texting, and a car wreck. He didn't need or want to know anything more. With a pillow over his head, he'd managed to survive the first month on sips of air and water. Now, almost a year later, reality was slapping him in the face. "I..." He swallowed, or tried to. "I guess I..."

"I know you probably don't want to talk about it, but if you ask me, it was an accident. The P-Skulls didn't seek her out. Think about it. They were on a joy ride. But you know how this thing goes. The Hides of Hell took care of business, payback style, by cutting the patch off a dead guy. So guess who wants payback for the payback?"

"The Pulver Skulls," Will said and shook his head. "All the more reason to get home. We shouldn't be in the middle of this. You go to your mom's, and I'll lock myself in my house. No problem. No one will even know I'm there."

"Don't you want to find Bill and Liam?" Miki gaped at him like his pores were oozing green sludge or something. She shook her head with disgust and rocked back on her flip flops. "Let me guess. This is the part where you endorse the law of least effort, right? What a selfish jackass. You're exactly the type of guy I can't stand." She crawled toward the tent flaps. "I'm outta here."

95

"Wait." He tried to grab her ankle with his fingertips, but his cast got in the way. "Hang on a minute!" She turned, giving him the squinty eyes, so he pleaded. "Miki, I'm lost here. I don't know what to do. What if I never see my dad again or...oh, God. Or my brother?" His eyes welled up, and from previous experience he knew he was about to rupture. Will lowered his jaw and stared at the green cast in his lap. How could he make her understand? "One minute I feel tore up and raw like there's no hope, and the next, I feel nothing...like I'm dead inside." A rogue tear rolled down his cheek, and with a quick hand, he smudged it into his skin. He couldn't lose anymore people, pets...family. He wasn't strong enough to deal—

A lump the size of Alaska climbed up his throat. He couldn't swallow...couldn't breathe. Something had to give.

"Will." He looked up, and Miki's face crumpled with distress. She lunged toward him, sat in his lap with her legs on either side, and pulled him into a full-body koala hug. "I'm sorry. I'm so sorry," she whispered.

He took it all in—her warmth, her touch, her emotion—and squeezed her back tightly, not even caring how he didn't have a shirt on or how a couple more tears escaped. He'd been drowning earlier, but this connection was saving him like the floating dock in the middle of Lake Judy. He pressed his nose against her warm neck and held on. Don't let go, Miki.

After a long moment, she spoke softly into his ear, "I have a plan." His skin prickled with electricity.

Her plans always left him uninspired.

Or maybe inspired but underwhelmed.

More like *over*whelmed in a closet with five of his peers looking on. Yeah. So, Miki had a plan? Hey, call him dubious, but for some reason he was turned on.

"Later," she whispered in a soothing voice with her hands on his upper back. "When the guys ride to Burnout, we'll pretend to follow along, slow and easy. Then, when Caboose passes us, we can turn around and head home, like last time. Just the two of us."

Her body was pressed into his, and he felt safe for the moment, all wrapped up with Miki in her t-shirt and jeans. He didn't want to feel the chill of her moving away. Not when they were together like this, bonding. His skin warmed like a pilot light somewhere inside had flicked on. She was the only one who could make him forget why he was here. His good hand slipped around to her lower back. Instead of all the tension and drama, maybe this thing between them could start being easy, right here, right now. His palm slid farther down to cover her back pockets.

"Uh…" She leaned back with a frown. "What are you doing?"

"Miki, I wanna be with you." Will lifted his cast, and his free fingers combed a blue strand away from her temple. He traced the shell of her ear where she wore black pearls and silver studs, nothing fancy but cool. He leaned forward and gently pressed his lips to her throat.

"Will, would you get serious? We're in a tent. This isn't the time or the place." She pushed away from him, and goosebumps sprang up on his naked chest.

"Why are you even here?" He scowled and reached for his t-shirt, bending his leg to hide himself. Who could figure her out? One minute she was breathing heavy in his ear, then boom! Chill factor five. It was the same old story: she sought him out, broke through his defenses, and riled him up. Then, when he was about to say yes, she'd already left him behind.

Except in the hotel room. He'd definitely said no that time. Otherwise, what would have happened? Thank God, she hadn't been carrying condoms.

"I'm here because..." Her voice trailed off like she had no more words. See? Even she didn't know why she was in his tent, tormenting him.

"Hey, you're the one who said you were the easiest person I could get. I only thought—" She gaped at him, her eyes filling with water. Was she going to cry? He closed his eyes and let his head fall forward. Dude, just shut up. You stupid—

But those were her words, weren't they?

"God, pathetic," she whispered, and he looked up. Her face turned pink. "Forget I *ever* said that." She turned away and pulled up the zipper.

"Where're you going, huh, Miki? What am I missing this time? You're the one who came in here, jumped in my lap, and started whispering in my ear. If you don't like me the way I am, then why don't you leave me alone?"

"You're right...I will leave you alone," she said in a weird defeatist tone very unlike Miki. She slipped out of the tent, and the ground tarp rustled as she walked away.

What the hell? Will crawled to the open flap to call her back, but instead, he watched as she ran across the campsite, past a group of milling bikers, straight to Owen.

Figures. Nothing but trouble.

What was she up to this time?

Will leaned back inside the flaps and pulled the zipper down slowly. What was he up to? He went from slamming beers to popping pills to forgetting why he even existed. Earlier he felt hollow and worthless, but now—could he find his dad and brother like Miki said? Was it within his power to save them? How? He didn't even know where to start.

What did the Pulver Skulls want with his family? According to Miki, it was one of their guys driving the truck. One of their guys killed his mom. Now, those bastards had Dad and Liam. Was murder part of the escalating retaliation?

Who knew? What he did know was he couldn't sit in this festering tent, sweating like a pimp in church while Dad and Liam were being beaten down by a bunch of thugs. His mom would want him to do all he could for them, wouldn't she?

Yes, Will.

Right. It was time to get off his ass and do something.

CHAPTER 10

CRUMBS

"How many times do I have to tell you? He's an inferior shit. You don't need to chase after crumbs, Mik." Owen's face was dirty from the wind, dust, and last night's bonfire smoke, which made his dark eyes glint. He looked past her and snapped a twig. "Looks like lover boy's finally back. I'm hitting the showers."

Miki glanced toward the trail leading to the bathrooms where Will walked along with a thin towel slung around his neck. He'd been gone nearly an hour and probably went through a roll of quarters paying for hot water. Even though she was still ticked off, she hoped he didn't get his cast wet. Why didn't he get a waterproof one? Maybe making the decision required an effort. Oh, no...couldn't do that!

His dark hair hung damply past his shoulders, and his brown eyes searched the campsite until they met hers. He held her gaze, then nodded his chin toward the tent as if he wanted her to meet him there.

"And...if I see you in his tent again, I'll break his other arm." Owen snapped the poor twig into another piece and threw it into the cold fire pit before marching off.

What a blowhard. Miki turned on the picnic bench to face Trip, who had his chrome prosthesis propped up on the metal grate. He had a hot body and wore black athletic shorts, proud to show off his fake limb. The rest of him was all muscle. Why couldn't she like him? He was quiet and gorgeous, and if one caught him in the right mood, he'd drop nuggets of pure wisdom. He was like her personal Magic 8 Ball.

"Why do I have to be related to Owen again?" And the answer is…?

"He's only looking out for you," Trip said. "Better to have him be with you than against you. Count 'em… small blessings."

"Right." She smiled. "Well, Trip. This has been fun, but now I'm off to talk to Will," she whispered dramatically, "*in his tent.*"

"You're asking for trouble," Trip said, pulling a hunting knife out of its leather sheath. He felt the blade with his thumb and pursed his lips.

"Why does everyone always tell me that?"

He laughed softly, rolling a green branch between his fingers. "I think you know why," he said and cut off the broad leaves.

"No." Miki rubbed hands over her face and growled into her palms. "I really don't."

"Miki…" He turned toward her and gave her a thoughtful look. "You're a beautiful girl."

"I am?" She straightened. This could be it. He was about to drop a nugget. She searched his face. His five o'clock shadow was right on time, and his skin was tanned under his buzzcut. Enlighten me, Oh, Wise One.

"And not only on the outside." He nodded in a shy sort of way, carving off a strip of bark. He murmured, "No crumbs for you."

"Trip," Miki said softly and smiled as she stood. "Thank you. No one's ever said anything so…nice to me before."

"I bet they have," he said and cut another strip off like he was peeling a raw potato. "Only, you don't listen."

Maybe she didn't, but she'd keep her ears open from now on because those few words—wow! They warmed her. Her dad should take lessons from Trip because why couldn't he say something like that to her?

"I guess I should go pack, huh? It's getting kind of late. Shouldn't we be leaving for Burnout?"

"We're chilling here for another night. Club business, yadda, yadda. You might as well settle in."

"Where's my dad?"

Trip chuckled. "Nope, not going there."

She blew out a long breath and automatically headed toward Will's tent flaps, but she made a hard right and crawled inside her own instead. No matter how much she wanted to tell him their plan was shot to hell, to snuggle and be with him, he wasn't her boyfriend, or her buddy, and she wasn't accepting crumbs anymore. She didn't owe him anything...and after what he said to her? Basically throwing her own words back in her face—so embarrassing! She wasn't one of those easy, needy girls. She was beautiful, like Trip said, inside and out...and strong, too, dammit!

Why'd she dye her hair blue? Because she could. It was wild and new and hers. She didn't need her dad's approval then, and she didn't need it now. Starting at this moment, she wasn't going to care where he was or who he was with.

She dropped onto her sleeping bag and stared at the rain flap. It was green.

Green like an old survival bracelet...like a cast...like a track suit.

Miki sat up and squeezed her temples; it was hard being a new person. It was hard not to care.

The tarp crinkled as she crawled across the tent floor. Yes, she was an idiot, but she had to see Will.

"Finally! What took you so long?" Will scooted aside as she climbed in. "I've been waiting forever," he groused, pulling a deck of cards from his pack.

His sleeping bag had been smoothed out, and his stuff was picked up and orderly. Even though it looked as if he'd been busy with housekeeping, it still smelled like mildew and camp smoke.

"You could've come to my tent." Why did she always have to go to him? If he wanted to talk to her, he could have made the effort.

Effort. She hated that word.

"And get my ass kicked? No thanks." He shuffled the cards.

"You're going to get it kicked anyway, so brace yourself. Are we playing?" She picked up the cards he'd dealt her. "What's the game?"

"Rummy. Jokers wild," he said. "It's getting late, and we haven't talked about the plan. When are we heading out?"

"Things have changed. The guys are staying another night," Miki said while organizing her hand. What a sucky shuffle job! If they were playing poker, she'd wipe the tent floor with him. "But maybe this works out to our advantage anyway. I mean, we could still leave, sneak off on our own when it gets dark, like around nine-ish. We'll push my bike to the end of the loop, and ride it on out of here. How does that sound?"

Will studied her over the top of his cards to the point of awkwardness. Why was he giving her the smoky-brown eyes? She wiped the side of her mouth in case there was something on her face, then shifted uneasily on his sleeping bag. He looked away, pulling a card from the draw pile.

"I...your turn," he said and scratched his brow. "I also, uh...I'm sorry for what I said, you know, about you being the easiest person. I was being a smartass. However, I do stand by my earlier comment about how being with you is *not* easy." He blushed, and normally she would have found that absolutely adorable. But he sucked at apologies, so she imagined smacking him alongside the head instead.

"Keep digging that hole, Sullivan, and you'll end up walking to the Powerhouse Inn." She drew and discarded.

"Powerhouse what? No. We are not going back there."

"Yes…we are. I want to see Pinecone, Will. She knows something. When she heard your name, she got all fumble-fingered. My gut says we need to check it out, and it's on the way home. Right where you want to go, remember…to hide?" She glared him down. She wasn't taking no for an answer. He was going to the Powerhouse Inn, whether he liked it or not.

"Truce, alright?" He held up his green cast like a white flag. "I won't throw what you say back in your face if you'll do the same for me. I want to find my Dad and my brother, okay? I need to find them alive. I have to, and I trust your instincts. If you think Pinecone has answers, I'm there."

Were the stars aligned? Because she'd gotten two ginormous compliments in less than an hour. She didn't know what to say but it seemed like a precious thing to have Will's trust because he was so stingy with it.

"Royal flush." She spread her cards out into an arc as wide as her winning smile and tossed the other cards aside.

"Dude…" He shook his head. "We're playing rummy."

"*You're* playing rummy, and how's that working out for ya?" She laughed.

"Miki!" Owen's voice barked on the other side of the tent's wall. Okay, fun's over. Her brother either had the worst timing or the best, she couldn't decide.

"I'm in Will's tent, playing poker," she yelled over her shoulder. She lifted her brows at Will. "My gut says it's time for me to leave."

He leaned back against his pack, and on a scale between bored and resolved, he still looked like a ten. Sexy devil.

"Please do," he said and tossed his cards onto the pile.

God it felt good to leave. She could annoy the hell out of him, still be herself, and not worry that he didn't like her. She released herself from his tent, from his clutches, and glided out into the open air.

I'm my own woman!

* * *

Will surveyed the smooth stick Trip had carved for him. It was like a flat wooden spoon the size of a pencil. It slid easily between his forearm and cast, so he could finally reach the mind-numbing itch. Thank you, baby Jesus. It...felt...cosmic. He groaned as he shimmied the scratching stick back and forth, in and out, while taking in the puny campfire.

It was a dainty H.O.H. gathering tonight since, according to Miki, a majority of the guys had left for Burnout after a late breakfast. A few more peeled away at their own pace, leaving the prospects on clean up duty and Dad's motley crew behind. Well, everyone except the good ol' prez and his new gal pal, Val. Will hadn't seen them since this morning. Leo the Lion: president, father, friend, *brother*...what a huge a-hole.

The rest—Flossy, Trip, and Owen—didn't make up a very rowdy crowd tonight. They were putting off a weird vibe of somber, mostly sober, and unusually alert. They'd even offered Will a beer, ignoring Uncle Shorty's edict: No drinking for Willy Boy.

It had been hard saying no as he chewed through a spicy chili dog laden with onions and cheddar cheese, but he did, and he felt like he deserved a pat on the back for good behavior. Although, what he really wanted was to pop some pain pills and grab a catnap. He should have done it back when he had the chance. Now, it was too late. The sun was setting, the fire was crackling, and very soon, he'd be riding off with Miki, chasing the pain again.

He stole another glance at her through the wavering heat and smoke. Boots instead of flip flops, jeans instead of the obvious I'm-going-for-a-ride leather pants, and a snug t-shirt. She was busy laughing it up with Trip.

So yeah, no booze, no pills, only aches and Miki, which was synonymous with pain…as in a pain in the ass.

She'd said she didn't like him anymore. Why? What'd he ever do to her? She'd liked him for as long as he could remember, then in a snap, it's done. All from his one lame comment? C'mon, he was fairly sure he'd made plenty of 'em before, and it hadn't meant anything. Only showed she couldn't be loyal if she tried.

Will, this is your mother speaking, and that is the most inane argument I've ever—

Yeah, yeah. The whole thing was stupid. They weren't going out, and they weren't really friends, just stuck in a cycle of her flirting and him trying to keep up without getting hurt. She waffled hot and cold from a ray of sun on his face to a bucket of ice down his pants. Boom. Not easy. Not in the slightest.

Last year's closet scene was a huge eye-opener. She'd made up the rules, she'd selected him, she'd rolled the erotic dice.

Bite and Butt

Will tried not to blush in front of the others, but he felt like a monk at a biker rally with the words Bite and Butt staring back at him, black on white. Miki threw her shoulders into the couch and laughed, her teeth showing brightly against her tan skin. No zombie lips tonight. No black licorice.

"At least I didn't roll Bite your Nipples because sometimes I get feisty. I wouldn't wanna hurt you," she said and wagged her brows.

Jesus. I am a gentleman. I repeat: I am a gentleman. Wait…who was biting who again? He didn't really know how the game worked since he hadn't been paying attention. His mind had been wrapped around debugging the Grand Theft Auto game. It kept crashing at the start—

Miki crooked her finger at him, so he automatically pushed off the couch and followed her, willing and kind of eager to leave behind the video game and the four others in their group. When the closet door closed, everything turned black and surreal. He couldn't see anything, yet his imagination went wild as his senses prickled with awareness. Delicate fingers skated up his elbows and biceps, and he stooped to feel her warm breath on his neck. She pressed her body into his, and her hands explored his back. His heart ratcheted up and felt like it might explode. He inhaled the scent of her skin; she licked his. He groaned. She sighed. They were like crickets, their legs rubbing together.

Only a few hours earlier, he'd bought her an ice cream cone, and she'd asked for his number. A big moment, right? This was big, too. In the back of his mind, a voice chirped to slow things down because seven minutes wasn't nearly long enough to get where they were heading. Did this mean they were going out, or was something more formal required to make it legit? He wouldn't mind holding Miki's hand and kissing her in public. He could call her his

GF when he introduced her to his non-biker friends. *This is Miki Holtz...my girlfriend.*

The whole thing felt right...her hands on him, his lips on hers...them being together.

"Miki," he whispered next to her ear, "I like y—"

Ding-ding-ding!

With a gust, the door whipped open, throwing in shards of light. He jerked back into the leather coat sleeves, and before his eyes could adjust, Miki pulled away. Everyone clustered around, chattering excitedly for details.

"Did you bite his butt or did he bite yours?"

"Oh, my God. How far did you go?"

"Which buttons are undone?"

"Will! Stay in the closet because I'm next."

He blinked in a daze while Miki stood with her back to him. One of the girls, Izzy with the weird last name, tried to push past Miki, but she cocked her elbow out to block the doorway. Then, Miki flapped a hand under her nose with dramatic flare.

"Game over," she said and wrinkled her nose with humorous disgust. "Will here just filled the closet with the aroma of Mona's bean dip." Someone made a farting noise, and Miki laughed. "It totally reeks."

He blinked and opened his mouth to defend himself, but he was too stunned. What should he say? He'd been about to ask her out, and all she had on her mind was making fun of him in front of everyone. His whole body flooded with the burn of humiliation.

In the span of a day, he'd gone from being one cool dude to feeling like a gullible loser. If only the closet would swallow him whole and spit out the pieces...

...far, far away from here.

Will shook himself out of his reverie and searched Miki out. She wasn't hard to find, straight blue hair glinting by the fire, still grinning up at Trip, who apparently was a comedian. So what, right? It didn't matter. The fun and games were long over. With the darkening sky, it had to be nine o'clock by now.

It was time to ride.

CHAPTER 11

THE DARK SIDE

"Hey, Miki, how about another hand of poker?" Will nudged her with his hip while giving Trip the standard chin-nod. Dude, this isn't the girl you're looking for...go about your business. Trip returned the gesture. Chill, bro. Everything's cool.

"A glutton for punishment?" She smiled, and Will nodded.

When he breathed in, he felt an internal shift, which had him resting a hand over his guts. Sure, he had a bruised spleen, but the ache seemed more mental than medical at the moment. His insides churned and scraped like a glacier ready for the big thaw; he was coming alive. It's how he envisioned the getting-off-his-ass-and-doing-something part.

Hang on, Dad, Liam. I'm coming for you. I don't know where or when or how. I don't know anything really, but...hang on.

"Hear that, Owen?" She faced her brother with hands on her hips. "I'm playing cards with Will and guess where? In his tent." She poised for his reaction, but Owen merely crossed his arms and glanced at the sky as if searching for something violent to say. He took too long, and Miki was done. She turned to Will. "Texas hold'em sound good?"

"Sure." Will touched her elbow. Move along, move along.

"What's poker without beer, Gadget?" Flossy lobbed a cold one at Will. The bottle clanked against his cast, and he fumbled with it down the length of his shirt. Finally in his possession, he held it up. Brown glass, no label. It had a flip-top lid and was sealed with a rubber gasket.

"What's this?"

"Mook's home brew. He left a few behind, so there's plenty." Flossy dug through the cooler for another one and graciously wiped off the melting ice before handing it to Miki. "There ya go. Knock yourselves out."

"Why are you giving them Mook's beer?" Trip asked with a frown.

"Don't forget," Flossy murmured. "You're a prospect."

"I'll ask, then." Owen pulled his shoulders up and glowered. "Is it necessary? Why waste it on them?"

Flossy tilted his head back and looked down the length of his nose at Owen, whose lip curled like a dog. Their fists were clenched ready for blows. Flossy didn't like explaining himself, and Owen didn't know how to stand down.

Will took a step back, ready for a brawl. What was the big deal about a couple beers anyway? Talk about unwarranted aggression.

"You want another hotel incident? I don't," Flossy muttered through his whiskers. His voice was low and hard to hear. Then, he spoke louder. "Leo said keep everyone in camp. What better way to do it?" He stepped away from Owen, ending the testosterone challenge. "Right, kids? Let's have a beer and relax." He nodded his beard at Will and Miki while Owen visibly fought to simmer down. Will wanted to yell at him, *Hey, Anger Management called, and they're missing their biggest meathead.* But instead, he turned away to follow Miki to his tent. She had a way of shrugging her brother off, which he admired immensely.

She unzipped the flaps and climbed inside as Flossy laughed and said, "It's called Babysitting 101." Will scoffed, clicking on the electric lantern. They didn't need to be babysat. He wanted to flip 'em all off, but more important things lay in wait. The sooner the horde forgot about them and got back to drinking, the faster he and Miki could breeze on out of here.

Will made a seat on his sleeping bag and studied the beer. One sip would taste so good. Maybe two. If he downed the bottle, he'd be "right as rain," as Uncle Shorty would say. He could still ride bitch, one beer wouldn't kill him.

"If you touch that beer, I'll kill you," Miki said softly.

Will looked at her. No frown, no posing, she was only stating the facts. Her big brown eyes didn't waver from his, leaving no doubt she'd use the row of silver skull rings on her fingers to knock his lights out. His brow furrowed.

"Calm down. I wasn't going to," he muttered and reached for his backpack. Mook's home brew was definitely coming along, a celebratory drink to share with Dad and Liam.

"Don't you know you're never supposed to tell a woman to 'calm down'?"

Sure, you catch more flies with vinegar. No...wait. Honey. Where had he heard that before? He took out the deck of cards, a water bottle, and his survival kit to make room for the beer beside Mom's ashes and the apple pie. There was room for one more, and Miki didn't balk when he crammed her bottle into his bag, too.

There were no pockets in his Ghetto Gramps, so he pulled the green hoodie over his head, his cast sliding easily through the cut sleeve. He tucked his folding knife, his new scratching stick, and a Mini Mag-Lite into his long front pocket. Everything was shipshape and ready to go. He turned to her.

She sat quietly, watching him, the bright lantern casting long shadows across her face. Her skin looked like brown sugar, smooth, tan, and she smelled good, too. Anise and vanilla and flowery shampoo...

"Your blue hair is growing on me," he said. See? Add some honey. He could be sweet.

"So," Miki said and shrugged, giving him the bored look, one he, himself, perfected over a year ago. Two words sat on the tip of his tongue: What's changed? But he kept his mouth shut. Did he want to show her his weak and needy side? Not really.

The guys were being awfully quiet out there, so Will leaned forward to slowly lift the flap, but ended up catching Flossy's eye. Those guys were way too attentive for his liking.

Will gave him the *Yo, bro* chin-nod, then lowered the fabric back down.

"We're never going to get out of here," he muttered while Miki shuffled the cards. "And, I don't feel like playing, so now what?"

"Small talk. I'll start," Miki said, dealing out a hand of solitaire. "What do you wanna be when you grow up?"

"I don't know, but I know what you should be...a nurse." He watched her fingers flip through the cards. "Remember when we used to play doctor? You had a dolphin scarf you used to wrap around my leg like a cast. Man, I loved it." He nudged her foot with his, but she didn't look up.

"I wanna be a mechanic," she said. "Instead of saving lives, I'll save one bike at a time."

"Because of your dad or is it something you really want to do?" Will waited a beat, but she didn't answer. "You always had a wrench in your hand. My favorite part was when you'd pretend to crank on my ankles and knee caps. God, it tickled, and it was all I could do not to flinch." He had a hard time imagining her in baggy overalls with grease under her nails. "Because if I flinched, I knew you'd rack me in the nuts or something."

Finally, she wiped off the serious look and grinned down at her two of clubs. "That doesn't sound very doctorly. Besides, people are gross. Pus, crap, spit, blood. Then, there's the smell of vomit. Gag. No thanks." She flicked the end of her card with her thumbnail. "I think you should be a counselor."

"What?" Will laughed. He couldn't even picture caring about someone else's problems.

A loud crash echoed off the circle of trees, and Leo's voice bellowed into the campsite. "Look what I dug up! A pulverized piece of..."

There was a loud grunt.

Will whipped open the tent flap in time to see a bald-headed dude skid into camp on his face, his shirt and mouth filling with dirt. The guy's tattooed arms were held behind his back with several bands of duct tape, and his black leather vest had an ugly patch, Pulver Skulls MC. His face was swollen on one side like he'd taken a serious beating at the hands of Leo the Lion, and blood dribbled from his split lip and busted nose.

"Oh...shit," Will whispered, and Miki gasped. She covered her mouth and stared at her dad with wide eyes.

"You're gonna pay!" The dude spat blood out of his mouth as he eased up on his knees. One of his eyes had puffed shut, but the other looked around, searching the faces. Across the campsite, his one crystal blue eye met Will's. The guy didn't look away.

A shiver crawled up Will's spine. He shifted back into the shadows and lowered the tent flap a tad, hiding his face, yet still able to peer around it.

Owen kicked the pulverized P-skull between the shoulder blades, planting him back in the dirt. Then, Leo knelt on one knee. "You shut up. You're in a world of hurt. Where'd your buddies go, huh? Left you for the wolves, did they?"

The guy gave a harsh laugh as in, *You wish*, then howled up to the tree tops—"He's here!"—like a coyote calling to his pack.

The camp fell quiet.

"Tape him to the tree," Leo said in a low voice. "Someone get me a baseball bat. Maybe we get answers, maybe we don't, but we can have fun while we're swinging."

Will dropped his arm, and the tent flap swished closed. His heart knocked hard against his ribcage like a hammering motor ready to throw a rod. Engine failure was imminent. He did not, *could* not be around for this, and neither should Miki, which meant they both needed to check out. He rubbed a soothing hand over his

115

eyebrow, but it trembled uselessly, so he dropped it. His eyes searched for hers.

"That dude..." Will murmured. "I'm almost positive he was in my room. At the hospital."

"My gut says it's time to go," she said, looking scared out of her wits as she eased into her leather coat. Everything was in place. Her saddle bags had been packed earlier and were cinched onto her bike, ready and waiting. Will shrugged into his backpack as swiftly and silently as he could while heavy boots and sharp voices bounced around camp on the other side of the tent flaps.

He pulled his knife from his hoodie pocket and flipped it open. With a gentle pop, he pierced the fabric at the back of the tent, slicing the wall open from top to bottom and across, making an "L" shape. He held a finger to his lips. *Be quiet.* Then he stepped out into the darkness.

CHAPTER 12

NOCTURNAL

Miki's scalp tingled from the chilly air that ran through her hair at eighty miles per hour. Putting their helmets on wasn't part of their last minute plan when she and Will ran for her bike. She'd jumped on, revved the engine, and alerted the entire camp they were leaving. Dad had roared, "Miki! No!" and raced toward her like a raging bull, but she'd gunned it out of there with only one problem: They had a tail.

It was probably Owen or Trip, maybe even Flossy. Who knew? After wasting an hour taking lefts and rights on the backroads, they finally hit pavement. Now, they were free, racing back toward Trout Lake to the Powerhouse Inn where they'd find answers, save Bill and Liam, and go home.

This time the ride was easy since she was pumped full of adrenaline. She couldn't slouch if she wanted to, and she doubted Will could either. He held onto her with a firm grip that said he was alert and alive. Hours of riding seemed like minutes as she geared down into the Powerhouse Inn's full parking lot. The engine purred beneath her until she turned off the ignition in front of the main office. Silence, yet her body vibrated like it was still on the road.

Miki pushed the glass door open. *Ding!* An electronic bell signaled to someone behind the front counter. A young man with fuzzy brown sideburns from ear to chin stood. He had a cell phone to his ear, and he murmured, "I've got company," before clicking off and setting it down.

"Hey." He nodded and glanced at the clock in the lobby. Straight up midnight. He fiddled with his pencil, bouncing the eraser end against the desk impatiently. The room temperature was cool, but the air was stale and smelled like the inside of a refrigerator.

"Uh…" Suddenly, Miki's adrenaline took a nose dive, and her body went limp with fatigue. She shook her head, clearing it. "Do you work here?"

His thick brows went up as he held out his hands— *I'm here aren't I?*—and with a lofty tone asked, "What do you want?"

The guy didn't have a name badge or an official uniform. Didn't hotel clerks used to wear polyester vests over white dress shirts? This guy had on a wrinkled black tee and had a bad case of bed-head. It was late, so maybe he'd been resting, although he looked bright-eyed with those green laser beams.

"We're friends with Pinecone and, uh…a guy named Smiley." Miki tried for a grin and looped arms with Will. Yeah, she had a memory on her. Besides, who could forget a name like Smiley? "So when does she work—"

"You're *friends* with Smiley?" The guy had a high pitched laugh. He looked past her shoulder to someone behind them. "You know these two?"

A chair creaked and Miki let go of Will's arm to turn around. A good-lookin' boy around their age with an obvious Viking heritage closed a magazine he'd been holding and rolled it into a tube. Wow. Spiky blond hair and brilliant blue eyes. He was startlingly gorgeous—

"No," Smiley said, his eyes flicking back and forth between her and Will with no recognition. "No, I don't."

"You sure? I think I've seen you before." Miki squinted, imagining him with his plaid shirt in her neighborhood. "Have you ever been to Overdale?"

"What do you want with Pinecone?" Smiley tapped the magazine tube against his faded denim leg.

"She works here, right? We were in the other day, and she was behind the counter. She offered us a discount and mentioned a password."

"Pinecone's helpful like that," the desk clerk said, drawing the attention back to himself. He leaned his bony elbows on the lobby desk and smiled while his gaze roved over Miki's body, openly checking her out.

Will straightened, pulling his shoulders out of a slouch. "Hey—"

"As luck would have it," the hotel guy went on, "...she's in tomorrow. If you stop by in the morning, I'll let you know when she starts." He wagged his brows at her.

Creep.

And pretty stingy with the details, too.

"Okay." Miki nodded. "But we need a room for the night. Any chance the uh...Honeysuckle is available?"

"What a coincidence. It's under construction. The only thing available is the Shooting Star, and it's hourly. We don't rent hourly to minors, unfortunately. But I'll see you in the morning, right?" he asked.

"Uh, right. To see Pinecone," Miki said slowly and nodded. He seemed a little too eager, which didn't sit right in the pit of her stomach. She turned to Will. "Let's go—you." She'd almost called him by his name, but thankfully caught herself. She could be stingy with the details, too.

Smiley unfurled his magazine while he watched them without saying a word.

"Looking forward to it," the furry hotel clerk said, but Miki didn't look back. When Will pushed the door open, she kept close to his heels.

Once in the parking lot, he scanned the area, his hands jiggling the things he'd put in his hoodie pocket earlier. He looked tall under the stars and calm. "This place looks full tonight," he said casually, like a young man who had it together without a worry in the world.

"I got a very weird vibe from that guy. Didn't you?" Miki touched Will's arm, stopping him.

"Yeah…I did." He frowned. "From both of 'em, but I think we should stick it out and see if Pinecone shows. At this point, she's our only connection to finding my dad and Liam."

"You're right." Miki bit her lip with a quick glance back over her shoulder.

"We can leave your bike in the corner of the parking lot over there by the tree. See? It's hidden from the streetlight and besides, everyone'll think it's a guest's. Then, we can sleep undercover in the thicket." Will pointed to the tree line behind the hotel. "We'll be out of sight and right where we need to be for a meet and greet. If there's a whiff of trouble in the morning, we're gone."

"Okay, sounds like a plan." She nodded." But what if I freeze to death?"

"I've got a thermal blanket." Will patted the shoulder strap to his pack.

Miki studied the fringe of his black eyelashes and wished he'd be the one to take her hand, hold it, and say, *Don't worry, I've got this.* Or how about, *I'll keep you warm, baby.*

"I'm pretty hungry, too," Miki murmured, shifting her gaze to the sparse stubble on his jaw, then away. She straddled her bike. "What if I starve to death?" she asked, turning the key. The engine purred loudly into the night, and she waited, hoping he'd tell her something memorable. Something like, *Baby, I'm packing all the things you like.*

He dropped on behind her and wrapped his good arm around her waist.

"I've got two granola bars and two beers. Snacks for champions. Any other problems I can solve for you?" He put his chin on her shoulder. "What're you waiting for?"

She sighed. Always something more, it seemed.

* * *

Will felt like he was robbing a bank, looking over his shoulder, tip-toeing in the shadows, and crawling on all fours through bracken ferns and skunk cabbage. But the red osier dogwoods were a thick shrub and would be worth the trouble. No one would see them hanging out here for the night.

"It's damp," Miki grumbled, dropping her saddle bags on a pile of wet leaves. "I'm thirsty, I'm not digging this situation, and you better not tell me to 'calm down,' either."

Will grinned, pulling his backpack open. "I was going to say *relax*...here." He handed her a beer, and while she quenched her thirst, he dug in his hoodie pocket for his flashlight, and after clipping it to his sleeve, he got down to the serious business of setting up camp. He tugged and shuffled with the narrow tarp to get it unfolded and as close to the thicket as possible. Even the simplest thing turned out to be ten times harder with a casted arm and thumb.

"Why am I doing all the work while you're standing around, chugging beer?" Will grunted as he smoothed out the corners.

"It looks like a one-man job," she said and made another round of slurpy noises. "Mook makes a good brew."

"But does it look like a one-armed one-man job? I'm sweating here." He nudged her saddle bags under the brush with the toe of his boot and dropped his thermal blanket onto the tarp. With awkward movements, he unwrapped one of the granola bars, ready to devour it in three...two...one.

The tarp crinkled as he sprawled across it. This was no peach floral couch, no hotel mattress, and no foam camping mat. He was going to freeze his balls off. He looked up at Miki, standing above him, taking another swig. She wiped her mouth, and knelt beside him.

"Granola bar?" He held one out to her, but she waved it away.

"Thish beer's...taking the edge off. I'm sho tired I could fall over."

"Here." He sat up and made room for her. What was going on? Why was she slurring? "Are you okay? Hey, drop the beer and lie down. You seem a little—"

"I can't do anything with you, Will," she mumbled in a low voice.

"Do what? Oh…hey, I'm not asking, okay? Miki?" He held up his good palm. It was too dark to see her eyes, and he didn't want to rudely shine his flashlight in her face. He kept the beam down, but he could still see the outline of her. "I only meant it's cold out, so—"

"Please, please…" She crawled to him and collapsed against his chest. "Pleash don't be mad at me anymore." She sighed, going limp in his arms.

"Miki." Will patted her on the back with his cast and fingers. "Miki." He rolled her off and down onto the tarp. When he jostled her, she was like a boneless chicken, legs bent and arms floppy. What the hell was wrong with her? "Miki can you hear me? Oh, my God." He put his cheek down next to her mouth and nose and felt her warm, even breaths, like she was sleeping hard, dead to the world.

Sleeping? Passed out from half a beer? Home brew or not, it was seriously lightweight. But then again, Flossy had said, "Knock yourselves out."

Wait a minute…

What did he mean? Then, he'd said something about a hotel incident and staying in camp. *Have a beer and relax.* Did those guys…would they…? Yes, they would.

Unbelievable!

"Miki? Man, I think you got roofied." This time, Will did shine the light in her face. Her lids weren't closed all the way, and it looked freaky, showing the bottom half of her brown eyes. He gently pushed them closed with the tip of his finger, so her lashes rested on her cheeks. No dried eyeballs on his watch. He sat up to cover their bodies with the mere scrap of fabric

123

called a thermal blanket, then shifted and lifted and pulled and broke another sweat trying to get Miki's head to rest on his arm and her body tucked in close in a quasi-comfortable state.

"I can't believe they'd give us spiked beer," he murmured next to her hair. "These are the people we call family, you know? Our dads, our brothers, I mean our *real* brothers."

Why did Miki want to hang out with the Hides of Hell? She said she wanted to be a mechanic but why? For herself? His guess...it was for President Daddy's approval. They were thugs. Every last one of 'em.

"I should have known something was up after the jab about babysitting. Why are those guys drugging us when they should be out there looking for my dad and Liam? What if I had drunk the other beer? We'd both be lying out here like cougar bait. It's effed-up, man.

"Don't worry, Miki. I'll take care of you. Nothing bad's going to happen to you, understand?" She wore her leather coat, but he draped his arm across her midriff anyway, hoping to add an extra layer of warmth. It felt good to be here like this, cuddled up with her, nice and snug. He could chat about anything he wanted to with Miki or with his mom or even to the stars, and it would only be a benefit. Let go of some of his negative energy. Talk to someone who might understand—but more importantly, who wouldn't remember anything in the morning. Win-win.

Will searched the dark sky filled with stars and tried to pick out the end of the Little Dipper.

"Okay, so I've been wondering..." His voice broke the silence. "Why don't you like me anymore? I liked it when you liked me because I liked you and...but then your meathead brother is always around like a junkyard dog, all hackles and fangs. I'm one who appreciates a good bout of loyalty, believe me. But c'mon, you know? How's a guy supposed to get close when he has to worry about getting his face punched in at every turn?

"Then there's the whole closet thing. Yeah, yeah, I yelled at you and told you to delete my number, but I never understood why you cried about it. We were hooking up in the closet, and I thought we were going somewhere. Then out of the blue, you told everyone I frickin' farted and laughed. Why the grief? I felt stupid."

Man, he'd felt more than stupid. Not only the pointing and snickering bummed him out that night. It was all the energy he'd invested in getting to the ledge, gearing up to take the plunge into Relationship Land, and throwing caution to the wind by saying, *I like you!* out loud to Miki and the universe...only to have her lie to everyone and laugh in his face. It was a horror show.

"Afterwards, you threw your bikini in my face, all flirty again..." Will sighed and listened to the silence.

Where was the night life?

It seemed too quiet.

"Yeah, I don't get you. I mean, I feel like you're only messing with my head, playing games. But if you really think we've got something...why don't you tell me, straight up? You could show me a sign, you know, something small like flexing your elbow." Will waited. There was nothing. "Miki? Can you hear me?"

The night was ominous with no rustling leaves and no answers. Hopefully, the stillness meant the nocturnal animals were busy elsewhere and not crouching in the shrubs. His pocket knife might stop a small raccoon, but it wouldn't do much against a hungry mountain lion.

"What's with Leo?" Will whispered next to Miki's ear. "What kind of dad leaves his daughter with a bunch of roofie-packing drunks who apparently carry baseball bats to a rally? Jesus, Miki, they're all crazy, so I don't get why you want to be a part of it."

On the surface, he still wanted to blame Miki for her mixed-up signals, if only to keep things simple. He could hold a massive grudge, but while he'd been busy doing that, she'd become more fearless and more...spunky. Sure, it was kind of a grandma word—

Will, this is your mother speaking. FYI, your grandmother would never say spunky. Spirit is a better choice. It shows flare and independence. Miki's a girl who makes things happen.

Spirit. Definitely. Miki had it in spades.

And she's rocking the blue hair, Will. She looks good, as in REAL good—

Yes she does. Wait...what?

His mom would never say that. So whose voice was it? His own? Was this part of the big thaw? Part of moving on? Oh, God, he was losing her. He squeezed his eyes shut and searched for the singsong voice she used when she wanted help with something.

Will, my love. Where are you? My computer screen turned blue again.

There she was. Mom, can you hear me? I love you.

He listened intently, but nothing more came. After a while, he drifted off. When he awoke some time later, it wasn't to complimentary coffee and doughnuts.

CHAPTER 13

FRIENDS

"Help me. I'm going to puke."

The soft voice pulled Will out of a dead sleep. He couldn't see anything, but he kicked and paddled harder to get to the surface. Blub, blub, blub. Here I come! His eyelids peeled open to a dusky sky and to Miki on her belly, crawling off the tarp into the wet grass. She whimpered like a whipped pup.

"Shh. It's okay, Miki." He crawled to her and patted her back as she retched up last night's chili dog. Sick. He snapped off a broad leaf from a skunk cabbage and covered the chunky mess. "How ya doing? Feeling okay?"

"I can't move my legs." She gulped, then wiped her mouth weakly and lifted her head to glance around. "Where are we?"

"Remember the beer last night? You drank it and passed out cold. I think you got roofied."

"Roofied? What does that mean? Like the date-rape drug? Oh my G—I don't remember anything!" She cried and rolled over clumsily to examine her clothes.

"Don't worry, okay." He patted down the air in front of him. "Nothing happened. We spent the night out here, so we could meet up with Pinecone. What's the last thing you remember?"

"The bike ride. Being in the hotel lobby. The crazy-haired guy behind the desk." Miki's eyes were watery, and she sniffed, then frowned. "The beer was drugged?"

"It must've been. There's no other explanation. You drank almost half, and within ten minutes, you fell on your face. You don't remember anything else?"

She shook her head and rubbed her eyes with the tips of her fingers.

He tried not to blow out a relieved breath, but thank God. Forget being a mechanic, she should be the counselor the way he'd downloaded last night. Pitiful. What if she'd heard him rambling on about his feelings and remembered it?

Deny or die, plain and simple.

Miki covered her face, and her shoulders trembled as a sob escaped.

"I feel funny, like I'm scared, but I don't know why." She unzipped her coat, and pulled the hem of her shirt up to wipe her nose.

"Hey, it's probably the drug wearing off, which is good. But you know, it's still early. Let's chill out for a bit and wake up slow. Come here." He helped her scoot across the tarp and put his arm down for her to use as a pillow. "We can small talk, and this time I'll start. Like tell me...do you like to bake? You know...cookies, pies?" Her blue hair fanned over his shoulder, and instead of answering, she hugged him.

"If one of us had to drink Mook's spiked beer, I'm glad it was you and not me, so I could be here for you, you know?" He wrapped his arm around her waist and squeezed. "The knight in shining armor stuff. While you were busy napping, I had to fend off the wild animals. If it were the other way around, my cool-card might've taken a hit."

"You're pretty lame," she murmured, and the strength in her voice made his heart calm. She sounded okay. Maybe in another hour, she'd be back to her normal, annoying self. He pulled her in close and kissed the side of her head.

"I don't want to sound like some kind of macho dude—you know what? Never mind. But what if we'd both drunk it, you know? God…makes me want to kill those guys."

"I think you should stop talking now," she whispered, her eyes wide and staring up into the branches. The dogwood leaves rustled, and Will jerked as an upside down face with bushy brown hair came into focus.

"Why, hello there," a tenor voice said from above and chuckled.

Who the…? Will's heart gunned as he scrambled to disentangle himself from Miki.

"Found 'em!" The guy turned his whiskered jaw to holler over his shoulder while tucking his gun into a holster belted to his pants. It was the guy from the Powerhouse Inn. The one behind the desk. Now he was wearing a worn leather jacket, and he pulled at the front zipper to cover the gun's grip. "Heard all that moaning and thought it might be a cougar but nope. Only horny teenagers hiding in the woods." He cocked his head to the murmuring voices echoing behind the trees. "Over here, guys!"

Will stood, keeping his back toward the shrubby dogwood and scanned the faces emerging from the foliage. In total, there were three, all adorned in some form of black leather, worn denim, whiskers, and ink. Will's guts roiled. Were these guys Pulver Skulls? If so, he and Miki were screwed.

Will stepped over Miki's slack legs and off the edge of the tarp. He squared his shoulders as he perched his hands on his hips, but his cast made it awkward, so instead, he held it out in front of him and rubbed it as if he were polishing a club. The pre-dawn air chilled his face, but adrenaline flushed his body with heat.

"Who are you guys?" Will looked down at the short one, the wolverine from the hotel with the high voice. He had green eyes the color of snap peas and resembled an overgrown elf with those teased-out sideburns and little black boots.

"Don't worry." The elf-guy flashed his palms. "We're friends, remember?"

"Oh, yeah? How so?" asked Will, glancing at one face, then the other.

"You're friends with Smiley. You said so yourself, and any friend of his is a friend of mine. We keep things close. So..." The elf rubbed his hands together. "I know who you are, Will Sullivan, but who's your girl?"

"You better step back." Will straightened, easing his arms down to his sides to flex his fingers. He was a lot taller than the elf. But this was a biker scene, and Will was no biker. What would Liam do? His brother was always prepared, as in Boy Scout material. Whenever he left the house, he shoved mint gum and a love glove in one pocket and cash, plastic, and a knife in the other. Will swallowed hard, forcing his anxiety down. Okay, he was ready. No problem. He had a knife, too.

"I need water....bad," Miki croaked, then groaned behind him like her stomach was agitating again.

"So, what's with your poor girl, here? What's her name?" Elf gazed at Miki with interest.

"What does it matter?" Will squinted.

"I like to know who my friends are. Besides, do we leave her in the woods for a big cat to gnaw on, or does she come with us?" Elf shrugged.

"Us?" Will widened his stance and casually shoved his hands in the front pocket of his hoodie. His fingers traced the scratching stick, then the pocket knife. It wasn't much, but there was no way in hell they were touching Miki or taking her anywhere.

"You're kind of a tall one. How old are you anyway? No, no. Let me guess." Elf rubbed the scruff on his jaw, and his eyes roved over Will's forehead and chin. "Baby face..."

What the hell was this guy talking about? Will looked at the grubby gang again. He knew elf-guy hid a gun under his coat and seemed a little off his rocker. The old, greasy-haired one to the left kept sneaking glances over his shoulder—edgy—while the biggun on the right looked bored out of his mind. Will gripped the pocket knife a little tighter. What'd they want with him? What'd he do to draw the Pulver Skulls' attention? Nothing! He went to school, hung out at bonfires with his buddies, and slept on his beloved couch.

"So I'm guessing fourteen." Elf nodded like he had it all figured out.

"Hardly." Will scoffed.

Miki groaned again, and Will *really* hoped she was faking it because he could use her help here. With the row of rings on her fingers, she could take the elf down with a good wallop, no doubt. Knock him right into the holiday season.

"Hmm. Not too scrawny, either. Probably not a day over seventeen, then. Am I right?" He nodded to the old dude, the one with long, limp hair. The guy's lower lip was packed full with dipping tobacco. "What do you think, Greer?" Elf asked him.

"Who gives a rat's corn-hole?" Greer said in a gravelly voice and spat in the dirt. "Shut your clap trap and grab the girl. She's luggage until we figure this out. Pitty..." He motioned to the giant. "Pack up the camp. I want no evidence these two were here. Too close to home for my liking."

Greer's jacket blared some vintage rock, a little "Iron Man" by Black Sabbath. He jerked his phone out and held it to his ear like a clam. "Yep? Uh-huh, uh-huh. No, we got him right here. Uh-huh. What...you got two? You sure?" Greer's beady black eyes frowned and pinned Will in his place. "Well, hell. How many William Sullivans are there?"

Will's heart thudded heavily in his chest. Was Greer talking about *his* William Sullivans? Or somebody else's? There had to be two hundred or so in the phone book for Washington alone, not including Oregon. Dad and Liam were still alive, right? Nope, don't even question it. Of course they were.

Greer ran his fingers through the stringy length of his hair and turned away. The dude wore an ugly biker patch on his back. He walked to the tree line, nodding —"Uh-huh, uh-huh"—like he was taking orders, and spat off to the side.

This was not good.

"Pulver Skulls gang, huh?" Will tipped his head back, trying for the savvy-chill-and-bored look. He could take the elf, *mano a mano*. Maybe even Greer. Although there would definitely be pain and a lot of blood involved. But no way in hell could he get the giant Pitty down...and all three at once? Not even a contest. His hands were still in his hoodie pocket around his knife. He worked it back and forth with slow movements in between his skin and his cast, being careful while maintaining eye contact with elf-man and Pitty. Everything's casual—nothing to see here.

"We're not a gang. We're a brotherhood," Elf said, smiling like a lunatic.

"It's a club," Pitty chanted tiredly, as if on autopilot. He crossed his beefy biceps over his denim jacket. Yeah, he had no mind for this. Pitty was either a disenchanted prospect, a lazy hang-around, or someone's cousin who owed a favor. The guy might be phoning it in, but he was a big dude, like a Scottish caber tosser. He even wore a man bun. What self-respecting biker wears a man bun? A barbarian with ham hands and a pit bull jawbone, that's who.

"Oh, right. A club where everyone carries guns and kidnaps people," Will muttered. He'd ride his bike and love every minute of it, but he'd never live the thug's life. He'd never be a brother.

He quickly glanced behind him to check on Miki. Their eyes met briefly before he turned away. She was tough. He could tell her cogs were working overtime like his. They'd get out of this. They would.

"Where's the respect? No one's getting kidnapped, right, Pit?" Elf didn't look at his comrade but waited for the grunt of acknowledgement. "We're just hanging out with friends."

133

The older dude, Greer, crammed his phone in his jacket and walked back to join the fray. He held his hands out like a preacher.

"What'd I tell you, Pitty?" he asked in a begging tone. "I said to pick up the tarp and leave no evidence. What're you standing around doing nothin' for? Let's move! We need to get out of here before we're surrounded by a cow herd, ya damn idiots."

Pitty rolled his eyes and stomped to Will's backpack in a huff. He picked up the granola bar wrappers and kicked the beer bottle into the shrubs while Greer pulled out a zip tie.

"Turn around, boy, and let's make this easy. I hate beating on kids. Hands behind your back. Okay, that's not gonna work with your cast." Greer sighed like he was seriously put out. Will slowly turned back around, and Greer scratched his dirty head.

"Cut it off, why don't ya?" Pitty said, jerking the blanket off Miki while Elf leered down at her.

He nudged her leg with his boot. "Why don't you get up?" he asked softly.

"I...I can't stand. My legs are like gummy worms," she said and threw a worried glance at Will as if to say, *Now they know.* Or...*Now what?* Or...*We're up shit creek with a hole in our boat.*

Will's gut said to keep her close. These guys wouldn't leave her behind, not when she was a witness. How many more P-Skulls were hiding in the woods? Will's mind scrambled for a directive...stay calm, say something.

"How about you guys leave her alone? She took a bad hit and now—uh, you know, you can't tie my wrists, so I could just carry her out. No funny business." Will held out his cast and his open palm. *See how I'm injured* and can't do any harm? He cleared his throat to keep his voice steady. "Sound good?"

"A bad hit? You guys packing dust or something?" Greer asked. He nodded his chin to Pitty. "Check his bag."

Pitty tugged at the zipper, then rifled through Will's backpack. "Beer. Underwear. What's this?" He pulled out a Tupperware container and Will's heartbeat revved. His slice.

"Dude, it's just apple pie."

"My favorite," Elf murmured and patted his stomach. His green eyes widened when Pitty pulled out the double zip-locked bag of ashes. It had been secured with clear packaging tape for travel. "Holy shit. Is that... what is that, two kilos?"

Will touched his chest and could feel his heart hammering against his ribs. He was two seconds shy of a heart attack. Should he correct them, let the guys know they were holding the remains of his mother and not a hefty bag of powder? Jesus. Or should he keep his mouth shut and let them think—

"I don't know what it is but shove it back in his bag, and let's hustle outta here. We'll check it out later. You got a bullet in the chamber?" Greer asked, not taking his eyes off Will.

"I sure do," Elf said in a perky voice.

"Empty your pockets, boy, then pick up Hot Stuff over there. Anything goes wrong..." Greer narrowed his eyes. "It'll get ugly fast. You don't want to see ugly, do ya?"

Okay, okay. Calm down, and don't rock the boat in shit creek. Go with it. Will tossed his Mini Mag-Lite on the ground, then pulled out his scratching stick. He stopped and stared at it. Trip had spent hours honing this thing to perfection, because he knew the hell of wearing a cast. Trip was a good guy; he was like—okay, so there was one biker who was like family. Will gripped it tighter as his arm tingled, getting its big itch on.

"Dude, I need this thing for scratching." Will knocked the carved stick against his cast and pasted on an urgent look. "I gotta keep this."

Pitty blinked as if surprised by the size of Will's cojones for making such a demand. His jaw clenched into a solid square, and he leaned forward to ever-so-gently pluck the scratcher from Will's hand. With a woebegone expression etched on his face, Pitty squeezed his fist.

Snap!

Will sucked in a breath and held it as Pitty opened his fingers, letting the two pieces fall into the grass. It's okay. Stay calm. Will turned away and blew his bangs out of his face, then knelt next to the tarp. He leaned over to whisper next to her ear. "Watch the elf. He's the one—"

Pitty's monster boot swung out and kicked Will in the calf. Pain zapped his leg, and Will hissed. When he looked up, the giant pulled an imaginary zipper across his mouth. "Shut it."

"Right, gotcha. Miki, it has to be piggy back, okay? Can you get up on your knees at least?"

She rolled around with a lot of grunts and struggles before Pitty swore under his breath and picked her up like a cat, attaching her to Will's back. The others waited while Will fumbled around, getting her legs hooked over his good arm and cast. She was small, so it didn't matter how flabby and out of shape he was or how he had a broken arm and bruised guts...no. He had height and weight on his side; he could totally do this. Will straightened and nodded. He was good to go.

While she warmed his back and hugged his shoulders, he pressed her legs into his sides, hoping to reassure her. They would get through this. Her legs would start working, he'd drop her to her feet, and they'd run. At least Pitty didn't look like the type to exert too much energy engaging in a chase. The big guy looked bored with the whole operation. He'd checked-out. Finally, there was a plus.

Greer blazed through the brush away from the Powerhouse Inn, and Will followed with Miki on his back. The elf tailgated them, clipping the backs of Will's boots every other step or so, and Pitty tromped along behind with Will's backpack slung over one shoulder. He grunted whenever elf-man said something stupid, which seemed often enough for the two miles they must've hiked.

When Miki joined in, Will knew she was starting to feel better.

"I have to go to the bathroom, so sue me," Miki said from over Will's shoulder.

"You know what's amazing to me?" Greer sniped at her as he pushed a branch out of the way, then let it fly, snapping Will in the face. *Ow! That stung, asshole.* "It's amazing your mouth still works when nothing else seems to."

"Listen, Greer." Will chimed in. "I'm sweating here...and I got aches and pains...all over, dude. You don't know this...but I was in a serious accident...last... week...and my meds are in my backpack...the one Pitty's carrying...and if we could just take...a break—"

"That's it!" Greer stopped short, flinging his arms out.

"Dude..." Will leaned forward and panted. He could feel rivers of sweat running between his shoulder blades. Jesus, he was out of shape. A year of beer drinking had made him soft and weak. Of course, he had Miki on his back. She was a small fry, but with each step, she felt more like a two-ton Tony. Before he lost any more strength, it was time to vacate the situation.

Miki pressed her knee caps into Will's waist, a sign she could feel her legs again. He signaled back with a gentle squeeze. They were on the same page; it's go time.

"I bet we've walked for all of ten minutes," Greer complained. "So if you two whiners don't shut up, I'll stick my boot in your arses and kick your lazy carcasses down the ravine. Got it? Now, let's move, because if our ride drives off and leaves us, I'll kill you straight up. I really will. I don't care what Ham says." Greer turned and stormed through the trees with renewed angry energy, muttering under his breath. "I think the bastard has lost his ever-lovin' mind. 'Bring William Sullivan to the cabin,' he says. 'In one piece,' he says. What a damn idiot."

He grumbled some more, but Will stopped listening and let more distance grow between them. Elf passed on his left, and Pitty came up on his right. He towered over Will and jabbed him in the bicep with a finger as unyielding as a tire iron. What was one more fat bruise on his already black and blue body?

"Ow." Will scowled and loosened his arms from around Miki's legs, so she could slip to the ground. Her arms went slack at his neck, and she eased down his back to stand on both legs. "Pitty, let me take my pain meds, dude. I'm dying here." Will squeezed Miki's shoulder to steady her, but more importantly, to put her on high alert.

Get ready to bolt because this was it!

With his feet planted in the dirt, Pitty remained stoic, his deep-set eyes looking down the length of his nose.

He didn't show an ounce of surprise when he saw Miki could stand.

Will braced himself, half-expecting Pitty to put the backpack down, but he didn't. Miki took a short step to the side.

Get set…

Wait!

Will's eyes widened. He hadn't thought the plan through. Mom's ashes were in the bag. The apple pie! He wanted to swipe it out of Pitty's hands on the run, but—the giant was an unmoving wall.

Mom?

Oh, God, now what?

Miki took another step. Leaves crunched.

Will turned when Miki yelled, "Go!" and lunged off the trail into the thick shrubs. His heart shifted into overdrive, and his breaths went shallow. She did it; Miki ran. His eyes met Pitty's hard face, and in a split second, Will snapped to attention.

He charged into the bramble, barely feeling the branches as they lashed across his face and snagged at his Ghetto Gramps. He hurdled through the brush with a burn tearing through his chest. Forget the broken toe. Don't slow down. Keep moving. There was only one direction to go—straight ahead toward the Powerhouse Inn. The crashing and hollering behind him barely touched his consciousness.

Go…go…go!

One foot in front of the other.

Push it.

Get to Miki—to her bike and to safety.

But the farther he ran, the more distance he put between him and his backpack. He didn't have the ashes. He didn't have the apple pie. He didn't have his mom. His thoughts grabbed at his mind, like the thorny blackberry vine wrapped around his ankle.

He stumbled.

CHAPTER 14

LIGHTS OUT

"I like you, Will. You know I do, right?" The elf said calmly.

"I...don't like the way you like me," Will said, staring into the unwavering black hole of a Smith & Wesson revolver. Turns out, Pitty had some motivation after all. He apparently played a little college football and charged after Will like he was playing to win. Sacked at twenty yards.

He and Miki never stood a chance.

"I can respect your point of view. I'm a reasonable man. But you..." Elf chuckled and lowered the barrel, pointing it at the dirt. "You ran. We're friends, remember? Friends should trust each other." He nodded to Pitty, who jerked Will onto his feet by his shoulder seams. "Do we want a walking man or a dead weight?"

"Kids..." Greer sighed and tightened his lower lip over the bulge of snuff while he rubbed his forehead. "At this juncture, let's try dead weight. We need to get outta here. I ain't missing my ride and walking up Heart Attack Hill for nobody. I don't care whose plans are what."

Pitty turned Will to face him, then rolled his fingers into a fist the size of a pork roast and ratcheted it back.

"Not his face!" Greer barked. "I don't want blood all over the place."

"Hey, now!" Will's eyes widened, and his hands flew up. "Wait—"

Clunk.

Lights out.

* * *

Miki froze with shock.

"Not so hard! We're not lookin' to kill him." Greer glanced at the sky and threw his hands up in exasperation. "My circus...my monkeys," he muttered.

"Will!" Miki dropped to her knees in the damp grass and made a mad scramble to crawl to him, but a hand gripped the hair at the back of her head and snapped her upright until she skimmed the earth on tippy toes. Her neck was cranked back at a sharp angle to the point it was painful to swallow, and her scalp burned where her hair held on for dear life.

"Looks like those legs of yours are working now," hot breath whispered next to her ear, and the balmy scent of stale coffee and tobacco drifted past her nose. "So walk. No more boyfriend to carry you, and I ain't doin' it. I'm a patched member for God sakes. Not some giddy prospect." Greer shoved her, and she stumbled, falling forward on her knees, back where she started. "Get up and get to movin'."

A wave of hopelessness washed over her, and she squeezed her eyelids shut, but the salty tears pushed passed the seams. Not only did she have vomit breath, but she had mud in her teeth and leaves in her hair from her failed getaway attempt. She'd darted off with quivering limbs and clown feet. Needless to say, it turned into an immediate face plant.

Within ten minutes, Pitty had hauled Will back only for the hotel guy, the elf, to cold-cock him with the butt-end of his gun, dropping Will like a bag of wet sand. Was Will alive? God, if his skull wasn't cracked, he'd have a goose egg the size of Mount Rainier for sure. How much more could his poor body take?

Miki stared at Will's green sweatshirt, looking for signs of life. The fold of fabric across his chest moved slightly, and his eyelashes fluttered against his cheekbones. He was breathing.

With her hands in the mud, she pushed off and struggled to stand. There was no point in wiping her eyes; she was already a train wreck, so why bother? Besides, she was being controlled by these mongrels and no longer her own woman. There was no need to put on a pretty face. God. What would they do to her? To Will? Beat, rape, torture…what did they want? She groaned weakly, and more tears fell.

Greer studied Pitty, then the short elf. He glanced down at Will before lifting his dark brows in a question, Which one of you is carrying the kid?

"Let's see…" the elf scratched his pork chop sideburn and looked up at the pine boughs. "I'm only five-nine, which puts Sullivan at six feet, easily. We wanna make good time, right?" He looked at Pitty and grinned. "You gettin' this?"

Pitty closed his deep-set eyes and slowly inhaled and exhaled as if he were trying to find his calming center. When his lids finally opened, he dropped Will's backpack and leaned down to manhandle Will's limp body up over his shoulders. All Miki could do was watch from the sidelines and leak tears while she screamed in her head, *Careful, you f-ugly bastard. He has a bruised spleen!* She wanted to step forward with arms swinging, but she was a watered-down version of herself, weak and dirty and pathetic.

"Let's go…" Pitty gasped. "Fast! He's heavy." He grunted and bent his knees to take Will's weight.

"Well, he's gotta be a buck ninety…two-hundred pounds tops," the elf said with his unusually high voice as he shrugged into Will's backpack and adjusted the straps. "What do you think, Greer?" he asked over his shoulder ready to get his chitchat on. Then, he sauntered through the brush, following Pitty, who had Will slumped over his back.

"I've got one of those *feelings* again, like we've made a humongous mistake with these two." Greer clamped his hand around Miki's bicep, propelled her in front of him, and prodded her to keep walking. "What's this Sullivan kid packing, and how is he worth anything? Why, he's so green behind the ears, it's embarrassing."

"Green like his track suit," the elf said.

"Sure, whatever. Just hustle, would ya? Pitty's hauling balls with our prisoner," Greer said, giving Miki another jab between her shoulder blades.

She stumbled and more tears of frustration spilled from her eyes. She sniffed. The word hopeless echoed against her temples. Will was unconscious, she hadn't talked to her mom in days, and the guys didn't even know where she was. A jarring sob escaped her lips.

"Here we go," Greer muttered with disdain.

"You're cute, considering." The elf turned and walked backwards while he studied her. His green eyes glinted in the rays of light, which flickered through the heavy branches. "I like your hair. Blue's my favorite color. What's your name?"

What did she know about kidnappings? The first rule was don't ever be in a position to get caught...duh. The second? Be a nice human, not a target. Create a bond. Miki wiped under her eyes with her finger tips, then put on a brave front. "Michelle," she said with forced friendliness. "What's yours?"

He looked down at the toes of his boots and chuffed out a breath like it would be absurd to give her his real name. He lifted his gaze and smiled. "You can call me Honey Bunny."

"I..." Miki covered her mouth with her hand and tried to choke back yet another sob. She was alone with these two men. Pitty and Will were no longer in sight. This was not going as planned. Think! What was rule number three?

"Shut your clap trap before she turns this into a full-fledged crying jag," Greer said. "Chafes worse than wiping your arse with forty-grit. Now, I haven't tried it, but I know not to go there." He chuckled and spat somewhere behind her. "Besides, nothing's worse than an ugly crier."

Ugly crier! Was that even true? Normally, she wasn't big on wallowing in self-pity, so any waterworks had a narrow time slot. Squirt, sniff, and be done. But today marked the first time she could remember feeling completely feeble and powerless. She couldn't help it; the wimpy tears overwhelmed her.

So now who should she believe? Trip, who'd told her she was beautiful and not to accept crumbs, or the greasy creep behind her? An ugly crier...

She pulled up the hem of her shirt and wiped her nose on top of where she'd wiped it before. The more she walked, the less her leg muscles trembled. Not only was her strength returning, step by step, but she had thick-soled biker boots on her side. When the opportunity presented itself, the toe of her foot was going to meet Greer's privates in a hostile greeting. She was going to put a lot of effort into ringing those berries, and like her dad said, *Maybe we get answers, maybe we don't, but we can have fun while we're swinging.*

Miki pulled her shoulders back and straightened. She was a lot like her dad, tough and single minded. Her brain worked like a bear trap. Once she got an idea in her head, she couldn't shake it free. Dad was like that, too. It's how he became president of the Hides of Hell. It was his goal, so he chiseled away at it nonstop, then drove it home. She could do the same, couldn't she?

Yes, she could, for Will's sake and her own. Miki forcibly blinked, squelching back the tears. Watch it, you dip-sucking, P-skull. Because you're mine.

Wow, that felt good. She couldn't say it out loud, but thinking it was enough to fuel her strength.

As they trudged along single file, crunching twigs and pushing branches aside, Miki's mind sped through the weapons inventory. It was possible there were no bullets in the chambers of *Honey Bunny's* gun. Fortunately, he hadn't pointed the revolver at her, so she didn't get a good look. Would the green-eyed goon have risked cold-cocking Will with the grip if it had? Maybe it didn't even have bullets. Then again...

Maybe it did.

Where was Will's knife? He'd sliced the tent open with it the night before, yet he didn't throw it on the ground when Greer told him to empty his pockets. Pitty had patted Will down, but the only comment he'd made was calling dibs on the twenty folded up in the cuff of Will's sock. Miki stared at Will's backpack in front of her. Was his knife in the side pocket?

All her stuff was packed neatly in her saddle bags: cell phone, pepper spray, wallet, and a first aid kit. Oh, and a box of Good & Plenty, the candy Will bought for her at the gas station a couple days ago. A matter of no consequence since Will had shoved her stuff under the shrubs, sight unseen back at the Powerhouse Inn.

The only things she had on her were biker boots, a row of silver rings on her right hand, and a black survival bracelet. As for weapons, she always carried knees, elbows, and fists. She'd thrown several punches in her life, but only one had actually connected. A guy was on the receiving end of a fat lip for getting grabby on the dance floor. Otherwise, throwing an upper cut was all new territory.

Greer grabbed her arm, jerking her to a stop. "Our ride's here." He swung her around to face him and looked beyond her shoulder. "Zip her up," he said.

The elf, Oh Short One—there was no way she was calling him Honey Bunny—grabbed one wrist, then the other, and cranked them both behind her back, cinching them together with a thick zip tic that cut into her skin.

"Don't worry," his light voice whispered from over her shoulder, and he cupped her biceps. It was meant to be intimate, and warning goosebumps rippled down the length of her arms under her coat sleeves. "You're safe with me. I'll keep my eyes on you."

Miki swallowed and opened her mouth to suck in more air. She felt short of breath as her heart thrummed

147

in her chest. Fight or flight…fight or flight. Could she run with her arms tied behind her back? Should she knee Greer in the nuts right now? How could she save Will? If she escaped, would they kill him? What if this opportunity turned out to be the only one that came along?

Greer brushed his friend aside and walked Miki backwards while grinning into her face. He was disgusting with that fine cut chew stuck in his teeth. She looked away as the backs of her thighs hit something hard.

She fell into a van, crushing her fingers beneath her. The back was completely cleaned out with no spare parts, tools, or seats. Only a scrap of tan carpet on the floor, and it smelled like wet dog and gasoline. Will was folded up on his side, lying motionless with closed eyes. His arms looked like they'd been secured behind his back.

Greer grabbed her ankles and shoved her legs in before slamming the double doors. It was dark except for the light crisscrossing above them from the windows.

She inched onto her side to study Will's pale face, his dark lashes, the mole on his cheek, his beauty mark. She pushed her foot against his shin, and his eyes opened. Melty-licious brown.

"Will," Miki mouthed, but he closed his lids as someone clambered into the van from the passenger side.

It rocked back and forth, but before the door shut, Greer's heavy metal ring tone cut through the cab. He answered it gruffly, then fell silent as a muffled voice squawked into his ear.

"Uh-huh. Uh-huh. We're at the van ready to head up —Well, the hill's a bitch, and the kid—" Greer's annoying drawl cut off as the van's engine turned over. "Uh-huh. I tell ya this whole thing seems—Ham said what? I thought he was supposed to be here—Oh...I didn't know. Uh-huh, later."

Gravel crunched, and the van rocked again as the other guys clambered in.

"Criminy," Greer said. "Can't get a word in edgewise. Alright, guys. Apparently, The Almighty Ham is stuck in a Mexican standoff with the other William Sullivans. Tough crowd, but relief is on its way. We'll throw the kids in the tank and hold 'em there 'til tonight."

Miki glanced at Will to find his eyes locked on hers, open and alert. He'd heard it, too. Bill and Liam were alive—but for how long? Where were they, and what was going to happen tonight?

The van lurched forward and rumbled up a steep incline, bouncing off rocks and sinking in holes. The gravel crunched under the tires, and the undercarriage squeaked and groaned from the slow, uneven drive.

A guitar-riff blared from the front seat...Greer's ringtone.

"Yep? Well, hello there, Val." Greer's voice glided like Chiffon silk as he spoke into his phone.

Did he say Val as in Just Val? As in the Valentina who declared she'd been climbing all over Dad for six straight weeks? She looked at Will, and they frowned at each other. Why the hell was Val calling Greer?

"Uh-huh. I like where this is going...but tonight? I thought I told you I'm with the guys. I'm busy. No, no, no. Listen, how 'bout I meet you at Knotty Knolls later...no, it's like I said, just busy. Uh-huh. Later, Val." Greer dropped his smooth phone voice in exchange for his usual surly one. "I got one of those *feelings* again."

"It's your beer gut talking," Pitty said from somewhere above Miki's head.

"No doubt." Greer sighed heavily. "I was sweatin' bullets out in those trees. Thought I was gonna have a coronary."

"Eat in moderation. It isn't rocket science," Pitty muttered.

"Let's see..." The elf guy paused like he was doing mental math. "I'm guessing you need to lose about fifty—"

"My *feelings* aren't about my spare tire. Got it, wise guy? It's about Val. I like my women loyal. Not ones I have to wonder about, and lately, I've been thinking she's up to no good."

"You saw her whispering in Smiley's ear. So? He's a kid. She was probably giving him his first hard-on. I could use one of those myself. Right, Michelle?"

Miki gnawed on the inside of her lip and kept her wide eyes trained on Will. His brows lowered, and he shook his head slightly, Never gonna happen.

"Shut your clap trap, McCord," Greer grumbled. "And before you say I'm jealous, I'm not. I'm only wondering."

So *Honey Bunny* had a real name, McCord, a name she wasn't likely to forget any time soon. To calm her nerves, she envisioned the toe of her boot finding its mark. Revenge served cold and right in the junk. But it was quickly clouded by how disappointed her dad would be. She closed her eyes and could hear his voice bellowing, "Miki-Lou! What do I always tell you? Communicate your destination, never get in a car with strangers, and know when to say 'no.' But most importantly, keep the bad guys guessing."

Self-defense. It was a lecture he'd drilled into her and Owen's heads at a young age. Now look at her...zip tied.

"So what's the plan for tonight?" Pitty asked when the van lurched to a stop.

The driver cut the engine, and all went silent. Greer sighed heavily followed by an unpleasant creak as the passenger door opened.

"I don't wanna talk about it," he said. "I hate beating on kids."

CHAPTER 15

PICNIC TIME

Miki blinked against the sudden head rush after being jerked out of the van and planted upright. The sun glinted brightly off the chrome bumper and was warm enough to dry the morning dew. Birds chirped in the trees, and normally, this would be the start of a gorgeous summer day.

Miki's heart thumped heavily in her chest as Greer frog-marched her across a beautifully manicured lawn bordered with yellow flowers. Without any words exchanged, the Pulver Skulls acted in unison. They were a choreographed trio, all on the same page, most likely from kidnapping people many times before.

Don't talk. Poke and shove your victims past someone's home, a peaceful-looking log cabin with a broad deck and a rocking chair. Then, whip open a metal side door to a large shop and rush the little prisoners down a narrow flight of stairs. Don't give them a chance to focus on the motorcycle parts, the gasoline cans, and the tools littering the concrete floor. Nope. Don't let them get any bright ideas.

In the basement, things were even more bleak. It was cold and dusky.

The ten-foot cement walls formed a spacious room cut in half by a chain-link fence, which spanned from the bare floor to the ceiling. The fence was held taut by steel pipes that were dropped into holes in the floor. Probably, so it could be put up easily for "guests" or taken down for parties. More likely, if Miki knew her bikers, it was for the quick take-down in case the cops came snooping around.

The metal cage rattled as Greer opened the fence door and shoved her into the cell. With her hands bound behind her back, she lurched forward to keep her balance. Pitty pushed Will inside, pulled the door shut, and secured it with a padlock. He handed the key to Greer, who poked it into the little watch pocket on the front of his dirty jeans. Greer gave it a comforting pat.

"You two look after the kids. I need to head over to Ham's cabin," he murmured, and the hair on Miki's arms prickled at the name—Ham, the man in charge, the biker hunting Bill and Liam.

Will stepped farther into the dark cell as the three Pulver Skulls formed a loose huddle. They stood in front of her, talking, like she didn't exist or wasn't considered a threat.

Typical. In the backs of their minds, they probably thought she was some bubblegum chewing high schooler who only cared about the state of her blue hair and the chips in her pink nails. The less they focused on her, the better. Miki took her cue from Will and slowly drifted back into the shadows until her hands met solid concrete.

"I'll order us a couple of Knotty pizzas for later. Remember, no news is good news, which means, as far as I'm concerned, the deed is done." Greer wiped a palm across his sweaty brow while sucking tobacco juice hard against his lower lip. "Ham'll be on his way back, and then...then, it's show time. Got it?"

"What deed?" Will asked hoarsely from his post near the wall. "What's going on with my family?"

"The Sullivans are toast, boy." Greer bashed the chain-link fence with the side of his fist. "Soon, you will be, too, because you tangled with a Pulver Skull, and we're going to see you live just long enough to regret it. Capiche?" Greer pulled his narrow shoulders back and expanded his chest while he glared between the wire links, trying for fierce. Miki narrowed her eyes at him and noticed he relaxed too soon. His machismo ebbed away and left only a hygiene-challenged fatso in a leather vest.

Was this the best the Pulver Skulls could do? She stood by, only imagining the pleasure of rolling her eyes at Greer's pathetic show of force. It was obvious he didn't have the energy or the talent for the big bad biker routine. Seriously, low-rent.

"Greer..." McCord started, his eyes searching out Miki's. A tense breath caught in her throat.

As she struggled to keep her cool, Will lunged past her. He was lit up by the beam of light pouring in from a basement window as well as his anger. His leg kicked out and rattled the chain-link fence, sending the P-skulls back a step.

Will's dark bangs flew forward, and amazingly enough, he didn't fall on his butt, even though his arms were banded behind his back with duct tape. His feet were planted wide, and he snarled, "You murdering bastards killed my mom!"

"Now, you listen here..." Greer trembled with anger. He stabbed a finger in Will's direction. "Your guys killed my boy, Barrel, and cut the patch off his dead body. He was a brother, and I won't live in a world where you sons of—"

"Boo hoo." Will sneered. "Your dead brother was drunk driving and killed an innocent woman, Cindy Sullivan! She loved animals and old people and cared about life—"

"Barrel was an innocent man!" Greer thundered and spittle flung from his lips. "...sitting in the passenger seat."

"Passenger seat? I call bullshit," Will whispered vehemently, his chest heaving with exertion.

"Come on, kid. You know as well as I do the driver took off. Nobody knows where she went, but believe me..." His voice trailed off, and it seemed to take a moment for Greer's brain to engage, telling him to shut his own clap-trap.

"She?" Will straightened.

A woman was driving? Miki's general rule was to keep her ears open at all times, and because of it, she knew things a lot of other people didn't. But apparently, the full story had alluded even her. Good job provoking Greer, Will.

"Who?" Will demanded.

Pitty closed his eyes and snorted with disgust. He seemed jaded, but he might be the only smart one around. Maybe she could sway him to the Hides of Hell way of thinking...offer him money or a chance to talk to her dad. Maybe he'd consider changing sides.

Greer would leave soon to get pizza and meet up with the two-timer, Valentina. Miki's only real worry was McCord. She could feel him watching her even though she avoided his gaze. He was a loose cannon with a gun and green eyes that shone with perversion. How could she fight him off without taking a bullet in the chest?

"Uh-huh. I hate beating on kids, but I'm sure going to like beating on you." Greer nodded his whiskered chin at Will, then turned to his cohorts. "Who's got the backpack? Let's check the goods and see what we're dealing with here."

"Greer," McCord said again, peeling Will's bag off his shoulder. He walked to the opposite corner of the room and with a thud, dropped it on a thick coffee table. "While you're handling the kid, I'll handle the girl, okay?" McCord's eyes sought hers again, and they crinkled warmly while putting the chill on her insides. *Handle her?* His words sent a skittering wave of creepy critters up her spine. He was on the small side, yet wiry and strong like a ranch hand. Behind the mutton-chop whiskers, he had a young, fresh face, and behind that squirmed something sinister and twisted. McCord was dangerous.

Will turned to face her, blocking McCord's line of vision. His brown eyes were intense as he glanced up at the hopper window near the ceiling. He mouthed silently, *Our way out of here*, then nodded as if asking, You with me?

It was narrow, probably nine feet off the floor, and their arms were tied, not to mention they had an audience. Hell, yeah—she was with him. He stepped to the wall, and she followed, inching down beside him, cross-legged on the cold cement. Her shoulder touching his... his knee touching hers. Two points of connection that kept her secure and hopeful.

A ray of sunlight filled with dust motes filtered down through the narrow window. It was brightest where the P-skulls stood, hovering over Will's backpack. Pitty sat on an orange burlap couch covered in burn holes, and what Miki hoped were beer stains.

Interior decorating at its finest. What a dump.

"Nothing happens to these two…" Greer sliced the air with both hands. "Not until I see the whites of Ham's eyes. Got it? This thing could go sideways at any—" He stopped to rub the back of his neck and gave a labored sigh. "I don't want any problems. Just…leave it for now, and let's take a look in the bag."

"Right. Leave it," McCord muttered sourly and ripped the zipper open with one smooth jerk. He reached in and pulled out a brown bottle. "Twenty-two ounces of stale beer," he said and plunked it down on the scarred wood.

"Kids." Greer scoffed.

"Mook's home brew," Will called out. "It shouldn't be flat, but if it is, I don't mind. I'd still drink it. In fact, we're kinda thirsty over here."

"Oh, I care. I really do," Greer said. "I bet you'd like a cloth napkin with your grilled swordfish, too." He raised his black eyebrow. "No? Good…because you're gettin' nothing. Now, shut up."

"I know what I'm hungry for…" McCord pulled out the container of apple pie and tossed it on the table beside the beer. "Now, we're ready for a picnic. Look here, our friend even packed a spork."

Pitty held the container up to the light and chuckled. "It's all yours. Pie looks like it took a pounding."

Will moaned softly beside her and squeezed his eyes shut. When he opened them, he panted like his breath caught. Was he in pain? Miki nudged him with her knee, but he only stared across the room at the trio. They laughed at their running commentary about pounding pie and limp suds. They continued to make jokes as they unpacked a rain jacket, dirty socks, pain meds, and a tube of ointment. When they pulled out the plastic wrapped brick—what they thought was powder—the room went quiet. The only thing Miki could hear was Will swearing under his breath.

McCord broke the silence by popping the lid off the pie container. He worked the spork back and forth, then tilted the container up to his mouth and raked in a ginormous bite. His cheeks were rounded while his jaw worked up and down. "Hmm." He nodded with a thoughtful frown, then swallowed. "Hmm. Tastes… different," he said. He scooped in a more civilized piece and chewed. "Like apples and dirt," he said around a mouthful. "…and cheese with a hint of freezer burn. I thought he meant homemade pie, but I'm guessing store-bought."

"Sounds delicious," Pitty muttered and slid the beer to his side of the table.

"It sure isn't how my mama makes it." McCord inhaled the last bit and forced out a gurgling belch like an amateur comedian.

"Dude's a monster," Will whispered unevenly.

While McCord brushed crumbs off his black t-shirt, Greer fished a switchblade out of his front pocket and stabbed it through the clear packaging tape. Using the tip of his knife as a spoon, he dipped it into the powder and brought it up to his tongue.

"Wait!" Will scrambled to his feet. He crossed the cell and leaned his face on the chain-link fence. His fingers were rolled up tight behind his back. "Those are my mom's ashes."

"Christ!" Greer sputtered, shaking the dust off his knife. He spat on the floor, then wiped his arm across his mouth, his neck blooming with red heat. Pitty tried to smother a laugh behind his large hand, and McCord grinned.

"Wait'll the guys hear how Greer sucked ash," he said and tossed the empty pie container onto the coffee table.

"Sometimes, I wish—" Greer's lips pulled back tight, and he shook his fist at eye level, so everyone got the gist. But the lack of reaction told Miki all she needed to know: Greer was an inflated inner tube. No traction... just a pocket of hot air. "I'm headin' to the cabin. You guys have first watch. I'll let you know when Ham rolls in."

"Ham rolls," McCord tittered.

"I'm so done," Greer muttered and strode to the door. His heavy boots thudded against the wooden stairs as he slowly trudged up each one to ground level.

"What should we do now, Pitty?"

Pitty grabbed the beer bottle off the table with one hand and pulled his phone out of his pocket with the other. "I'm going to savor Mr. Mook's home brew while I sext with my lady friend. You can do whatever the hell you want...just don't bug me."

McCord grunted and busied himself by reading the label on Will's prescription drugs. He snapped his fingers. "Idea. How about I get us a couple frosted mugs from the party fridge, huh?" He disappeared behind the corner of the stairwell where an unseen door squeaked and glassware clanked.

Miki sat quietly next to Will, who rested his head on his raised knees. It was either a gesture of defeat, a pain induced fold-over, or a cat nap. She hoped it was the latter. Miki sighed. It must be late afternoon by now. She hadn't seen her dad or her brother in nearly—she tapped her fingers against the cement floor, counting. They'd left camp thirteen hours ago.

Pitty lounged quietly on the couch, making intermittent happy noises while tapping and swiping at his phone screen. After a while, McCord returned with a small box in one hand, two glasses pinched in the other, and a bottle of beer tucked under his arm.

"Wanna play Exploding Kittens?" he asked, tossing the game box on the table. "I found it in the backroom." He slid the glass across the table to Pitty before popping the top on his own beer. He filled the mug and took a sip. Pitty picked up Mook's home brew and followed suit while they got down to the business of divvying out cards, but instead of playing, they took turns reading them to each other.

"Here's a good one…" Pitty murmured. "Beard Cat."

"Nope Ninja." McCord laughed.

"I have a knife," Will whispered into his knees, and Miki jerked her eyes away from the bumbling duo to study Will's hair. So he was awake and prepared. He'd had the knife all along.

"I think I love you," she murmured.

Will leaned back against the wall and studied her as if he thought she were serious. She squelched the need to explain it as a joke, and left the words to hang out there, nice and awkward-like. One side of her psyche enjoyed the personal torment; the other side enjoyed his.

She gazed into his brown eyes and let the time pass. He looked back into hers, and a sense of comfort washed over her. His guard was down, and he seemed open and lost and approachable and ready. If she ever wanted to know anything, reach out to him, now was the time. This was the closest she'd ever been to the "real" Will. She moved her leg to touch his.

"Will," she said quietly.

"You're killing my zen," Pitty griped from across the room, setting his drink on the table with a clunk.

"What's a little silent-but-deadly between friends?" McCord tilted in his chair to cut another one loose. "I blame the pie. It tasted like shit."

"Here." Pitty tossed the cards into the center of the table. "I'm done."

"Oh, no." McCord stood abruptly, and the dining chair he'd been lounging on scraped back loudly. He clutched at his guts and groaned through his teeth. "I gotta hit the head."

"Your departure would be my pleasure," Pitty murmured as his interest returned to the phone in his hand. "Take your time. I'm not going anywhere." He picked up the beer glass and took a long swig.

"Will..." Miki tried again, keeping her voice low and soft. "Whatever happened with us?"

His eyes left hers to watch McCord hobble through a door on the other side of the couch. A fan clicked on and a muffled whirring noise filled the basement. Will looked back at her.

"Us?" He shifted forward and squirmed like he was trying to pull his arms out of a pair of coat sleeves. "What do you mean?"

Pitty took another swig of beer and grinned at his phone.

"Remember the 'spicy dice' from last summer? I picked you, and I thought..."

Will rolled up onto his knees, gyrating his elbows and shoulders with a furrowed brow. He struggled, pausing only to check on Pitty's progress with Mook's beer.

Another satisfied gulp. Ahh.

Will turned his attention back to her. "You thought...what?"

"I thought..." Was he really going to make her spell it out? "I thought we had something, like there was chemistry. Like we'd connected."

"Really?" He stopped moving and frowned with disbelief. "Because you humiliated me in front of everyone. Do you know how many rump-ripper jokes I had to listen to? There was never an 'us.'"

"I've apologized for the farting comment at least twenty times," she murmured. "Guys joke about it all the time. Proudly, I might add—"

"Not in the middle of hooking up." He rocked his shoulders again, contorting up and down.

"I know. I'm sorry. If I could hit replay, I'd keep my big mouth shut, and I wouldn't be jealous of a girl like Izzy—"

"Come on. Jealous? I wasn't in the closet with her, was I? No, I was there with you." Will's lips tightened into a line as he continued to jostle his arms behind his back.

"She liked you, Will, and I knew she wanted to get with you in the closet. When I chose you, she gave me one of her looks like 'game on.' It sounds dumb now, but at the time I just...I felt...you know, I had to think fast, so she wouldn't get you alone. It worked, didn't it? A little too well. You said some pretty horrible things to me. I was never supposed to look at you, talk to you, or call you...ever again."

"I was mad." Will sighed. "Listen. Forget it, and let's concentrate on the here and now. We've gotta move fast. McCord's in the bathroom, and in about ten minutes, Pitty's gonna hit R.E.M. like a freight train. I finally got the knife out of my cast, but with this broken thumb, I don't think I can cut myself free. Let's sit back to back, and you take the knife. Getting through the duct tape should be easy, but be careful. Don't slit my wrist, alright?" He turned, facing away from her with the folded pocket knife clutched in his fingers.

The fan still whirred behind the closed door, and Pitty slouched deeper into the couch while blinking at his phone. When he rubbed his eyes, Miki decided it was safe. She shimmied around until her backside met Will's. Her fingers walked along his cast to his palm to the knife handle.

"Got a hold of it?" Will asked. "It's really sharp, okay?"

"Calm down." She opened the blade with a click and walked her fingers up the thick bands of duct tape.

"Did you tell me to calm down?"

"Yeah, I did." She smiled at their inside joke while slowly maneuvering the knife back and forth. It was sharp and after a few see-saw motions, it cut through the tape's adhesive like butter.

"Don't you know you never tell a guy to—"

A low, animalistic moan reverberated off the bathroom walls. McCord! She jumped, and the knife sliced upward.

CHAPTER 16

KARMA

The blade of the knife zipped through the duct tape and thudded to a stop against Will's cast. Miki froze even though she was sweating bullets. She could have cut him. Oh, God. She could have stabbed Will with his own knife!

Behind her, she could hear Will's heavy breathing and the soles of his shoes scrambling on the concrete floor. He took the open blade from her grip and touched her wrist.

"They've got the zip tie on tight. Let me get this out of the way." He pushed her woven bracelet up her arm and tucked it under the cuff of her jacket. "Don't flinch, okay? I'm going to slide the blade underneath the plastic band, like this..." The cold steel pressed against her skin, and Miki clenched her teeth, waiting for the pinch of pain or the warmth of drawn blood. She closed her eyes. Please-please-*please* don't cut me, Will. What if I faint?

"I'm, uh..." Miki bit the inside of her lip. "I'm not good with the sight of my own blood. I thought I'd put it out there since you think I should be a nurse, which is never gonna happen, by the way."

"I'm sorry I have to—"

The zip tie jerked hard and bit into her wrist.

"Half way, Miki. One more slice, and it's done."

Her arms went numb at the pressure, and she could barely feel the flat of the knife or Will's fingers touching her skin. "You're strong, Miki. It's what I like most about you. You can do this." The zip tie jerked again, and her shoulders fell forward with release.

A hot wave of adrenaline, fear, and anxiety surged through Miki's body all at once. The weight of her leather jacket felt smothering, so she jerked her arms out of the long sleeves and let it fall to the ground behind her. Sweet relief. The air was dank and cooled the skin on her arms and the sweat on her back...

Until the blood started circulating again. The skin where the zip tie had been tingled painfully while glowing an angry red. Her paracord bracelet rubbed against the raw skin, so she unclipped it to massage her wrist gently while Will hovered. She knew she needed to get up, to move. McCord could whip the bathroom door open at any moment, and she was pretty sure he wouldn't let a fiery case of rot gut get in the way of his trigger finger.

Will knelt in front of her and held his palm out. "You okay?"

She nodded, grabbed his hand to pull herself to standing and crammed the bracelet into her front pocket. He surprised her by wrapping his arms around her. His cast rested hard at her waist, and his free hand pressed at her nape. He squished her cheek against his chest and held on tight.

"I'm sorry," he said.

"Are you hug-bombing me?" she asked breathlessly into his green sweatshirt. He didn't answer, which was totally fine. She felt safe and needed in his arms.

"I hate goodbyes," he whispered fiercely, not letting go.

"It'll all work out. Don't worry." Miki rubbed circles over his back and murmured, "I'm here for you."

He dropped his arms and dipped his chin to look down at her. "Not for long, though," he said. "Only one of us can get out, and it's all you. Here, keep the knife folded, and when you're up there, whack the window with this steel point. It breaks glass. Okay?" She took the folded knife out of his hand.

He gave her a quick nod and slid the fingers of his good hand along her jaw, tilting Miki's universe. He seemed far away and kind of lost, like the gears were churning and grinding away at some thought. Maybe he was worried about being left behind or about her getting caught. His thumb went under her chin, and slowly, he dropped his lips onto hers. The kiss started as tender and tentative, then quickly became urgent.

Her heart and head were off balance as conflicting emotions bounced from one side to the other—He's kissing me. What about the law of least effort? Who cares! Savor the moment. But we're in a cell, idiot! We have to hurry. What if Greer comes back? Will's lips are touching mine. Please-please-*please* don't stop…

He pulled away and rested his forehead against hers. "Ready, Zombie Lips?" he asked with a shaky breath.

Great. Why'd he have to act all cute and sweet and turn things mushy right when she was preparing to leave him, to escape? The tearing sound was her heart being pulled apart. She wanted to stay with him, but she needed to go in order to save him—in order to save herself.

Without waiting for an answer, he took her cool hand and led her to the wall under the basement window.

"You're gonna hop on my back and work your way up to my shoulders. Use the wall for support—"

The toilet flushed, and Miki gasped as Will clutched her shirt and dragged her down until her butt hit the concrete. He slid her leather jacket across the floor and crammed it between them. "Hands behind your back," he ordered in a low voice. Her chest heaved out of control, and she bit her lip hard to keep from whimpering as the bathroom door opened a crack and light glowed from behind it.

"Pitty?" McCord said weakly. "Pitty, I think I'm dying. My stomach—I don't know if I have the flu or what, but could you—Oh, God." The door clicked shut and an agonizing groan was drowned out by a muffled splashing sound.

"Sick," Will said under his breath.

All went quiet again after the blur of excitement, except for the bathroom fan, which continued to hum in the background. Miki strained her vision on Pitty, a gigantic spud sprawled on the couch. There was no peep, no snore, not even a twitch. Her shoulders fell with relief, and she sagged against Will.

"You know, I saved Mom's pie. Now, after all this time, it's been eaten by a P-Skull who looks like an elf. No, a hobgoblin." Will dropped his chin. "I can't believe it's gone."

"Will…" Miki gently placed her palm on his forearm and squeezed, drawing his attention. "It all worked out, though. Didn't it? I mean he ate it, and now look, he's paying the price. Karma's a bitch, right? Serving up just desserts, one slice at a time. Maybe this is Cindy's way of looking out for you. Her way of giving you a second chance."

He stilled for a moment. "Maybe."

"Come on, Will." Miki stood. "Get up, and let's do this. The sooner I'm out, the sooner I'm back with help. I don't want to leave you alone with Greer."

"I don't want you to either, so when you're right, you're right." He stood with his knees bent and curtly told her to climb on. Miki pounced on his back, and after a quick jostle into position, she pulled her feet up, careful not to grind them into his spine. He hissed and grunted as she floundered clumsily. What would his skin look like now, after she'd stepped all over his healing wounds with the soles of her boots? He panted while walking his palm and cast up the wall, leveraging her up to the window.

While teetering on Will's shoulders, her heart raced, and her mind spun. She was up in the nose-bleed section, clutching at the window frame as goosebumps rippled down her forearms. Will was six-foot something, so looking down was probably not the best idea, but she did it anyway. Wow. Big mistake. There was nothing to catch her fall except a slab of cold concrete.

Miki lifted her eyes to her target while running through the Goldilocks scenarios. A hit too soft might not break it. A hit too hard might send her hand through the glass. Visions of blood splattered against the gray floor made her a little woozy. She shook off the thought —it's now or never—and reared the knife back. With a strong grip and some added control, she hit it just right, and the glass splintered. She opened the blade, used the tip to pry the shards out of the frame, then tossed them outward, off to the side.

"Hurry." Will grunted.

"There's too many little pieces. I can't crawl out without my jacket for protection."

He looked off to the side where the black bundle sat beyond his reach and swore forcibly under his breath. "Come on down. We'll try it again."

* * *

Sweat dribbled along Will's back, his front, his brow, his neck, his butt-crack. Jesus. With his hoodie on, he was a hot, steamy mess. But if he'd taken it off, he'd only have a thin t-shirt between Miki's hard boots and the crunchy cornflakes on his back. Sick. Maybe it wasn't sweat dripping off his shoulder blades. Maybe it was blood from torn off scabs.

Miki kicked him in the side of the head as she flailed to get half-in half-out of the window. He stepped back, grinding small bits of glass under his feet, and watched her rock on her belly over the leather jacket. The only thing left to see were her denim legs sticking out of the frame, which turned into the top of her boots, the tread, the heels....

She was gone.

Free as a bird.

He almost cried out, but the word "wait" was trapped behind his teeth. What if this was the last time he saw her? Greer could come back...cut off his head, spit in the hole, and the last thing Will would remember was her biker boot clocking his melon.

It was their last touch.

Suddenly, there was her face and blue hair, blocking the sunlight. "I'm coming back for you," she said, lobbing the folded knife through the frame. It skittered across the floor.

"No." Will ran and scooped it up. "Keep it!" He turned, holding it toward the window; it was empty. This time, she really was gone. "Miki?" Will said softly and let his arm drop. If she was still there…

Nothing.

There was only the whirring fan and the put-put-puttering of Pitty's lips as he started to snore softly.

Stay safe, Miki.

How long would it take her to get down the mountain? Would she meet any of the Hides of Hell boys on her way? Did the guys even know they were kidnapped? What if she ran into the Pulver Skulls? What would they do to her?

Will bit at the skin on his chapped lips. He wouldn't be able to get to her; he wouldn't know if she made it or if they killed her.

A scorching ball of pain the size of the sun rose out of Will's chest, and his windpipe burned with loss. No more Miki. Tears leaked out of his eyes. Snot dripped from his nose. Shortly after came the sweat and the slobber. Everything hurt, inside and out.

He closed his lids, slid down the gritty wall, and choked while trying to hold it all in.

After a long, catatonic state of nothingness, a buzzing sound brought him back into consciousness. *Buzz-buzz-buzz.* Silence. On again, off again. He slapped at his hip, expecting to feel a vibrating phone in a denim pocket but found neither. Instead, he was flat on his back in his Ghetto Gramps ready to make angels on the dirty floor. The sun sat low in the sky and reflected off the busted glass still stuck in the window frame. How long had he been out? Twenty minutes? An hour? His adrenaline had worn off, and everything throbbed—his broken pinkie toe, his cracked arm, and his bruised guts—thanks to the gymnastics he did while helping Miki escape. If only he could reach his pain meds.

Buzz-buzz-buzz.

It was Pitty's phone on vibrate. It wasn't set to ring— karma again?—otherwise, it might have alerted McCord or perhaps if there were someone upstairs in the shop…

Was Greer calling?

Will sat up and slipped his hand into his hoodie pocket. He had his knife. If there were guns involved, he was dead meat. If not, he might have a microscopic chance of busting out of here. In one hand, he had a sharp blade, and in the other, he had a green cast, a club. He'd beg to use the bathroom, and when Greer opened the chain-link door, Will would turn on his inner ape and get primal.

Creak.

The hair on the back of his neck flared. What was that? *Creak…creak.* Someone was in the stairwell, methodically making their way down. Will curled his fingers into a tight fist until the edge of the knife's handle bit into his palm.

It's go time.

Get ready.

The wooden stairs creaked and groaned as weight shifted on each step. Will's hoodie filled with furnace heat, and he inhaled three quick breaths to chill himself out. He leaned his shoulder into the wire fence and held his hands behind his back.

Someone fumbled with the door knob, then the door pushed open. A waft of greasy pizza with green peppers flooded the room, and Will's stomach churned with hunger and acid. First, there was a white cardboard pizza box. Then, there was a forearm...blond hair...a face. It was the kid from the hotel lobby, the kid who was friends with the elf and some chick called Pinecone. What was his name again?

Grins. No...Grinly?

He pushed into the room, all white tee and clean denim like he hadn't been soiled by the Pulver Skulls yet. He placed the box on the coffee table between the card game, the beer glasses, and Will's emptied backpack before surveying the room slowly. His piercing blue eyes landed on Will. They studied each other for a moment before the kid turned away, not seeming to care another human being was in a pen, contained like an animal.

"Pitty," the blond kid said in a low voice and waited while perusing the items sitting on the coffee table. What was he looking for? He seemed tense and focused, coiled like a spring ready for action. Was he supposed to be down here? Every movement he made seemed slow and calculating, like he was up to no good.

Miles. No...Smiles?

What was he looking for?

Another low moan escaped the bathroom, and the kid froze, cocking his ear to listen. He quietly stepped around the table corner to knock on the bathroom door.

"Yo," he murmured into the painted wood. "You in there, McCord?"

"Hey, man. I'm sicker than a dog..." His muffled voice sounded shaky and frail. "Can you help me, bro?"

"Sure," the kid said but walked away to pick through Will's things. He unrolled the rain jacket and shook it out, seeming to find something of interest. He held up the brick of ashes.

Will's brows jerked up, and he clutched the fence, forgetting, then not caring, how his hands were supposed to be tied behind his back. "Dude, those aren't drugs. Those are ashes. They're cremated remains!"

The kid gave him an impassive look as he tucked the bundle under his arm. He stepped toward the door to the staircase.

"Don't go!" Will banged his cast against the fence. "Smiles. No...Smiley! Wait!"

The kid didn't look back or even pause. He strode across the room to the exit and closed the door behind him. The wood stairs creaked with his departure. He left the same way he'd come, quickly and quietly.

"No!" The word ripped out Will's throat, leaving his insides tattered and raw. "No." He shrank to the floor. No.

CHAPTER 17

BITS AND PIECES

Miki almost couldn't tear herself away from the broken window. She lingered outside against the concrete wall with her leather jacket clutched to her chest. She needed to catch her breath, get her bearings, and accept the fact that she was free and Will was not. She had to leave him behind, and sort of like plucking her eyebrows or ripping off a Band Aid, the separation had to be quick because without a doubt, there would be extreme pain.

She had tossed the knife back into the cell, so Will would be armed and maybe a little less vulnerable. *Take it*, he'd yelled up to her, but she'd stepped out of sight, so he'd think she'd left. Of course, that would require a modicum of intelligence. For some reason, being a glutton for punishment called to her, and she hesitated long enough to hear him tentatively ask, *Miki?*

The soft lilt he'd added at the end of her name sounded so pathetic, so alone, it undid her. With a fist pressed to her mouth, she kept silent while her heart exploded into micro-bits against her ribs. What evil world was this? She'd wanted him—heart, mind, and soul —for as long as she could remember. Everything about him meshed with everything about her, and at each turn in their developing relationship, something catastrophic happened to keep them apart: a faux "fart" in the closet, an over-protective big brother, Cindy's death...

Now, throw in kidnapping. What next? The planet would probably jerk to a stop on its axis if she ever got together with her soul crush, Will Sullivan. If you love something, set it free. It's exactly what she had to do.

She pulled away from the broken window and skirted the concrete wall until it became beige siding, then she paused to jam her arms into her black leather jacket. Once again, adrenaline, fear, and anxiety pushed heat and sweat out of her pores. It didn't matter because there was no way in hell she was taking this coat off. With it on, she transformed into a Hides of Hell biker; she turned into one of the guys. She didn't have the big Hides of Hell patch on her back or the rocker for Washington underneath, but she was a legitimate tough girl, a biker brat ready to kick it.

What would her guys do right now?

Flossy was the observant type, so he'd case the perimeter, looking for weak spots. Ironically, Trip with his fake leg was a tracker and would tune into footprints, doughnut crumbs, and errant cigarette butts. Dad would head straight for Bill—who lived on his bike, always on standby—to rally a vengeful comeback. Owen would tap his anger and charge anything that moved like a strapped bull, tossing fists and busting chops. Liam carried anything and everything in his pockets...aside from his usual Zippo lighter and Leatherman multi-tool, he'd surprise her with a hairband if she needed one, a cough drop, and without fail, a working ballpoint pen. He was a regular yes-man. Liam, do you have an oil rag? Yes. Do you have the time? Yes. Are you ready? Yes…always.

But she wasn't a man with bulging muscles or a gun-toting biker. She wasn't her dad or her brother. She was a slim girl without any combat experience or weapons. She crouched and darted across the short expanse of grass to the tree line. Under the cover of blackberry brambles and tree shadows, her heart hardened and her confidence grew. She had a job to do.

Focus, girl. You're Miki "Hot Bod" Holtz. What's it gonna be?

Run.

The ground was springy with a mass of needles, twigs, and pinecones, and it crunched under her boots with each step. It was deafening in light of other sounds. Even the birds had gone quiet as they watched her clumsy efforts from the branches above.

All she had to do was follow the road back down the mountain, short-cutting across all the switch backs. How many miles had they driven? What if she got lost in the woods? Never mind all that. Once at the Powerhouse Inn, she'd find her saddlebags, her phone, her bike, and someone to help. But…did she have enough time? Where was Greer? Where were the other P-Skulls? The heat of the day felt like four in the afternoon. Did Greer leave to meet Valentina already? Would he ride a motorbike to Knotty Knolls or take the van?

The van.

Maybe running wasn't the best plan after all.

Miki searched for the cabin's tin roof above the thicket while she pushed through the dense foliage. She slipped in between the branches and with a shaky hand, tipped a broad leaf to the side.

There stood the log cabin bordered with yellow flowers. The white van had been backed into the driveway. Was it locked? What were the chances of finding keys in the ignition? A loaded gun in the glovebox? A hunting knife under the seat? Maybe some rope?

Miki's heart surged and swayed like it might fly out of her mouth. Oh, God. Failure was not an option. She clamped her lips together and swallowed the rising panic.

Calm down.

She pulled in a deep breath and focused.

The closest windows on the building were dark, but the place was a large rambler, so it was hard to tell if someone were milling around on the far side or if it had been locked up, cold and empty.

It was awfully quiet over there.

She dropped her hand, and the leafy branch sprung back into place, blocking her view. Okay, new plan. She'd sneak to the van, stay low, and check the doors. If they were unlocked, she'd sweep it for weapons or keys, never forgetting: elbows, knees, and boots. Those were the strongest points on her body.

She pulled the branch down again to gauge the distance and to visualize everything working out. See how easy? It's a no-brainer. You're a girl, not a chicken. Get going! Get over there, and do it. There's no more time to waste.

Like now!

Right. Elbows, knees, and boots. She sucked in a deep breath and held it as she jogged across the lawn— doing it—doing it—doing it! At the van, she leaned against the solid metal and clutched at her heaving chest with both hands. Having...a...heart attack.

Sweat trickled down her back, and her tongue darted out nervously to lick her lips as she turned to spy in the van's passenger window. Through the cab, she could make out the shadowy front porch of the cabin but little else. There was no movement, no lights on, no faces in the window, and—her eyes dropped to the ignition—no keys.

Open the door.

It was unlocked. Okay, doing it.

Her hand shook as she scanned the oily carpet under the seat with her finger tips. Crumbs, wrappers, small screws, a little thing that was smooth and round...

A shelled peanut.

She flicked it aside and bent to peer under the seat. Score. A plastic box. What is it, a gun case? Please-please-*please* don't be a first aid kit.

She reached under again, her fingers searching for a handle. Before she could tug it free, gravel crunched on the other side of the van, and the driver's side door opened quickly, pulling a breeze through Miki's hair. Her eyes flew up and met with Greer's across the cab. There was an odd moment of silence where the only thing that could be heard was her loud gulp as she painfully swallowed back a terrified scream.

His eyes went wide with surprise, and his whiskery mouth hung open, inviting a sparrow to take roost. When his lips slowly closed, he took on a shifty look. Miki waited. If he went left, she'd run right. If he dove straight ahead over the seat cushions, she'd slam the door in his face. Her hand was still hidden, clutching the plastic handle. Her breathing came faster as anticipation for his move hung in the air. She wiggled the box back and forth, finally dislodging it. When he lunged into the van, she pulled it free.

Miki screamed and bolted across the lawn. It was back to her original plan. Run!

The black box swung at her side, and by its weight, she was fairly certain it held a gun. Her legs shook, her chest was on fire, yet her body felt bionic. She flew through the air, her feet touching the earth twice before the tree line was within reach. She sprang up again. Only this time, Greer was right beside her. He grasped her leather sleeve and jerked, spinning her in a one-eighty. She let the box follow the momentum and clocked him right in the temple. The box opened and silver drill bits sprayed out like buckshot onto the grass.

He fell to his knees beside a corded hand drill, but his grip remained strong, and he used it to quickly right himself. Miki screamed louder this time with equal parts fear and frustration and brought the empty box up again. The plastic edge clipped his cheek and sent his long greasy hair to one side. She reared back to dispense another blow.

But Greer gripped her wrist with vice-like fingers and twisted until her flimsy weapon dropped to the ground. His black eyes glinted like a coiling snake, ready to strike. He twisted her wrist again until she whimpered. If she didn't act, he'd break it, and probably her neck, too, and all with that dip-in-his-lip smile.

Elbows, knees, and boots. Now! Do it!

She bent her leg, ready to administer damage, but he pulled her into his broad belly, so instead, she raked the sole of her boot down his shin with as much force as she could muster.

"Son of a bitch!" he roared. She pushed into him, and when he stepped back, she drove her knee up to the moon. Wham! A sharp pain surged through her knee cap as her joint met the vertex of his legs. His grip went limp and slid away as he folded in half next to her feet, squirming and gasping for air.

Should she kick him again while he's down?

She stepped back and wiped a sweaty palm through her hair. Part of her wanted to, harder this time, but the other part screamed, *Get the hell out of there while you can!* His eyes were pinched tight as he rolled to his side.

"I'm a…kill…you," he choked out and spittle flew from his mouth with some clinging to the stubble on his unshaven chin.

Kill? A second nut shot wasn't worth it. She flung herself into the trees and ran as fast as she could, dodging low branches and jumping over roots.

She didn't stop to catch her breath or look over her shoulder. She sped through the mishmash of leaves and limbs like he was hot on her heels. Her fuel tank was filled to the brim with adrenaline, and it drove her straight down the mountain in survival mode, mindless of where the road was.

Time was elusive, and what felt like thirty minutes could easily have been eight seconds for all she knew.

Her bionic powers had left her a mile back, and now her feet were finding every gopher hole in the vicinity. God, she needed a break. She stepped behind a broad tree trunk and in between gulping breaths, listened to the forest noises: mosquitoes humming, squirrels jumping in the branches, a crow cawing. The muscles in her legs quivered, so she took a moment to lean against the bark, to wait before peering back. When she did, there was nothing.

No crunching and crashing of twigs.

No thundering feet.

No Greer.

It was eerily quiet after the horrible excitement she'd endured, but if she stood here and thought about it too much longer, she'd lose her mojo and have an epic meltdown. Will was still locked up, and once Greer recovered from getting kneed in the speed bag, he might go gonzo for Will.

Run. Keep running. Run and run and run. Don't stop. Don't ever stop. Will's life depended on it. She pointed herself downward, hoping that if she went straight and to the left, somehow she would wind up on the road or close to the Powerhouse—

A peripheral movement caught her attention, and she stumbled as a hand lurched out of the shrubs to grip her leather collar. She went airborne, her body flying in a downward arc. Her hands skidded in the damp soil, and a shocked breath was knocked out of her middle. She grunted on impact, then thrashed wildly to escape the grip. Oh God! It was Greer! He was going to kill her!

Before she could claw at the dirt and leaves and scream bloody murder, someone straddled her backside. Strong hands pushed her shoulders down and a deep voice hissed next to her ear, "Shut up! Or I'll kill you myself."

CHAPTER 18

UNRAVELING

Thirsty. Dirty. Hungry. Face-down in the muck. Completely exhausted. Miki's hands were free, buried under a blanket of dead leaves, and even though she could push off the ground anytime she pleased, she didn't. A single moment to process her life was required. Her muscles ached. They were limp. Shaky. Yet overall, she was supremely relieved to be in the position she was in.

"Have I told you lately that I love you?" she whispered hoarsely to the weight on her back.

"I told you to shut up," Owen growled, still sitting on her rump, pinning her down. "Listen. Hear that?" he asked with a strained voice. She could hear jack squat, only the blood pumping in her ears.

"All clear," someone whispered loudly from another hiding spot. It had to be Flossy. Was Trip here, too?

The sudden release of anxiety and fear gushed through her system, and tears flooded her eyes. They spilled over and flowed warmly across her skin, plip-plipping off the end of her nose. She was surrounded by her men, her family. She'd found help.

"Thank God." Owen rolled away from her, then pulled her upright. "Hey, you okay? Are you hurt? Who do I have to kill? Mik, look at me." She lifted her watery eyes to her brother's dark brown gaze.

Normally, she would have laughed at the sight of him, all concerned and gentle. She might have even called him an emotional weenie for a guaranteed reaction. This time, it made her cry harder. What was one more crying jag? Might as well do it in front of her big brother, too.

"This summer sucks!" She choked on a sob, and he pulled her into his pin-striped vest for a rough hug.

"Don't get snot on my lapel," he murmured, patting the middle of her back with a heavy hand. He dropped his arm to dig a phone out of his rear pocket.

"We have to go get Will." She raked the hair away from her face and swept the grit off the front of her leather jacket. She could really use one of Will's hug-bombs right now. His arms around her. Cozy. Safe. Connected. "He's still trapped in the basement, and that Greer guy will kill him."

"We're on it," Flossy said as he crouched beside her. He assessed her with his brown eyes, doing a full body scan from the top of her head to the toes of her boots. His polished turquoise ring glinted against his wiry beard as he stroked the length of it out of habit. "You good to go?"

She sniffed and nodded, finger-swiping under each eye.

"'Atta girl. At least you don't bounce like a dead cat," Flossy said.

No crumbs and no dead cat bouncing. Dig deep, Miki "Hot Bod" Holtz. Find your inner strength. Ignore the blisters, the sweaty pits, and the dirty hair. Ignore the thick tongue and dry mouth. Don't you dare think about a drink of water or a Badger Paw cheeseburger until Will is out. Now, get your ass back *up* that mountain and find the cabin. Go save Will!

Doing it.

"Okay. I'm ready, but we should hurry." Ignore those aching joints, too.

Flossy stood and searched the trees with his hands resting on his hips. "Any word from Trip?" he asked, not looking down.

Owen slid his finger over the length of his phone, reading a text message. "Let's see…he says, 'I don't have the right foot screwed on. Kept slipping on the rocks. Turned back. Yadda-yadda.' I guess that part means he'll hide down there and wait for the drive by."

"Drive by? You mean Dad?"

"Get up, Mik. You always wanted to be one of the guys, so now it's your lucky day. You lead the way." Owen held out a calloused hand, and when she took it, he jerked her to standing with a fast pull that set the pace. With each step toward Will, she felt stronger. God, she couldn't wait to see his face! His brown eyes, his long brown hair, that beauty mark on his cheek. *Where does it hurt, Will? Looks like you've got a bad case of hairy-mole-itis—*

"Dad and the guys are with Bill and Liam," Owen said. "They're heading this way, thanks to Trip. He found your saddlebags in the shrubs and part of a scratching stick, something he'd carved for Will." He jabbed her in the back forcefully and muttered, "I'm pissed at you, as usual, but glad we found you in one piece."

"Bill and Liam are alive?" she asked over her shoulder. Her heart lightened at the good news causing the pain from her blisters to melt away. She trudged up the incline step by step with renewed energy.

"You put too much faith in the P-Scums," Flossy murmured. "Hides of Hell are chasing their pipes all the way here. Bill wants to see his kid alive, so we'll make it happen."

"The guys were surrounded and stuck in BFE with no cell coverage...still doesn't keep a brother down," Owen said. "Apparently, Liam played bait, while Bill out-maneuvered the P's to put the call out. He's wily for an old dude."

"Old dude." Flossy chuffed out a laugh. "Tell it to his face when he shows up. Then, watch out. Bill knows how to make things turn and burn. A sight to see, and one you don't wanna be here for," he said to Miki.

"Nope." Owen agreed.

No, she didn't. Not if it involved baseball bats and duct tape. Besides, once she had Will in her grasp, she'd get as far away from this town as possible.

"I just want Will out, safe. Then, he and I'll be on our way," she said. "Is my bike still parked at the Powerhouse Inn?"

"We doubled up and hid our bikes down below. Trip'll ride it," Owen said. "Don't worry. We called Shorty for backup, and he's on his way, too. Give us the low-down on the sitch. What can we expect?"

"Four guys that I know of," Miki said, ducking under the mossy branches. "One's in a roofie slumber down in the basement with Will. One's bogarting the bathroom with a bad case of the green-apple-quick-step, and Greer is the one I kneed in the junk—

"Jesus," Owen muttered and hissed in a breath between his teeth.

"I left him praying to God on the lawn, and there was another guy who drove the van, but he's an unknown. I haven't seen or heard of him since they dropped us off."

"Sounds like a cakewalk," Flossy said. "Let's step it up. I wanna be done in time for happy hour."

* * *

Will pulled on his green hood and rested his forehead on his cast, ready for a mind-numbing doze. The rough texture pressed into his skin and would probably leave an angry imprint, but he didn't care. Pain was familiar to him, whether physical or emotional. He was truly alone, and the chill went bone-deep.

There were no ashes, and the running bathroom fan reminded him there was no apple pie.

Will leaned his head back against the concrete to study the crack in the opposite wall. Mom used to put grated cheddar cheese in the crust, just the way he liked it. It was the very last thing she'd ever baked, so he could never imagine eating it, and later, he couldn't bring himself to throw it away. For months, he'd stared at the clear plastic container in the middle of the kitchen table. When it started getting black spots, Liam snapped. He'd tossed the entire thing in the garbage can, throwing her away along with empty egg cartons and used coffee grounds.

Mom? I dug you back out. I'm the one who hid you in the back of the freezer. I saved you. I saved the pie...

Saved...for all the good it did him. His head felt heavy, so he dropped it onto his hard cast again. No pie, no ashes, no Mom. Dad and Liam—even Miki—may or

186

may not be alive. No Helmet. He hadn't heard his mom's voice in his head for what seemed like days, and he never thought he'd live to say he missed it. It's the reason why he drank. To get Mom off his mind, literally. Now, he missed her more than ever.

Mom?

See? Nothing. It was like he was losing her all over again. Was she tied to the pie? The ashes? Was he going crazy? Maybe she knew he was going to be dead soon, so she figured, why bother? She'd see him soon enough.

He couldn't shake the *why* of it. Why did the kid, Smiley, steal his mom's ashes? What was the point? To torment him as part of the P-Skull torture technique? The very least the punk could have done was to toss Will's pain meds within reach. His arm was killing him, and his mid-section felt like jelly, like he'd cranked out two-hundred sit ups on the hard gym floor. Actually, it felt worse. It was more like he'd been run over by a nine-hundred-pound Harley Road King. Fully loaded, of course.

Will would've popped three pain pills with no hesitation. Maybe even four for the pain in his guts, for the throb in his arm, for the misery, for the silence.

He closed his eyes and pictured Miki with strands of cropped blue hair tucked behind her ears. She still wore those delicate pearls, and he wished he could touch one. Touch her. Trace the shell of her ear. Man, she was beautiful.

Last year, he'd been pissed at her for implying he'd dropped an air biscuit in the closet, especially since he'd been seconds away from throwing his heart at her feet, something he'd never done before. At least he'd been spared that gory mess.

He'd given her a dose of the Chill Will and tried to stay strong through her tears and profuse apologies. A couple days later at the lake, he'd already thawed and was on the verge of forgiveness when she'd flung her swimsuit in his face. She was mischievous and the laugh she'd laid on him…oh, yeah. He'd wanted to work things out.

But how could he when Owen showed up? Aggressive as usual, putting a stop to the fun and games.

Then, his mom died, and there was no forgiving anyone. Not Miki. Not Leo and the Hides of Hell bikers. Not Dad or Liam and certainly not Mom.

Mom? I'd forgive you now if you'd only talk to me.

Nothing.

No Mom…no Miki.

She was lucky to be free of him—a beauty with blue hair and brown eyes. He was much too pitiful to keep a girl like her happy.

Will, this is your mother speaking. Go find—

"Hey, jerkoff! Your white knight is here to save your ass. Wake up!"

Wait! Go find what, Mom? Mom! Please come back. I've missed you so much. I can't even begin to tell you how glad I am to hear your voice again. I'm listening. Tell me something…anything. Ground me. Yell at me. Just don't go.

Mom?

"Hey! You ignoring me down there? I mean that's some nerve, right? You think we've got all day?"

"Shut up!" Will squeezed his eyes shut so tightly he saw pressure spots dancing behind his eyelids. Owen was the ultimate nightmare. There was absolutely no peace with the guy around.

"Hallelujah," Flossy hollered. "Good, we've got a live one."

"Watch it, Little Willy. I have no problem leaving you to rot with the vermin. Doesn't matter to me because I was going to beat the tar out of you anyway. You're a worthless skin bag..."

Whatever. Getting saved by Owen was akin to getting his teeth kicked in. As far as he could tell, the animosity had started when he'd refused Owen's call to play flag football. It was as simple as leaving Owen's team short a member, and they'd lost. Naturally, Will was to blame. Not to mention he'd been caught playing video games with Miki in the clubhouse...alone. Owen's head had nearly exploded.

"...you listening to me, Gadget Freak? Get used to your new nickname. I can't wait for you to turn prospect. I will personally see to it..."

Will had been thirteen, and Miki a few months younger. Her hair had hung to her waist in a long, thick braid. It was shiny and black, and he'd taken a hold of it, tugging her toward him in a daring move. It was so she'd run her race car into the wall. How else could he win? When she returned the favor, her hand wrapped up in his hair, he'd been electrified. A tingling bolt had ripped through his body. It was horrible. It was exciting. It earned him his first bloody nose, thanks to Owen, who showed up like the hot-headed loser he was.

And...thanks again, Owen, for chasing off Mom right when she was about to dispense with some sage advice. Now, there was nothing but crickets and Owen's grating voice.

"...and I was just messing with you, man. I won't shove my dirty fist down your throat or ram your head through the beer fridge, okay? I like you well enough, and it's why I'm here...to help you. Will? Come on, throw me a bone. I'm really trying here, but we're running out of time. What's Bill going to say when we return without your hide? You're disappointing everyone...again."

"Oh, my God." Will jerked his head up and blinked. The sun beamed into his peripheral from the broken window. If Dad and Liam were alive, they'd be the ones standing out there. "They're dead...aren't they?" He stared at the wall's now familiar crack, the one he'd been assessing for the past two or three hours, and his heart splintered into jagged pieces. It scraped its way down to the pit of his belly, leaving him raw. "My entire family... gone. I'm all alone." He rubbed his fingertips over the arm of his sweatshirt and couldn't feel a thing. He was fading out, becoming—"I'm nothing."

"Are you done unraveling it yet?" Owen muttered to someone off to the side. "He's losing his mind, and I don't know how to deal with crazy."

"Hang in there, Gadget," Flossy said, his voice sounding distant. A shadow of movement flickered above.

"Why don't you get your dick out of your ear," Owen yelled into the basement. "I already said Bill and Liam are alive—"

"If they were alive, they'd be here...instead of you!" Will panted, trying not to cry. God, not in front of Owen. His diaphragm froze, and he couldn't pull in a full breath. "Shit. Leave me...the hell...alone. Let me... just...let me be."

"What a drama queen," Owen said off to the side.

"Way to talk him off a ledge. You ever get the feeling like you're *not* helping?" a feminine voice demanded. "Will! Here, grab on!"

"Miki?" A movement caught his attention. It was a kinked length of black paracord with a large loop tied on the end, and it swayed against the wall. He followed the line up to the window, but he couldn't make out her face. Everyone up there was back-lit, mere silhouettes.

"Will! Your dad and your brother are on their way here, so get off your Ghetto Gramps, already."

Her warm voice crashed over him like ice-water—They're alive!—and he jerked up to standing. His brain spun, so he leaned a shoulder against the wall to sort out his equilibrium. "My mom's ashes...they're gone."

"Hear that? We've got incoming," Flossy muttered tersely. "Step on it, Will."

"I told you I'd be here for you, and I am, and I forgive you. Now, please-please-*please* hurry!"

"Forgive me? For what?" His backside was stiff as he limped to the thin cord. He gave it a quick tug.

"For being the world's biggest idiot, but we can talk about it later." She slid her leather coat under the cord and over the sharp points of glass still stuck in the bottom of the window frame.

The black sleeve slapped the cement in front of his face, and the scent of leather and Miki's soap wafted up his nose. His chest nearly exploded with a tidal wave of emotion. She was close, safe. He was being freed from his hell hole by the Big Bad Biker Bunch, and Dad and Liam were speeding down the freeway, toward him. It was like this kidnapping had pushed him through some kind of time warp, and he hadn't seen anyone for years.

Whatever was out there, he was ready to face it, head on. He put his foot in the loop and gave it all his weight, half expecting it to slip free from its tether above. But it held and cinched tightly around his boot.

"I'm ready. Pull me out," Will said.

The line stretched tautly—*tzzz-tzzz-tzzz*—and Will zipped upward in three quick tugs. The cord friction-burned a hole in the back of Miki's jacket, leaving a pungent smelling cloud, the last barrier to the outside world. Both his biceps were gripped by strong hands, and he was pulled out of the dark basement and into the light.

CHAPTER 19

GUESS WHO

Will closed his eyes and faced the sun. The air was sweet with cottonwood pollen and warm sap. Owen and Flossy hauled him through the window frame and dropped him on his knees in the grass. They let his arms go, and his cast clunked against the earth. He was free.

"Long time, no see," he told Miki, pushing awkwardly off the ground to stand, but before he could bask in the glory of his surroundings, he was man-handled across the lawn to hide in the shadows of the tree line.

Growling engines echoed through the forest as bikes rolled two-by-two up the cabin's long driveway. Dread crawled along Will's spine. Black tires. Chrome pipes. Black and silver beards. There were a lot of Pulver Skulls pulling up.

"Where're the guys?" Will tore his eyes off the metal beast forming some distance away to scan the trees. Where was Dad? Liam? Where were Leo, Trip, Mook, even Caboose? Where was *anyone*? Jesus! "Things are looking serious over there. What's the plan? Hoofing it down the mountain? Because I think we'd better blow... as in five minutes ago."

193

Flossy nodded while he thoughtfully stroked his wiry beard like he was soothing a pet cat, but his eyes were dark and vigilant. The thick silver jewelry and his extra-white t-shirt snug across his torso were in direct contrast to his gnarly tatts, dirty fingernails, and torn jeans. The dude was unpredictable and scary as hell, which was why the three of them were looking at his red, hairy chops right now. He was the silent boss.

Flossy flicked his thumb over his shoulder, indicating they should move out in the opposite direction of their gathering "friends." He crouched, hot-footing it to a nestle of shrubs. Denim swished. Pinecones crunched. They stopped. Listened. The bikes rumbled about a quarter mile away. After a beat, Flossy pointed out his intent, then shuffled farther into the trees until they were on the backside of a downward slope. Will could no longer make out the shop, which also meant the Pulver Skulls couldn't put the make on them, either. Right?

Flossy waved them into a huddle.

"What's the word from Trip?" he muttered to Owen, who already had his phone out.

"The Hides passed him two minutes ago, so our guys are close. He's going to join them on Miki's ride, and that'll be the last we hear until show time," Owen said in a low voice. He knelt forward and shoved his phone into his back pocket.

"Make sure you got it on vibrate."

Owen's eye twitched at the directive, but he jerked his chin in answer. "These two need to vacate. Once the pyrotechnics show up, they'll be a distraction—"

"Dude," Will said. "Just say the word." Finally, Owen was saying something agreeable, something Will could get behind. He could practically see his mom throwing her hands up. *It's about time! Will wonders never cease?* He nudged Miki with his shoulder. Smudges of dirt marred her cheeks, and short pine needles stuck out of her hair like pins in a pincushion. *A new-age beauty queen.* All she needed was a camo bikini. "You ready?" he asked.

"Pyrotechnics?" Miki frowned at Owen. "You guys are going to burn another P-Skull building down?"

"Another?" Will raised his brows and looked at the other brown eyes in the bunch. *Was setting fire to real estate turning into some kind of Hides of Hell specialty?* This was the first he'd heard of it. *Wasn't arson a class-A felony? Prison...anyone hear of it?*

Flossy put a chokehold on his beard and narrowed his eyes. "Tooth for a tooth, eye for an eye. You think we're gonna let them get away with kidnapping our kids? Our families? It keeps going, Miki. The earth keeps turning, and the P-Scums keep burning. Everyday the Hides get stronger, those bastards get weaker. One day, they'll have to stop because there'll be nothing left. They'll be broken."

Jesus! Will widened his eyes and stepped back. *What happened to a good ol' fashioned bonfire with friends?* Someone might die here tonight, and he just...he didn't want any part of it.

"They're here." Owen's eyes lit up, and he cupped his ear as a sign to listen. Loud pipes growled in the distance, and everyone visibly tensed. Owen leaned forward to pull out his phone and with a shaky hand pecked out a fast message. "God, every time something like this goes down I feel sick to my stomach." His breath blew out in a tense laugh. "In a good way."

"Calm down," Flossy murmured, stretching his neck to get a good look through the trees.

Will nudged Miki again and whispered next to her ear, "He said 'calm down.'" Okay, so this probably wasn't the time for jokes. Then again, what if he were the one to die here tonight? Wasn't it better to laugh now while it can do some good? It seemed better than dying with a joke on his tongue. "Remember, oh, about a hundred years ago, when I said you were nothing but trouble? So is this what it's like to be on a date with you?" Ha, ha. Right?

"Why?" She scrutinized him from under her fringe of lashes. "Are you asking?"

He furrowed his brow. Was she joking or being serious? It felt like a trick question, one he couldn't really handle right now in the middle of their escape attempt. Besides, she always tried to move things along too fast. What was wrong with his pace? You know, a little dance first. He wanted to lead, yet she was always stepping on his toes.

"Figures," Miki said and turned away. "Same old story."

"Hey, now—"

A twig snapped behind him and the hair on the back of his neck flared. Two thick arms banded around his chest and squeezed. He was pulled back roughly against solid muscle. Fortunately, he'd had nothing to drink all day, or he probably would have sprung a leak, and pissing himself in front of everyone was not an option.

"Guess who?" said a gravelly voice in his ear and suddenly Will fell limp with relief. Okay, he wasn't captured—he was being man-hugged. But why play the stupid "guess who" game at a kidnapping rescue?

"Dad?" Will choked out. Then, he was spun in a circle and engulfed by leather and whiskers. Will held on like a baby possum; he was never going to let the old man go, even though his dad's shirt was damp with sweat, and he was pitting out like a steamy vat of onion soup. Will inhaled, relishing his dad's stink. It was proof-positive the man was alive.

Dad locked onto Will's shoulders and shoved him away while still holding on at arm's length. His dad rocked him to and fro with a stretched on grin and glittering eyes.

"You are a sight for sore eyes, son. You look like your mom. When I thought you'd been—" He shook his head and glanced at the ground cover before lifting his eyes again. "I'm happy to see you, Willy Boy." More rocking to and fro. Will swallowed hard against the mounting bubble of emotion pushing up his throat. His old man's beard hung down his front, banded together in a twenty-inch rope. Before Will could think twice about it, he yanked it like a pull cord, something he used to do when he was a kid and wasn't pissed off. It had been a long time.

Dad's grin got wider and his grip stronger and more firm. When he released one of Will's shoulders, it seemed to float there. Dad jerked Will into a circle with the guys, and whether on instinct or years of experience, they leaned in like a team ready to hear the play. Bill stepped into the coach role and all eyes were drawn to him.

"You owe me a beer for saving Baby Boy's butt," Flossy said and smirked.

His dad laughed and clapped Will on the back a little too hard—Will winced. What the hell was this "Baby Boy" crap about? Will's brows lowered into a straight line. Was it the name the guys called him behind his back? He wasn't even the youngest kid at the club house. He wasn't the shortest either, not by a long shot.

"Barely," Dad said. "I could've found you guys a hair earlier if Owen was smarter than his smart phone."

"Shee-it," Owen drawled. "Face it. You're slow, old man. You missed the whole thing…"

More jabs quickly went around, a little something for everyone, including Trip, who wasn't even here to defend himself. Will instantly felt the void growing between him and the brotherhood. He was nothing more than a package, the goal; he wasn't a part of them. Will pulled his shoulders back and his head left the huddle. He looked up, expecting to see Miki.

She wasn't there.

"…has got the Molotov cocktails and is going to…"

Will's pulse accelerated as he searched the trees, left, right—

"Guys, where's Miki?" He blinked frantically, trying to make out a form in the lacy shadows. They grunted and shifted their boot heels in the dirt to have a look around.

"I'm right here, jackass," Miki said, standing farther behind him. She was by herself. Alone. Her arms were crossed under her chest, and her denim hip was cocked to the side. "But I'm about to leave. I'm done here."

"Me, too," Will said, elbow-jabbing his dad and easing away from the pack to get closer to Miki. He crunched through the twigs toward her, then stood looking down and waiting…for something? A hint? A connection? Like we're in this together, right? He pulled a crunchy leaf out of her hair and showed it to her, but all she did was look him in the eye with an annoyed expression and said nothing. He dropped it and traced a strand behind her ear like he'd thought about doing in his cell. Had it been twenty minutes ago or twenty days?

"Miki-tiki-tavvy," he said, expecting a reaction like an eye roll or the way her lips used to twist into a half smile. None came. She blanketed him with a blasé, stony-faced glare, which made him feel silly for even thinking about calling her the juvenile name.

The void grew, this time between him and her, a distance he wasn't prepared for or necessarily liked very much. The last thing his mom had said to him rang in his ears...*Go find*— It was right before Owen saved his baby-butt. Will had wanted the sentence finished. Find what, Mom? Tell me! But now, he knew what she meant.

Go find a life. Time was elusive. There was too much on one side and not enough on the other. Find acceptance. Find solace. If it was finding love, it might be standing right in front of him. How would he know unless he moved forward? He tried again. "Miki—"

KA-BOOM!

Holy, mother of... A gasp left Will's lips, and his eyebrows flew up into his hairline. What the hell? He crouched and searched out Miki's hand with his own while looking to his dad. The look on Dad's face meant the gunshot was unexpected. No...the timing wasn't right. Wrong again, his face held the look of harnessed excitement. This was the Hides of Hell way.

"Go!" Dad hissed at Owen. "Mile marker eight. White truck. Don't stop for anything!"

Owen didn't question it; the plan had been set and agreed upon. The parties who needed to know had been informed. He ran to Will and Miki, bouncing on his boot soles. "Come on!" he shouted in Will's face. He grabbed Miki's other hand and tugged her into motion before dropping his grip and jaunting into the trees. He didn't look back, and he didn't have to. Will felt Miki loosen her fingers from around his, so he let go, and they crashed through the underbrush, following in Owen's wake.

* * *

Two idiots. Jackasses. Honestly, with no hydration and no sustenance in her stomach, how did they expect her to keep up? Bastards.

"I want my paracord back, too, *Will*." Miki huffed and puffed glaring holes into his butt cheeks. She'd been pissed off for a full hour, but it didn't mean she was above appreciating the swell and swish of his Ghetto Gramps. She was in the back of the line as usual, so might as well make the best of it even though she was getting the *hangry* shakes from lack of food. She hadn't eaten since dinner yesterday.

"You should carry a dog bone. You know how you get when you're hungry." Owen tossed over his shoulder smugly. His tone seemed smug to her, anyway.

"'Shut up, or I'll kill you myself,'" she mimicked her brother with a deep doofus-sounding voice.

"What a little ingrate." Owen had picked up a branch and was snapping it into pieces as they trudged along a deer trail they happened across. Maybe they were heading down to a meadow or a lake. "Here, I'm saving you like the big stud I am, and what do I get? A bunch of lip. Wait 'til Mom hears about this. Her little Miki-Lou—"

"She'll be on my side. She always is." She hadn't called her mom in days! She was probably worried sick.

"Can we play the silent game for a while?" Will muttered to Owen's back. "You two are driving me crazy."

Miki pursed her lips. Where was Dad, the great Leo the Lion? Why hadn't he come to save her or to see if she were all right? Bill had been in a life or death situation, escaped it, and immediately made his way into a dangerous predicament to reach his son. He even included Will in the group hug with Flossy and her own brother while she'd stood off to the side, ignored. They joked about saving Baby Boy...but what about her? What was she...chopped liver? Seriously.

She wasn't jealous of Will. Not at all, and she wasn't jealous of Owen. Not anymore. Not really. He was the son of a hardened biker. He knew the life and had made the choice to live it. Not to mention, he had one thing she never would...a penis. She would never be a part of her dad's world no matter what she looked like, what words she said, or what she did. It all boiled down to her not being a boy. She didn't have a P-card. In her dad's eyes, she would remain the sweet little thing that belonged in her mother's arms. Kisses on rosy cheeks, nibbling baked goods, and staying clear of the Hides of Hell way.

But, really, it didn't sound all that bad. Why had she been fighting it all this time? All those things sounded wonderful! Hugs and kisses from Mom, a cinnamon roll swimming in butter, and no men.

"Now you're being too quiet. You're not plotting to kill me, are you?" Will turned to look over his shoulder. "I've got your paracord in my pocket, if you're worried about it. I'll give it to you later when I'm sure you won't use it as a garrote to strangle me." He laughed softly and kept walking.

"Yeah." She tried to match his happy sound but couldn't. Will teasing her only made her think about the

Law of Least Effort. It reminded her of being too fast, wanting too much, and getting nothing in return. If her father were any indication, then she was a girl easily dismissed.

But she didn't *feel* that way! Why couldn't she be herself and like the girly things as well as the dirt and the grit? What was it Valentina told her in the campground bathroom so many days ago? Something to the effect of accepting what you can't change. But Miki had always liked the other side of the phrase better: change what you can't accept. Hiding in the middle was the answer to true happiness. It had to be in there somewhere.

She trudged along behind Will, lost in her own thoughts as coarse grass blades brushed against her jeans. The trail opened into a carpet of green, a meadow dappled with white foxgloves and pink bee balm. It was so vivid it took her breath away. A perfect pitstop.

"Wow. Look at all those flowers. My mom would've loved this place," Will said wistfully.

"This isn't a Sunday drive. Shorty's meeting us, so keep walking." Owen slapped at a mosquito on his neck and flicked the black speck off his fingers. "Skeeters are out. Must be getting close to dinnertime."

Miki's stomach growled low and mournful like a mama bear who'd lost her cubs. She dropped her head weakly. "Don't remind me," she groaned.

"I wonder how the guys are doing? You think everyone's okay?" Will asked Owen's back as he fell into line.

"Sure." Owen dismissed him with a wave. "Don't worry about it, Gadget. It was a regular day at the office, and now, the guys are having happy hour, off cracking peanuts, slamming beers, and making P-Scum jokes. It's all good."

"How would you know?" Miki felt the sting of a mosquito biting her forehead. Damned bugs!

"I'm connected, Mik. What are you?"

Disconnected. She scratched her temple and smeared a blood sucker down her face. Very disconnected.

CHAPTER 20

UNSPOKEN

Miki blinked hard at the mile marker. It said seven, right? She dragged her sorry butt closer and focused on it to make sure the universe wasn't playing some miserable joke on her. Don't you dare change back to a six. Once she passed the road sign, she breathed a sigh of relief. One more mile to go until they were picked up. So why did her feet suddenly feel like they were bagged in road tar? NOOooo! She wanted to shake her fist at the sky as each step became more and more difficult.

"You're P-Skull bait," Owen said, griping at her for walking on the side of the road while he was busy trailblazing through the gully grass in the ditch. With an empty fuel tank and zero energy, she needed a flat plane to walk on, a painted white line to follow, so her mind could wander with the breeze. No one was around. No traffic...no cars...no motorcycles. According to Owen, the bikers were done duking it out, and each side was probably off celebrating battle stories. Besides, Will was behind her. She could hear his boots hitting the asphalt. If he wasn't thinking about the P-Skulls and being bait, why should she?

What was on his mind, anyway? Was he as tired as she felt? Did his spleen hurt—or his broken arm? Was he staring at the white line, too...letting his thoughts drift? Where were his eyes right now? Maybe they were glued to her rear-end the way hers had been to his earlier. Was taking a sneak peek back at him considered an effort?

Probably.

Maybe it was better to not know. After all, she'd been tossed around in the muck and the mud, and if he were checking out her denim stitching, maybe it wasn't because he found her attractive but because there was a slimy wet leaf clinging to her butt. Ew.

God! She rolled her eyes. Who cared? If being dirty was a deal breaker after what she'd been through, then so be it. Consider the deal broken, *Will*. Talk about shallow! She could do so much better—

Her stomach twisted painfully with hunger, and she scowled—Men!—then brushed her hands over her back pockets in case there were any hang-ons. Surely, mile marker eight was around the next bend. One more step. Come on, girl...one more step.

Tail lights glowed ahead, and as she dragged herself closer, she could make out a white tailgate, which morphed into a truck with a monster bike tethered in the bed. I love you, Shorty! I really, really do.

"We made it, Miki." Will's good arm came around her waist, and he swept her along with him, whispering, "My God, we freakin' made it. Can you believe it? I can't believe it. Uncle Shorty!" He let go of her and jogged to the passenger side of the truck. "Aunt K! What are you doing here?"

"We're here for Cindy's memorial, Will. When it's done, you're coming home with us. Uncle Shorty brought his bike but will most likely—"

"I've changed my mind." Shorty interjected from the driver's side of the cab. "My knee feels fine."

"Okay, for all intents and purposes, he's riding to the rally, but after what's happened, I strongly encourage you and Miki to come home with me."

Miki leaned on the back fender and nodded. Yeah. She was ready to go home.

"No." Will frowned and shook his head. "There's not going to be another memorial. Mom's ashes were nabbed by some Pulver Skull, and there's no more apple pie." Will held his palms out like there was nothing else to say.

"Who took 'em?" Shorty demanded.

"Some young guy...a kid. His name is Smiley. He went straight for 'em—"

"Hey...it's okay, Willy Boy," Shorty's voice drifted through the window.

"Your uncle's right. We don't need those things to remember her. Physically, she's gone, but her energy, her spirit, it's in you and Liam. Okay? You're both a part of her. You look like her, and just imagine when you have kids of your own, you'll see her all over again. She'll always be with you, Will. Come here."

The passenger door swung open, and Karen slid out, wearing lavender Capri pants with bright canvas shoes. Her pewter curls swung above her shoulders as she rolled up on tippy-toes to bend Will like a reed into her embrace. Miki watched, feeling like a bystander.

"We're not saying goodbye, honey. We're celebrating the good she gave us. The way she made us feel. The love, okay?"

Will didn't verbally respond, but his eyes closed, and his cheeks warmed as he absorbed her sentiments and motherly comfort.

The tiniest trickle of jealousy poked at Miki's heart. She could really use a hug like that.

Owen appeared and slung his heavy arm across her bone-weary shoulders. He leaned down. "Nice day for a hike, huh?" and thunked her on the back, aiming for playful, maybe even affectionate. He missed the mark by a long shot. Miki swallowed hard against the disappointment.

"I haven't had that much fun in a long time," Owen said with a grin.

"Fun," she said in a bland voice. What was she missing? The whole day hadn't been fun. It had been harrowing! She could practically hear her dad say, *Toughen up!* Unfortunately, the tough stuff had been tapped, and she needed something more right now; she needed her mom.

Miki turned away from her clueless brother and sought Will...Karen. Someone who could replenish her positive energy.

Karen patted Will's cheek like only an aunt could before turning to face Miki. She pushed up her glasses and gasped.

"Oh, my gosh, look at you!" She pulled Miki into her floral t-shirt and murmured, "You poor thing."

Miki melted into Karen's protective arms, feeling like a mangy mutt. *Take me home with you, nice lady...take me home.* She slowly inhaled and was immediately rewarded with the sweet fragrance that had her picturing lemon pound cake covered lavishly with buttercream frosting... and sprinkles. Lots and lots of sprinkles.

Miki's stomach practically barked with angry hunger pangs. It was embarrassing, but she laughed and murmured into Karen's soft shirt, "I don't know what I need more, this hug, my mom, or a gigantic drink with a hamburger slathered in ketchup and mustard..." Karen made humming mama noises in her chest but didn't let go. "... and cheese. Lots and lots of cheese."

"Oh, dude..." Will rested his green cast against his big hoodie pocket. "I cannot un-see the billboard for Diablo's. A fat bean burrito, blowing up with carne asada—"

The truck's horn blared.

"Cogitating about food can happen on the road," Shorty hollered impatiently from behind the wheel. "Get in."

Miki squeezed into the back of the cab, knocking shoulders with Will and Owen. Shorty gunned it, churning loose gravel under the tires.

"You need to call Mom," Owen murmured to her but was probably checking out his reflection in the tinted glass since he didn't look her way. "I texted her, but she wants to hear your voice."

"I don't have my cell."

"I know. Safety last. Right, Mik?" Owen casually dropped his in her lap. "Throw in a good word for me, will ya?"

She tapped the phone screen, and the moment Mom answered, Miki sagged, all her muscle tension releasing at once. Mom's voice gushed with love and worry, and it spoke to Miki's heart. While she'd been chasing Dad's elusive and mythical love, her mom stayed in the background as solid as a rock. Miki's anger and resentment at nearly everything dissipated. Of course, seeing the sign "Burger Barn Drive Thru, Next Exit" helped a lot. "I love you, too, Mom," Miki said and felt revived. She swiped at a tear before handing the phone back to Owen.

Once at Burger Barn, they placed their orders, then pulled into the parking lot to wolf down their bounty: large sodas, burgers with bacon, tomato, cheese, and bags of salty fries. When she finished, Miki crinkled up her hamburger wrapper and tossed it into the bag. Her eyelids suddenly weighed a ton. When Shorty pulled back onto the road, her head bobbed like it sat on a spring. Will patted his bicep, and she fell limply against his side, grateful for the offer. She knew her lips were hanging slack, but she didn't care.

A warm hand touched the side of her face. Mom...no, it didn't feel quite right. Then, a roughened thumb slid along the slope of her nose. It was a man's hand, gentle, but the nose thing wasn't her dad's style. Miki's lashes fluttered open, and Will's grin filled her world. Even through the darkness of the cab, she could make out his lips, teeth, and the beauty mark on his cheek. He had a baby face, but a smattering of whiskers poked out along his chin and jaw. It was dark outside, late. What time was it? She pulled back and wiped a hand across her mouth.

"Sorry. I think I slobbered on you," she said hoarsely and blinked, trying to get oriented. She craned her neck to look out the side window. Where were they?

"We're alone," Will said. His mouth opened like he had something more to say, then closed it. Whatever was on his mind was left unspoken. Instead, he pulled the hood of his sweatshirt over his hair and leaned into the corner of the backseat to watch her.

The waking-up process was proving to be quite a show. His brown eyes followed her movements as she swiped under her lashes, combed chipped nails through her hair, and licked her dry lips. Not quite human, but getting there.

"You were so far gone…no one wanted to wake you. We had a whole conversation about—you didn't hear any of it? Amazing. Even with the truck doors slamming and the guys over there…" Will gave a nod to the back window. "I've never seen anyone sleep so hard."

"I have," she said. "You." She rolled her aching shoulders in an attempt to shake off the fog. The outside noises began to permeate—tinny music from a speaker, a crackling fire, deep-voiced murmurs.

"Ready?" he asked.

"Ready for what?"

"Anything," he said and looked away. He pushed the seat forward and reached for the handle on the passenger door. It opened, and he slipped into the night. He was gone but not for long. Fingers, palm-side up and jutting out of a green cast, entered the beam of overhead light. A dirty, broken arm beckoned her. "Let's go. Everyone's been waiting."

Waiting for what?

She placed her hand in his and let him play the gentleman card. He tightened his fingers and helped her out of the truck, which was a refreshing change from the time her dad forgot about her sitting in the back and nearly shut the door in her face. She shook her head, not in disbelief because it had been on her birthday but because it seemed like such a long time ago.

Will's hand fell away and rested on her back as he propelled her toward a substantial bonfire snapping and crackling in the fire pit. Tents, motorbikes, and beer coolers made up the outer ring, evidence that some of the guys had been here long enough to set up camp. The inner ring consisted of twenty to thirty Hides of Hell guys from the Overdale chapter. They were her guys, the ones she recognized. She easily picked out her favorites: Trip—a hottie who gave great advice, Flossy—a savvy mechanic who took the time to show her the ropes, her brother—nothing new to report there, and Liam—always ready to help.

Will left her to go have a hug-out with his brother on the other side of the fire. Will was tall and lanky like a rockstar—she could totally see him wearing a black, studded belt—where Liam had more of an athletic build. Seeing the Sullivan brothers together and laughing almost brought another tear to her eye. Will deserved to be happy. He really did.

On the other hand, she felt tired and scruffy and out of it. She needed two things to happen immediately: a volcanic hot shower and a lofty cloud to sleep on for the next five years. Was that too much to ask for?

Black and silver whiskers and blue tattoos glowed around the dancing flames. Most were men, but there were a few women. Her eyes dialed in on a big, busty blonde. Valentina. She looked like a giant pillow, all billowing white fabric and soft cleavage. She truly was a knock-out. How could a greasy headed, snoose-chewer like Greer even get on her radar? It just wasn't possible. It seemed more likely that Valentina used him. Yeah. Maybe to get answers? She called him when they were being hauled away in the van. Was she an informer? Was she somehow trying to determine her and Will's location? Interesting. She was probably one of Dad's rats. It was way more plausible than Big Val cuddling up to a disgusting P-Skull like Greer.

Valentina's long blonde hair fell back as she laughed at something Dad said. She caught Miki's eye. Her burgundy glossed lips quirked into a half smile, showing a *I know that you know* look. Or maybe it was a *I got what I wanted* look. Miki opted for her own blank slate, because honestly, she didn't know what to feel at the moment. A chamber in her heart was having a hard time caring.

She dropped her shoulders and glanced up at the smoke and the stars. She was alive. She'd saved Will, and she—

Why was everyone looking at her?

Suddenly, Trip was there, pushing a cold, wet beer into her hands. "Miki!"

Owen strapped his arm around her legs, and she shrieked with surprise as he scooped her up toward the sky. She grasped at his short hair, trying to keep balanced on his one broad shoulder while the guys cheered. Owen bounced her, and she laughed. What the hell was this all about?

Dad held up a bottle of beer across the blazing fire.

"To my daughter!" he bellowed to his men. "Most of the time, she's a pain in my ass!" The guys whooped and hollered. They quieted, and Dad continued. "She doesn't listen to a damn word I say and back-talks to beat the contraband." Laughter circled around the flames, and Owen jostled her above their heads.

Her eyes narrowed, but she managed to keep a smile in place. Where was he going with this speech? It better pick up, because so far, it was uninspired and unimpressive at best.

"To my little Miki-Lou, a beauty like her mother. But she's not so little anymore, right Will?" Chuckles went around, and all eyes shot to Will's stunned face. He looked like he either wanted to die or wanted to kill someone. Miki felt her cheeks glow with embarrassment. God…why?

"Okay, Dad…" Miki kicked her feet to get down, but Owen tilted his knees like he'd drop her head first if she didn't cooperate. "You've had your—"

"She's a brave young woman who kicks ass when it truly counts. I'm proud of you, girl. So tip your cups, and let's drink to Miki…she's got bigger balls than any damn P-skull out there!"

"Yee! Yee!" Flossy chanted and chugged half his drink before shaking it and spraying foam down her front.

Miki slapped at her wet t-shirt. "Floss—"

"Pass her around!" Dad's voice yelled above the crowd. Suddenly, the full beer was pulled out of her hand, and she went horizontal.

"No! Wait!"

Fingers walked along her back, pushing her forward, up and down. She flailed as beer sloshed on her face and soaked her hair. Hands patted at her and words of acceptance, the ones she'd always yearned for—from her dad, from the Hides of Hell brotherhood—coated her body along with the hops and barley.

"Way to go."

"Kick ass, babe."

"To Miki!"

She was dropped in front of her dad, drenched and laughing. She slicked the wet hair out of her face and waited for him to finish slamming his beer. His Adam's apple bobbed, and he dropped the bottle to his side with a loud "Ah!" His dark eyes sparkled, reflecting the fire, and he nodded at her before pulling her into a brief but tight hug.

This entire celebration was not necessary. He could have patted her on the back and said, You make me proud, and that would have been enough. It was as overwhelming as it was amazing, but it was her dad's way. Her cheek rested against his leather, and she murmured, "I love you, Dad."

"Miki-Lou..." he said and let her go. He didn't return the words, but she got it; they were there all the same. He straightened. "You've run off twice. Don't let there be a third time." He warned her with a stern face, before his lips crooked up into a smile, one she could see and appreciate since his face was clean shaven.

"You've got a great kid, Leo," Val said.

"I know." His arm snaked around Valentina's waist, and he pulled her in for a demonstrative nuzzle under her ear. She tilted her head back, exposing her neck, and gave a throaty giggle.

Oh, man, her dad was gone. Miki stepped back and lifted her brows with a message for Val: *You put the G in good'n'gross.*

Val grinned easily and pushed her puckered-up lips onto Leo the Lion's. Miki had been dismissed, but there was no longer the burn of rejection. Ultimately, she was in charge of her happiness—she had her way, and Dad had his—and taking a long, hot shower was job one. The couple before her grappled with each other's hair and moaned through sloppy kisses. Did they even remember she was standing here? Miki turned away. The creepy Greer had said it best. Who gives a rat's corn-hole?

CHAPTER 21

BACK IN BLACK

Twitter...what was the word his mom used to say? Some vintage romance thing. When Dad came home after a long ride, she'd clutch her heart and laugh. Right...twitterpated. Will's heart thrummed with it. He hadn't been able to take his eyes off Miki all night, not because her t-shirt was wet or because her eyes were dark and intoxicating or her skin sticky with beer. It was because he wanted to talk to her.

He had something to say, but in the cab she was barely awake, and with everyone shouting their names from the bonfire, the mood was off. Then, Leo had to go and call him out in front of everyone—*She's not so little anymore, right Will?*—and he'd wanted to skulk into the cool trees and away from the hot fire. Jesus, was he transparent? Sure, he'd always liked her, but he'd simultaneously disliked her, too, for making him feel like an out-of-control fool at her mercy. They were opposites. Her speed was fast; his was slow. She was a mover and a shaker; he liked his couch. Miki always seemed to get her way; she was lucky. Not him.

Not usually.

He'd always said she was synonymous with trouble, and without a doubt she'd proved it. If he'd had his way, he'd be at home, sulking under a growing layer of dust. She used to push him around—not physically but mentally—and he felt like a bear being poked by a stick, growling, Leave me the hell alone! But that was before.

He watched her blue crown weave through the mass of thick arms and wild man-hair to her usual green dome tent. She unzipped it and ducked inside. MS. TROUBLE with the caps on was out of sight, yet still on his mind.

Now, instead of wanting to be alone, he found himself searching for her. In the past week, he'd been shoved in and out of his comfort zone, yet through the whole experience, Miki was there, positive, bright. Like a ray of sunshine. He needed more of the same in his life. More of her.

Being with her made him stronger inside, like she had a square-to-spare through osmosis. No more alcohol, no more drugs, no more lounging on the peach floral couch. The deep, dark slumber was in the process of fading. Beside the residual aches and pains left over from his drunken motorcycle accident, renewed energy ignited in his limbs and his heart. It was sort of like Frankenwill was coming alive! All he needed was a bolt of positive electricity to get the party started. He needed Miki.

Will took a step in the direction of her tent as she crawled back out with a pink towel over her shoulder and a small toiletries bag in hand.

Oh, yeah. A shower. He couldn't talk to her. He was starting to smell like his old man after a long, hot ride. Sun, sweat, and leather…the whiff of death.

Will frowned not recognizing his tent. Plus, his backpack was gone, which meant…

No towel.

No soap.

No clean clothes.

And no freakin' plastic bag to cover his cast.

Damn, nothing was easy.

A heavy arm swung around his neck and spun him back toward the fire. "I love you, man," his dad muttered through a mist of beer breath. "I just wanted you to know that." He flexed his arm, giving Will's throat a firm hug.

"I know..." Will used his fingers to pry himself loose. "...love you, too."

"Hey, brothers! Looky here. I've got my boy back... both sons standing by my side. My sister and Shorty are here—"

"We're always here for you, Billy," Uncle Shorty said from across the fire. He blew cigarette smoke into the air while he rubbed Aunt K's shoulder with affection.

"Well, I got somethin' to say!"

"Hell, yeah," Owen grinned, roasting the sole of his boot on a hot boulder making up part of the fire ring. The flames had died down leaving a furnace of orange in the center of the pit.

"Dad, I thought we were gonna do this tomorrow." Liam shoved his hand in the pocket of his camo pants. He pulled out his phone and checked the time. "It's way late, and you're tanked."

"Why put off today what you can do tomorrow?" His dad's brows were pinched in the middle, and he patted his pockets like he'd lost a lighter or his cigarettes, but the man didn't smoke.

"Riiight," Liam rubbed his short hair and rolled his eyes at Will, who shook his head in return. Dad wasn't a drunk, but on the rare occasion when he did over-imbibe, he was a misquoting, love-you-man machine, and one annoying neck-hugger.

Dad rolled the first rubber band under his chin. It took five of 'em down the length of his beard to keep it clamped together in a rope. "See how long this is?" It hung, intertwined salt and pepper, down to his Hides of Hell belt buckle. "Your mom was twenty-two years old when she cornered me on the dance floor. Said she loved my beard—"

"Buckle up. Here we go." Flossy nodded his approval from the other side of Liam.

"Is this the memorial?" Will faced his dad with a frown. "Because everyone's drunk. Miki's not even here, and Trip is passed out on the picnic table." They basically forced him to be a part of this, and now it was turning into some kind of tacked-on, spur-of-the-moment, side show. This was important! "Dad, I don't want to do this now. I've been through hell and back, and I'm tired. What's wrong with tomorrow, huh?"

"Gone today and here tomorrow." Dad hooked his arm around Will's neck again and dragged him down, cheek meet leather. "I love you, man."

"I know, Dad…" Will said with squished lips before twisting out of his old man's grip. "Listen, I'm gonna take a shower and hit the sack." Maybe Miki'd let him borrow her girly soap to scrub off the past twenty-four hours of hard living. "See you in the morning, okay?"

"Hang on, Will, my son. What's the rush? How about waste makes haste." Dad and the guys laughed with unwarranted hilarity. There were a lot of bloodshot eyes in attendance from all kinds of smoke, squinting against the wind and the sun, and tipping back two too many.

"Anyone got a knife? I can't find mine…" Dad patted his back pockets again.

Liam held out a black-handled switchblade like it was a ball point pen.

"Thank you. I love you, man." Dad flicked the blade out and took a moment to admire the sharpness with his thumb. Then, he clutched the long hair at his chin, tucked the knife under it, and without a moment's hesitation, slashed out. His beard fell limp in his fist like a beheaded snake.

"Uh…" Will's mouth fell open. "What did you…?" Did he actually witness what he thought he did? He glanced at all the faces. Everyone was stunned. His dad —Bill—had finally lost it.

Caboose coughed. Owen rubbed his stubble while staring at the hairy rope with part fascination and part horror. Flossy splayed his fingers and took a sudden interest in his chunky turquoise ring. The party had turned unnaturally quiet.

"Dad?" Liam frowned at the dangling whip of hair.

Leo unwrapped his arm from around Val's waist to shake his fist in the air. He whooped—"Right on, brother!"—and the tension waned. Sighs of relief were followed by chuffs of nervous laughter. Then, there was the scraping ice and clinking of bottles as chilled beers started circulating.

"I grew my beard out for my wife, Cindy, because she loved it," Dad said soberly to the crowd. He shook the banded hair. "You guys know…this thing was a nuisance! It collected breadcrumbs, dust, motor oil. One time when I was riding my bike through Spokane, a grasshopper got caught up in it." Dad nodded to Leo.

"I remember you screamin'. You almost took out the guardrail," Leo said and grinned.

"I hate grasshoppers. Anyway, my point is this thing took a lot of extra care. But I was happy to do it since it put a smile on my wife's face. For me, it symbolized how we met—in a podunk diner outside of Shaniko. It was our start in this life together, the strength of our bond, and our two boys. I love you both so much."

"We know, Dad," Liam said.

"Yeah," Will whispered around a thick lump forming in his throat. He dropped his chin and stared down at the hem of his Ghetto Gramps while blinking hard to keep the tears at bay.

"Some of you might think I'm crazy, and some of you might understand...like you, Flossy. You lost your sister to cancer...and you, Caboose. Did you guys know he had an identical twin?" Some nodded, some looked around. "Well, he did. Now, I may not go to church or pray, but I am a spiritual man, and Cindy spoke to me."

What? Will looked up and studied his Dad's brown eyes, the crow's feet forming in the corners, and the bristly whiskers still making up the stubby beard on his face. Dad heard Mom's voice, too?

"She's the wind..." Dad swung his detached beard around his head like a lasso.

"The wind beneath your wings?" One of the biker's joked, and Dad's eyes crinkled as he laughed.

"The wind in the trees. All I'm saying is she wants my beard with her, and the only way I know how to send it, is through fire and smoke." He flung the snake into the hot coals. It hissed, coiled, and flared up brightly. "I love you, my Cindy!" He boomed at the night's sky.

As if on cue, AC/DC's "Back in Black" blared through the speakers, and a large red ice chest was dragged forward. Cindy's name was batted around along with stories and laughs, beers, and joints. Everyone geared up for a second wind to push 'em through to dawn. When Mook passed around his flip-topped home-brews in the big brown bottles, Will took it as a personal sign to check out.

He put his foot on the rock ring to see how his dad's beard was doing, but there was nothing left in the pit except a flickering orange glow. Too bad the apple pie was gone; he could have thrown it in the fire, too. Then again, maybe Mom didn't want to take the old, moldy slice into the afterworld.

"I miss you," Will murmured to the smoldering coals. "Big time." Then, he turned away. Forget the shower for now. He wanted to keep the smoke on his skin a little while longer.

CHAPTER 22

GO TIME

The next morning, thanks to Liam and the stash of hotel samples he kept in his pack, Will's mouth tasted minty, his hair was squeaky clean, and his skin smelled like a new pine air-freshener from his dad's old car. He rolled the rubber band and the plastic produce bag down his cast and dropped it in the garbage barrel holding the bathroom door ajar. He draped the thin, travel towel over his hair and scrubbed it dry with his good hand while sauntering across the road to the campsite.

It was time to talk to Miki.

Will stopped in front of the small green tent she'd slipped into late last night. Now, it was a sunny morning, he was freshly scrubbed, and decked out in his brother's clean basketball shorts and t-shirt. Throw in being well-rested, and he was ready to face the music.

Whenever it came to Miki, Will glanced over his shoulder, a habit from years of being on "Owen alert." A few of the guys huddled on top of the picnic table, smoking their morning cigarettes with puffy eyes and gravely voices as they busily reviewed the awesomeness of the night before. Will had no idea what transpired.

He'd gone to bed and slept like the dead. Most importantly, there was no sign of Leo or Val, no Aunt K, and no Owen —as if big bro could stop him this time. Will wouldn't give him the power, not anymore.

The coast was clear. This was his business and no one else's. Except now, his arm itched under the cast. He tapped on it, while staring at the tent's zipper pull. What was Miki's plan? Was she riding with the Hides of Hell to the Burnout Rally? Or was she heading north toward home?

After one more look back at the guys, he bent and slowly opened the zipper. He peeked inside at the spidery shadows of branches and leaves on the tent wall before crawling into Miki's lair. It was stuffy and hotter than a sauna, and in another five minutes, he'd lose his freshly showered feeling.

The tent was supposed to be a two-man, but she was sprawled diagonal, flat on her back inside a flannel-lined sleeping bag. Her arms were above her head like she was in a free-fall and loving every minute of it. Will paused. Should he give her a heart attack by jumping in the middle of her? Or should he sit in the corner with a wet towel around his neck and wait things out? What would Helmet do?

Right. Go for the heart attack.

"Don't even think about it," she murmured, looking from under her eyelashes.

"Hey...I, uh...I thought you were asleep."

"I was dozing, but FYI, you're not very sneaky. Zip-zip, rustle-rustle. Then, there's the heavy breathing. What are you doing in my tent, anyway?" She sat up and rubbed her eyes. She must have gone to bed with her hair wet because a raging blue and black octopus came to mind. Scary.

Will lifted his brows and stared.

"What?" She touched her hair. "Oh, no!" She raked her fingers through it or tried to. It was tangle central after an apparent night of tossing and turning.

"It's okay. Maybe a little distracting, but..." he waved the notion aside and debated whether he should pull the towel up like a hoodie. He might need the added protection in case this conversation went from a sure thing to hell-a-awkward. "I'm here because I wanted to talk to you...you know?"

He slowly draped the towel over his hair as if he needed to rub it dry again.

"Talk...now? I can't! I need to use the bathroom. I have to comb my hair, obviously..." she kicked her bare legs out of the sleeping bag and reached for a pair of denim cutoffs. "I need to get dressed and brush my teeth." She tugged the shorts on underneath her night t-shirt, and he tried to pull his eyes away, but he couldn't *unsee* the color of her underwear—neon pink.

Whoa.

Maybe she needed her privacy. Should he be here right now?

"Wait for me, okay, Will?"

I may or may not be a gentleman. I repeat: I may or may not—

"What? Oh, sure..." He nodded. "No problem." She smiled, gathered her things, and dove out. *Zip-Zip!* She was gone.

Will pulled the thin towel over his face while mentally preparing for some deep breathing until Miki returned. What should he say to her? Words definitely needed to be exchanged, but he didn't know the exact way to start. Maybe his buddy J.J.'s approach—"So…"—was the best bet to see where things went. There was timing and mood to consider…and effort, right? He should get extra points for visiting her on her territory and for initiating the conversation. But she ran off, and now, his stomach churned painfully, either from low food intake or from the impending feeling he was about to make a colossal fool of himself.

"Will!" His dad's voice bellowed from the campsite. "Liam! Anyone and everyone…wake up! It's go time. Cindy's here and waiting."

Huh? Will jerked the towel down. What did he mean, here and waiting?

Zip! He jerked the flap aside and crawled out, squinting against the sun. A power pack of muscle, bad hair, and black leather eased forward—some crawling out of tents, some stretching for the sky, and others scratching their bellies as they surrounded the dusty picnic table. Uncle Shorty rested his boot on the bench, lighting up his breakfast cigarette. He waved Will over.

"Willy Boy. Up and at 'em."

Will made his way to the table and elbowed in to be closer to his dad, who looked a whole lot cooler without the hair-whip hanging down his front. Will tore his eyes off his new and improved dad to frown at the roughhewn table. In the center sat Mom's ashes in the same taped up brick. The only difference was the strip of masking tape covering the hole Greer had cut into it. Next to it sat a stack of red plastic Solo cups and the switchblade, the one dad had used to cut off his beard.

"Dad, where…" Will shook his head. "How did you get Mom's ashes?"

"Not to worry, my son. Club business," Dad said, picking up the knife and glancing around the table. "We all here?"

"We're not talking about club business. We're talking about Mom. And no, we are *not* all here. Look around, do you see Miki? No you don't, and you know what? I'm not doing this. We did the whole memorial thing last night—"

"Miki!" Dad boomed and raised his palm in the air.

Will glanced over his shoulder to see her walking across the campsite. She wore her sleek leather riding pants with a clean t-shirt. The octopus hair had been tamed into a soft blue wave swinging along her jaw with each step. Her eyes were wide and questioning.

"Miki," Dad said. "We're getting ready to ride, and we're taking Cindy's ashes with us. Burnout Rally, here we come!"

"Yeah, man, let's do it," Flossy murmured.

"Ashes?" Miki asked. She stopped and looked at Will across the small gathering of Hides of Hell bikers.

"Dad...No!" Will yelled in front of everyone, not really caring about respect or the lack thereof. Screw them! He was being railroaded here. "I mean, dude, what's the freakin' rush, right? Last night you hacked off your beard, and I...I made my peace. I'm ready to move on. I'm ready to go back home." Will waved his casted arm at the brick. "With the ashes here...don't you see? She was stolen by a Pulver Skull, and I don't know how, but she's back. Isn't it like a message from the universe or something? A sign we should keep them?"

"It's a sign we're moving forward. Follow through, got it?" Dad's bearded chin jutted out, and he gripped the switchblade firmly, holding it up. "Nothing you can say is going to change the course of today. This ride is dedicated to Cindy Sullivan, and all of you standing before me are who I consider my family. It's an honor you're with me and my sons. All of us, we're spreading these ashes together." With a flick of his thumb, the blade sprang forward, pointing to the sky. The sharp metal glinted in the sunlight.

"You're not even giving me a chance to...to think things through." Will clutched his dad's forearm to keep the knife still. "The plan was for me to head home with Aunt K—"

Dad covered Will's hand with his free one. "Your Aunt K changed her mind. She's my sister, and this is family business. Right Karen? It means a lot to me." Aunt K nodded soberly, watching Will.

He jerked his hand from beneath his dad's. Un-freaking-believable. Aunt K had made it clear only yesterday how he would ride back with her. Now? She stood under the heavy arm of Uncle Shorty like a folded deck of cards. Mrs. Norton, his teacher and supposed role-model, his only aunt, couldn't stand her ground under the Hides of Hell pressure? Just great. Will inhaled a sharp breath. If they thought he'd buckle the same way, they could think again. Filthy—

"Hey, Will. You can ride with me, okay, bro?" Liam suggested helpfully as if he were pacifying a two-year-old.

"I'm not riding in your bitch seat." Will scowled. "I'm with Miki!" His insides churned with emotion. He felt rushed to say goodbye and panicked to say hello and cornered by time. Was he ready for this? Ready for a second chance at moving on? Hell, ready or not, the roller coaster had left the station, and he was duct taped to the front car. While his insides grappled with the momentum, Miki stood by, calm and quiet and as beautiful as ever...brown eyes, blue hair, and rockin' a pair of scuffed-up motorcycle boots. Her arms hung loose at her sides with fingers decorated in silver.

Go time. Now or never. He hated goodbyes, but to have peace, he needed to let go of the ashes for a second time. Goodbye, old life. Hello, new one. Hello, Miki. Wherever she decided to go—home, lake, rally—he'd follow. No more looking over his shoulder for the pin-striped vest. No more worrying about anger management's missing meathead. He'd confront Owen if he had to because Miki was worth it.

Will took a step closer, his eyes on hers.

"Miki..." He held out his hand. "I really need to talk to you."

"Will! We are doing this...right...now!" His dad bellowed behind him.

"Stop pushing me around!" Will shouted over his shoulder.

"Dad," Liam murmured. "Give him ten minutes to get sorted. We can all wait, right? It's not a big deal."

"Will! You've got ten minutes...No more! Then, we roll."

Will tilted his head in a "let's walk" way, and Miki nodded. She matched his stride past her tent, through a row of shrubs, across the paved walkway, and around the corner to the back of the bathrooms. Nobody could see them; nobody could hear them. He leaned his head and shoulders against the painted cinder blocks and looked up at the bird poop staining the roof beams. His heart idled high in his chest from too much pissed-off excitement.

Dude, calm down and talk.

Okay, but was this the right place? The right time? The right mood?

Anger, bird crap, and toilets. All signs pointed to no.

He leveled his gaze to watch Miki from under his lashes. They stood in silence, except for some chattering birds and the buzz of insects. He pulled his shoulders down and forced himself to relax. Finally, he could breathe normally.

"So..." he said, trying to come across all chill and casual. He waited for her to grab his first word and run with it. He started the conversation. Couldn't she drive it from here? Wasn't it her speed? Forward motion? God, he was screwing this up already.

Miki arched her brow. Will nodded with encouragement. Please say something...help a guy out. She didn't. Instead, she looked down to examine her fingernails.

Will blew out the breath he'd been holding. Shit. Forget it.

"So is it okay if I ride with you? I mean, I'd like to..." Will let his voice drift off. He was so lame.

"Sure." Miki shrugged. Her face pulled down with disappointment as she smoothed hair behind her ear. "Is that it? That's what you wanted to talk to me about, out here by the bathrooms?"

"I...I want to say goodbye in my own way," Will said and looked down at his bare calves sticking out of his brother's basketball shorts. The skin below his knee was bright pink. Scars to remind him of his drunken stupidity. Everything was changing, mending, moving on.

"Oh," she said, and he looked up.

"I can't believe my dad is going through with this. You know? Especially after the hotel kid, Smiley, nabbed the ashes. I mean, my dad and the rest of the guys must have gone through hell to get them back…only to toss them into the wind?"

"Through hell? I doubt it. I'm betting Valentina's the rat, and she sweet-talked the ashes right out of Smiley's clutches and hand-delivered them to your dad. She had to worm her way into the Hides of Hell hearts somehow."

Will studied her, a half grin tugging at his lips. "I love the way you have it all figured out." He pushed off the wall to stand close to her, not touching, but if he wanted to, he could…and if she wanted to, he sure as hell wouldn't stop her. "I wish…I wish we could go back to a time when everything was normal. My mom would be alive, of course, and I would have you in the closet playing twenty minutes of—

"Seven minutes, Will. The game is called Seven Minutes of Heaven." Miki smiled up at him, and Will inched closer, toe to toe, and traced a finger along her hand.

"We could do a lot more in twenty," he murmured. "Afterward, you'd probably still tell everyone I farted, because it's what you do…" Will held up his hand to keep Miki from interrupting, "…and I'd still get mad because it's what I do, but this time I'd answer your texts, Miki. I'd listen to you, and I'd forgive you, because I want to give us a chance, and I want…"

Miki waited, but impatience won out. "I want…?" She coaxed him.

"I want you to give me a chance."

"Yes, Will, and you can ride on my bitch seat." She closed her fingers around his.

Will smiled, squeezed her hand, and led her back to the campsite. His guts tumbled with nervous energy, but his mind and heart were at ease. They stopped beside the picnic table next to Owen, and biker conversations paused. Heads turned to openly assess them, but Will didn't let the scrutiny stop him from draping his good arm around Miki's shoulders.

"My girl," Will said, trying to stay chill. He shrugged like it was no big deal, but when Miki's arm snaked around his back, he couldn't stop the goofy smile from taking over his face. She hugged his waist while Owen studied them with narrowed eyes.

"Go, Gadget," Flossy said around his toothpick.

Ha! Suck it, Owen. Will kissed Miki's hair, and big brother didn't say a thing.

Dad stabbed the plastic brick with the switchblade and slit it open, exposing Mom's ashes to the slight breeze. Using the Solo cups, he scooped up small amounts and passed them to the brothers who formed their tight-knit family: Leo, Flossy, Trip, Owen, Mook, Caboose, Aunt K, Uncle Shorty, and Liam. Each person took a cup and chatted about a favorite memory. When Will accepted his cup, he didn't feel obliged to speak. His mom had been in his head, so she knew exactly what he thought.

Miki combed the blue hair away from her face and slipped on her helmet. She straddled the bike seat wearing a leather coat with a hole in the back. It had definitely seen better days.

"Hop on!" Miki hollered over her shoulder as she turned the key. Her black Suzuki cruiser roared to life— boom, boom, boom, boom. Will adjusted the helmet strap under his chin and bent his leg over the seat to sit reverse, his back pressing against Miki's. He rested the Solo cup on his thigh, covering the top with his good hand to keep the ashes inside.

They pulled away, nice and easy at the end of the line per usual. Will watched Caboose lean into a curve and open the throttle to pass them on the straightaway. Finally, a little privacy. Will studied the cotton clouds floating in the sky and actually felt everything click: the time, the place, the mood. He tipped a handful of ashes into his palm and squeezed his fist as hard as he could. When he slowly opened his fingers, the fragments and powdery grit joined the air, the exhaust, and in an instant, Mom was gone.

She was the wind in the trees.

CHAPTER 23

TWO POINT FIVE

Miki and Will coasted into Burnout sucking on the exhaust of the Hides of Hell horde but well ahead of Caboose this time. The group was two days late to the event due mostly to the P-Skull shenanigans. It was hard for the Overdale Chapter to be on time when they had to pull a rescue mission out of their crevasses en route. The kidnapping horror stories began at their arrival and grew bigger, badder, and more bizarre as the festivities wore on. It was a biker's version of a fishing tale.

Miki sipped on an iced lemonade outside The Dirty Nickel Saloon with Trip, Owen, and some other guys while she waited for Will. He was with Liam, walking through the tents of refurbished helmets and gas tanks. Those two were taking their sweet time, and patience wasn't one of her strengths. Miki waved her hand to cut through the lingering cloud of cigarette smoke. Nope... no patience. She was done.

"Leo's kid, right?" asked some skinny geezer with a lisp. Before she could respond, he poked her in the ribs, which seemed a little forward. She narrowed her gaze at him, and he wagged his grizzled eyebrows. "You're lucky the P-Skulls got ya. They can't do anything right. Why... when I was commandeered by the Hoolies, they had me for nearly a week. I was punched in the face so hard, I swallowed my two front teeth."

"Oh. Uh, that sounds...painful?" Miki stabbed at the ice in her cup with a red and white straw. She was done with the Hoolies, the P-Skulls, bodily injury stories, and all things kidnapping. *Where are you, Will? I wanna go home; I miss my mom, my clothes, my bed—*

"Check it out." The guy pulled back his hairy top lip to show off his toothless grin. Chuffs of laughter went around followed by, "You think that's bad..."

Miki turned away to roll her eyes in private and spotted Will jog-walking across the street toward her. Projectile happiness flew out of her chest, and she beamed like an idiot. She couldn't help it! She tossed her cup into the trash, and when he was close enough to grab, she hooked her elbow with his and pointed him in the direction he'd come from.

"My bike's that way, and I'm ready to ride. If we leave now, we'll be home before dark." She smiled up at him.

"Sounds like you want to get me alone..." Will quirked a brow, then gave her the heavy lids. "...again."

"You better not say 'Law of Least Effort,' or I'm gonna..." Miki shook a solid fist—all knuckle and silver —under his nose.

"Why don't you calm down?" he asked with a grin and hip checked her, sending her off a step. He scooped his good arm over her shoulders and reeled her to his side. In a suave move, he tilted her back, and planted his warm lips on hers.

It was the simplest, most natural, smooth-i-est, mind-meltiest kiss she'd ever had, and all she could do when he righted her was blink. Oh, my God. What just happened to me? She pressed fingertips to her lips and hoped like crazy that whatever this buzzing feeling was…that it kept on keeping on. Again and again.

Will's lips turned up into a smile. "Come on. Let's find Aunt K and Uncle Shorty and get out of here. I'm tired of this biker scene."

"Me, too."

"Really? I thought this was your thing. Isn't it why you want to be a mechanic?" He took her hand loosely in his and guided her back into the throng of tents where they were immediately engulfed by the aromas of beer, sausages, and carburetor cleaner.

"Yeah, at first. I wanted to hang out with my dad, and I thought if he needed me…" She shrugged. "You know, maybe he'd invite me to rides and rallies. Instead, I spend most of my time in the garage with Flossy, learning how to change oil and patch flats while my dad's…who knows?" She waved her hand through the air; her dad had his own thing going on.

They passed barbecue pits on one side and tents with buzzing tattoo needles on the other. In the distance, Twisted Sister blared through speakers, "Ride to Live, Live to Ride!" competing with the nearby laughter and revving motorcycle engines.

"I still want to be a mechanic, though. It's like a big puzzle but with dirt and grease." She wouldn't apologize for the things she liked: the rumbling noises, the black leather, the wind. "I love motorcycles, but believe me… even if those guys begged me to be a member, I wouldn't. I don't ever want to be that worried or scared again. Their world is not how I see my life. I just want to have fun."

"I know." Will swished his long bangs to the side to look at her. "There's no way I'm signing up for the club life. My dad knows it. Liam knows it. Everyone knows it. Doesn't stop me from wanting another bike, though. You and I can ride—"

He stopped dead in his tracks. "No way. Check it out." A big grin spread across his face as he nodded to a silver pull trailer with a mint-green sign that read, Cream Dream: Twenty Flavors. "Karma. I'm getting my second chance."

"How so?" she asked as an older woman with bleached blonde cornrows and a leather fringed bikini leaned out the window. "Happy Cream Dream. What can I get you two?"

Will's face warmed as he squeezed Miki's hand. "You carrying black licorice by any chance? Yeah? We'll take one scoop in a sugar cone."

"Only one?" The lady asked, taking Will's money.

"We're going to share. Right, Z-lips?"

"We are?" Miki asked, and Will wagged his eyebrows at her in a cute way, so… sure, she could share. Why not? This seemed like the perfect time to go with the flow.

The lady handed the cone through the window, and Will took it gingerly in his fingertips. He ran his tongue along the edges of the black scoop, catching the drips before he took a large bite off the top.

"Hmm." He frowned and handed the cone to Miki.

She was happy to repeat the process, licking each side, tasting the chilled anise with hints of vanilla. She smoothed her tongue over the scoop until it was flat. Yum, yum, and more yum. This was hitting the spot. She crunched into the side of the cone and looked up to see Will watching her.

His eyes had gone from melty-licious brown to dark and smokey. She held out the cone to him, and suddenly, it took flight into a wide garbage barrel sitting off to the side.

"Hey! I wasn't done."

He leaned toward her. "This is my second chance, right here. I'm gonna kiss those zombie lips," he said, and with a tilt of his head, his mouth touched hers. Even though his tongue tasted sweet and cool and refreshing, her entire body melted. His smooth lips slid, back and forth over hers, black licorice on top of black licorice. It was hot.

It was easy and effortless.

It was the stuff of dreams.

Miki sighed into his mouth before his lips traveled across her jaw.

"I'm totally digging this karma thing," he whispered and kissed the shell of her ear. When he pulled back, his cheeks were tinged with warmth. Absolutely adorable. "I'm glad you're here with me. I, uh...never got a chance to tell you this before, but I...Miki..." Will cleared his throat and shrugged sort of shyly. "I like you."

"Will..." Miki's heart revved. *Oh, my God. I'm in love with you, you idiot!* She laughed softly. "I like you, too. Now let's get outta here. I'm ready to go home."

They'd driven in one big loop: south to Shaniko for Cindy's Memorial Ride then northeast to Burnout Rally. Most of the miles were already behind them. Home was a mere two point five hours away.

"Me, too," he said, and when he smiled, she nearly fainted.

His teeth were gray. How sexy was that?

Once in the parking lot, Miki combed her hair back before sliding her helmet into place. She gave a thumbs up to Shorty and Karen, who backed their white truck out of the space next to them. Shorty claimed his knee was bothering him, but Miki suspected he didn't want Karen driving home alone. Old lovebirds. It suited Miki just fine. She'd have Will all to herself while following on her bike, caravan style.

Shorty tipped his chin and lifted his fingers, giving her the "peace on the road" sign as he pulled forward while Karen's palm waved fanatically out the back window.

Miki kicked her leg over the seat of her bike and turned the key. The motor rumbled loudly beneath her—boom, boom, boom, and her heart beat in unison. She braced the bike, steady and ready for Will to press his body behind hers. When his arm and cast wrapped around her mid-section, laughter bubbled up in her throat.

"Hold on!" she said, and nudged on the gas to follow Shorty's tailgate. Slow and easy was all right with her. There was absolutely no reason in the world to hurry, not with Will in her bitch seat.

Two point five hours of heaven coming right up.

Boom, boom, boom, boom.

Hell, yeah!

ACKNOWLEDGMENTS

I'm not much for fanfare or sugar-coating, and I'm not very good at adding a flourish. So I guess I'll stick with what I know and keep things succinct by saying I appreciate the people who offered early critiques as well as the words of encouragement and the writing wisdom. An all-cap THANK YOU goes to:

Kelly Vincent
Bev Katz Rosenbaum
Chase Nottingham
Kate Harold
Yvonne Bergholm
LaZetta Krause
Tina Wegner
Anna Hatlestad

Continue reading for a preview of Suzy and J.J.'s story…

Dealing
with Blue

Stacia Leigh

CHAPTER 1

SATURDAY SPECIAL

Everything was going along fine, which had Suzy relaxing against the vinyl booth cushion with a real smile tugging at her lips. The Platter Cafe served its usual, the best Saturday special in town: buttery eggs and syrupy french toast with a side of crispy bacon. The jukebox played "The Great Pretender," an old favorite and one she used as her personal mantra—fake it 'til you make it. Most importantly, her mom was staying the course, staying normal.

Suzy was about to wave her napkin in victory at another successful visit with Mom—yes!—when the gray-haired waitress appeared with the bill. She leaned into the booth and refilled Mom's brew, which had Mom straightening her yellow blouse with renewed energy as if the meal were just starting and not ending.

"I brought you something," Mom said and her blue eyes beamed across the cluttered diner table.

And just like that, normal took a downward turn. Suzy's smile waned, and she crumpled the napkin in her lap. Not this again. Just pretend it doesn't matter, Suz, and then it won't. *La la la.* Fake it 'til you make it, remember?

241

"Suzette." Mom clutched her fingers and searched Suzy's face. "This is our chance to start over, and I want things to be better between us." Her eyes were the color of the sky and swept up at the outer edges like a cat. She had cinnamon freckles on the bridge of her nose and a cap of beautiful auburn hair, not carroty red like Suzy's. She looked a lot like her mom, but would she turn out like her, too?

"Things have changed, I promise." Mom opened her hands, and her fingers were delicate, long, and bare; there was no wedding ring. She had always worn the gold band, even after the divorce, but today, it was gone. "I've changed, and I want to show you," she said, digging through her saddle bag of a purse. Car keys jangled in her hand as she scooted across the red booth cushion. "I left it in my car. I know you want to go meet your friends at the Butterhorn, but wait for me, okay? I'll be right back."

Why was Mom doing this now? In a few hours they'd be living together...so why bother? The muscles in Suzy's neck tightened as she watched her mom head to the glass doors, only stopping to make small talk with someone in the foyer. Great. It was J.J. Radborne.

They shared a class together, behavioral science, and yesterday, Mrs. Norton moved seats around, putting Suzy in a group with J.J. and his buddy, Will Sullivan. She'd wind up doing all the work because those two somehow managed to bluff their way through the school system. General rules need not apply.

J.J. grinned and nodded at something Mom said before glancing in Suzy's direction. She straightened at the eye contact and tossed her balled-up napkin onto her plate while watching J.J. swagger toward her with his arm draped casually over Gemma's shoulders.

Funny. Suzy hadn't noticed his girlfriend standing there, and it wasn't because she was plain or easy to ignore, not with that Nordic blonde hair hanging down her back. It was…what could she say? J.J. was an eye-full. His brown hair looked burnished by the wind, tousled like he'd just fallen off a surfboard and rolled in for brunch. He exuded charm and cheer and was everyone's friend, whether you were pompous, pimpled, short, or shy.

J.J. had the cute, wild, and carefree thing going on.

Not her type at *all*.

No, she liked her men like her hair, a little more contained. She touched the side of her updo and wove in a loose strand before pressing on a confident smile.

"Hey, it's The Professor." J.J. gave her a lopsided grin. "Guess I'll be seeing a lot of you from now on."

"Hi, Suzy. The Professor?" Gemma lifted her eyebrows at J.J. while sliding possessive arms around his waist.

"Grades, glasses. She's the nerd in our group, right Blue?" He laughed and held up his free hand in surrender. "Those were your words, not mine."

"I only wear my glasses for distance, and Will called me a nerd. I said I was smart." Suzy shifted uncomfortably under the weight of Gemma's gaze. Her dark eyes looked as if they'd been outlined with vine charcoal, and her heavy, cut bangs rested against her eyelids.

"You called us ignor-*anuses*, if I remember correctly."

"Classy," Gemma murmured.

"It was a joke." Suzy reached out and tapped the handles of her knife and fork into a parallel. She sat at a disadvantage behind a pile of dirty breakfast dishes while they scrutinized her from above. She could use a break here. What was taking her mom so long?

"A good one, too," J.J. said with an appreciative tone as he rocked back on his heels. "Did we even decide on a project? I don't remember—"

"Sounds like a lot of fun," Gemma drawled coolly. She shifted away from him and dropped her arms. "Come on, J.J., our table's ready."

"Yeah, okay. I'll be right there, Gem," he said, either oblivious to the sudden chill or pretending to be. He grazed her arm affectionately with his fingertips as he let her go and watched her trudge to a cozy table for two before turning back to Suzy. "There's a party in the meadow tonight and—Oh, hey, Mrs. Blue."

He cleared his throat and nodded to Mom as she slid into the booth with a gust and a sigh. "Hey, have a good one. Maybe we'll catch you later," he said and headed to his table and his waiting girlfriend. The "we" must be couple-speak for him and Gemma. They'd been going out all year long. Quite a haul by high school standards.

"I cannot believe his curls or those eyelashes," Mom said after J.J. was out of range. "No denying he's Gary Radborne's son. Looks just like him. I went to high school with Gary, and I remember he was voted 'Best Eyes' in our yearbook. If I can ever find it, I'll show you. But enough about him. Here." She placed a white envelope in the center of the table and pushed it across with both hands. Her face flushed with excitement.

Suzy reached for it and stopped. Was she ready for this? It felt like a rerun: Mom buys a gift, presents it graciously, then takes it back.

Of course, she would toss out a few lame excuses along the way like…It's not the right color, or…This reminds me of you, so I can't bear to let it go, or Suzy's all-time favorite…

244

I'll keep it at my house for you. Mom had done this so many times in the past that it *was* funny. So funny it made Suzy numb from the heart up. Her mom always had some reason why Suzy couldn't keep it. Always.

"What's the occasion?" Suzy asked, trying to keep the suspicion out of her voice.

"New beginnings." Mom nudged it closer. "Go ahead, Suzette. Open it."

She stared at the envelope before sliding it past the bowl of creamers to her side of the table. With slow fingers, she lifted the flap. Inside was a card and inside that, an ordinary brass house key.

"It's yours, okay?" Mom said brightly.

Mine? Suzy clasped the key in her hand like it was made of gold and squeezed it until the metal bit into her palm. She stood before her mom could backpedal and ruin the moment and shoved it deep into the front pocket of her jeans.

She was already late, but thankfully the Butterhorn Bakery was right across the street. She pushed the jellies and packets of honey aside to grab her glasses, but paused to soak in the moment. Her mom had actually given her something, and as crazy as it sounded, maybe Suzy didn't have to pretend like everything was fine anymore.

Maybe things had changed.

After several hours of shopping downtown with her friends, Suzy wandered toward her Mom's house with a belly full of coffee, two ears full of gossip, and one hand carrying a shoe bag with a new pair of flats in wild animal print. Normally, she would have selected black, something that went with everything. But if Mom could change, Suzy could, too.

Change was in the air.

She wasn't moving away from Overdale or going to a different school; all that stayed the same.

But yesterday her home was with Dad in the country. Gravel roads, pinecones, and croaking frogs. Nothing said freedom like a wide open yard in the Big Hack mountains. On a super clear day, they could make out the top of Mount Rainier in the distance, a jagged peak that kissed the starry Washington sky.

Simply put, it was beautiful.

Today, however, she would be at the Badger Court Trailer Park, which sat at the end of Main Street, a mere two blocks from school. Instead of the country, she'd be living with traffic, neighbors, and a country bar across the street.

But being in town again wouldn't be so bad. Who needed a car anyway? She could walk everywhere...the Butterhorn Bakery, Grubby's Burger Joint, even Moony's Theater if she felt like watching a cheap flick. Suzy kicked a bottle cap off the sidewalk. Was she the only junior in her class who didn't have a driver's license? Probably. Thanks, Dad. Thanks for being an over-protective control-freak who was halfway around the world right about now. She'd said her goodbyes to him early this morning at the airport—

Hey. No, pity party. Don't think about Dad, not yet.

Think about Mom. Things had changed.

Suzy cut through a vacant parking lot and entered the loop of trailer homes until she stood in front of #17, home-sweet-home.

Heavy yellowed curtains were shut, pressed up against the big front window, and large terra-cotta pots blocked the stairs on the sun-weathered porch. A sign, *Welcome! Please use other door*, was staked in one pot and surrounded by scraggly brown plants. Their stems stood tall, but their leaves had drooped from death and decay.

The sign said "welcome," but everything around it did not.

Rust seeped from the bolts, leaving sienna stains on the tin siding of the trailer house while the ornamental shutters had been given a fresh coat of teal paint. The glossy new color popped against the dingy tan, a sign of Dad's handiwork. He was the shine, the polish, while Mom was...Suzy shook her head.

Mom was the opposite.

But she'd said "new beginnings," right? Yes, she had. So the outside didn't matter; it was the change on the inside that counted most.

Suzy waded through the grass at the narrow end of the house to her old bedroom window. Straight white blinds were tilted open, inviting in what was left of the day's light.

She hadn't been inside since she was, what...eight... maybe nine? Her dad had moved all her stuff in, and she didn't even know if everything fit. But supposedly, all her personal stuff was in there, her current life meshing with old memories.

"Blue!"

She spun around to see J.J. clearing a short picket fence with sloughing paint in one easy move. He sauntered across the overgrown lawn toward her with grace in faded jeans and waving brown curls, all bad boy, all Mr. Cool.

Suzy groaned. She wanted to be alone to dig for the inner strength her dad assured her all Blues had before making the big entrance.

He pulled off his dirty work gloves while wearing one of his irresistible smiles, and stuffed them into the pockets of his open jacket. Wasn't he cold? Her nose threatened to drip, yet Mr. Ten Below here stood with his coat unzipped.

"I thought you had a party to go to," she said. "Which, by the way, it's a little cold for a cold brew."

"Geez, you're hard core. It's not even dark yet." J.J. laughed like she'd made a joke. "But soon enough. I just got done splitting logs for the bonfire."

"Still, it's freezing." She sniffed.

"That's why you bring a date. Someone to huddle with under a blanket, you know, to keep warm. You should come to the meadow tonight. You could snuggle with Will and debrief him on our group assignment."

She didn't ask, What meadow? She didn't want to seem clueless or interested. But she used to live fifteen minutes out, so what did she know about town parties?

"Will? I don't think so." Suzy looped the shoe bag over her wrist, jammed her hands into her fleece pockets, and did a tap dance to warm her popsicle toes. Will had never even quirked a brow in her direction. Just because they shared a group together didn't mean they had to get cozy. Mr. Cool was messing with her. "Besides, debrief him on what? We didn't agree on anything."

"I'm sure whatever you decide will be fine with us." J.J. gave her a cute weasel grin.

Cute plus weasel equaled huge headache.

"Except no rodents," he said. "No Skinner box, no maze, no rats...none of that. Let's stick with the law enforcement angle, the one Mrs. Norton suggested. Do interviews, read procedure manuals, you know, write a paper, call it done."

"Scared of rats, huh?" Suzy tilted her head back and studied him. A data point for the record: bad boy had a weak spot. "No raspy tailed pets at your house? No Mr. Nibbles?"

"I've never forgotten that movie, *Willard*. You seen it? All those rats..." He shuddered. "That was the last time I spied on Monty with a date. I cried behind the couch, and they both caught me. My brother never lets me forget."

"You were crying?" Suzy laughed. "I can't picture you—"

"Hey, I was in the third grade." His palms flew out. "It's not like it was yesterday. Anyway, I haven't seen you at your mom's place in a long time."

"Yeah. When my parents split—"

"Hold on." J.J. slapped at the front pocket of his jeans, scattering loose sawdust. He pulled out his phone. "It's Gemma," he murmured, and his green eyes sparked with warmth. "Later, Blue." He did some kind of man-club, chin wave thing and turned back to the short fence. "Gemma..." he growled into the phone.

Suzy chewed her bottom lip thoughtfully and watched him saunter away with his phone stuck to his ear. J.J. and Gemma…everyone said it had a nice ring to it, but Suzy didn't agree. Gemma seemed like a jealous cling-on.

He stomped his boots before entering his double-wide trailer, one that looked like a *real* house. It had a matching two-bay shop with brown siding, and dotting the perimeter were cute inside-out tire planters painted a bright white and filled with happy green plants, ready for spring. With a gnarled apple tree pinning down the other corner of the yard, the scene was one word: picturesque.

Suzy turned back to her bedroom window set in a small, rusty tin can and slowly breathed in some of her Blue strength.

Yes, she could totally do this.

She had to. She had no other choice.

She marched around the corner and up the deck stairs to the back door. It was time to enter the domain. Her fingers found the house key in her front pocket, and she rubbed it like a worry stone. The back door was locked.

Should she knock this first time or use the key? She had no idea what the protocol was—but this was her home now, right?

She pressed the key between her fingers before unlocking the door and stepping into the small mudroom.

The washer and dryer huddled together under a steep pile of mixed-up laundry. On the opposite wall was a coat tree sprouting with knit foliage. Scattered shoes lined the path like a breadcrumb trail through the room.

Suzy wrinkled her nose at the funky smell of old paper and boiled chicken while carefully avoiding a fashionable suede boot, blocking the entryway. Either

her mom had been cooking a vat of soup, or this place needed a good airing out.

"Hello?" She glanced warily around the door jamb into the kitchen where her mom opened her arms in a welcoming gesture.

Suzy's jaw dropped.

Oh. My. God.

STACIA LEIGH

…grew up in the Flathead Valley and is a graduate of Montana State University. She currently resides in the Seattle area with two cherrier-huahua mutts, two voracious readers, and one Star Wars nerd.

Riding with the Hides of Hell is a young adult finalist in the 2016 PNWA Literary Contest. Stacia's first independently published novel, *Dealing with Blue,* is a young adult finalist in the 2015 PNWA Literary Contest and a finalist for the 2016 Nancy Pearl Book Award.

She enjoys writing what she loves to read, a flirty romance, light on the angst and heavy on the fun.

Want to learn more about Stacia's upcoming books and latest projects or just want to swing by for a quick hello? Boom! Done. All you have to do is visit her here:

www.stacialeigh.com
www.goodreads.com/stacialeigh
www.facebook.com/stacialeighauthor
www.pinterest.com/stacia_leigh/rhoh/

* * *

Also, your opinion matters to independently published authors as well as other book enthusiasts, so please share it by leaving a quick review on Amazon, Goodreads, or another preferred site. Thank you!